ROOT AND BONE

ROOT AND BONE

JESSICA RANEY

Cursed Dragon Ship
PUBLISHING

For my Nan and Aunt Midge

Sheriff Ed Wagner held his hand over the coffee cup just as Leona went to freshen it. He shook his head and scowled.

"That pot's burned up."

Leona rolled her eyes. "I made it less than an hour ago, Ed, but suit yourself." She put the pot back on the warmer. It wasn't burned up, but Ed was persnickety. And he was especially persnickety when he was working on some worrisome case or, more frequently, in hot water with his wife, which Leona knew for a fact that he was. She would have known because of his order—only coffee and toast—but she also knew because his wife, Donna, had been to see Leona the day before yesterday to purchase a love charm. Donna was sure Ed was cheating on her.

He wasn't.

Leona had never known Ed to have the energy for philandering, but Donna was a worrier. The charm seemed to calm her nerves a bit, even if she was still mad at Ed. His mind was on that and likely other things, sheriff things. The combination of work and wife made him a bear to wait on that particular morning.

Leona didn't take it personally. Ed was a kind man and a good sheriff. She had known him since they were children and knew his surly wasn't about her.

Ed wasn't her only charge that chilly September morning. The diner was full of her regulars. Daniel Woodford and George Franklin catcalled to her from their booth. She brought them platters of eggs and bacon, and they gleefully attacked the food before heading back out to their delivery trucks. Dorval Ring sat in his usual place at the lunch counter. His gaunt face was shadowed and sallow, but his deep brown eyes were kind when they met Leona's.

Dorval was the skinniest man Leona had ever seen, so frail that it looked like a whisper of a breath would knock him over. His condition made Leona's heart hurt. Every day he hiked into town and looked for work, but nobody would hire him. Dorval smelled like rotten chicken, and his quiet and intense gaze gave everyone the creeps.

Leona was the only one who was kind to him. She knew what he really was, and she knew he couldn't help stinking and being so horribly thin. He sat at her counter every day and ordered a water, which he never drank. He needed something else that diners didn't sell.

Leona looked in the icebox and found the milk she'd been saving. It had gone bad three days ago. She caught a whiff of it and grimaced, then she poured it into a tall glass and set it in front of Dorval.

"Glass of buttermilk today. My treat."

Dorval sniffed at it and the color came back to his cheeks. He smiled a mite of a smile but then dropped his eyes, ashamed, and slid the glass back to Leona.

"I couldn't, ma'am."

Leona slid the glass back and patted his hand. "You know you can call me Leona, Dorval. And I said my treat. You need it. How long's it been since you ate?" she whispered it so nobody else could hear.

"A good long while," Dorval said. He looked at the spoiled milk and licked his lips.

"Go on then and have it. I've got something else too. I'll leave it out back. You come back around and get it later." Leona had saved out a chicken carcass for him. She would leave it by the garbage cans when she took the trash out at the end of her shift. He nodded at her and looked like he was about to cry.

Leona patted his hand again. "It's all right, Dorval. Go on now. Eat." She wiped the counter in front of him then left him to drink the lumpy milk.

At the far end of the counter, a handsome young man with sandy blond hair and gentle brown eyes sat still and stared ahead. He had no food or drink in front of him, and nobody else paid him any attention at all. Occasionally, a beam of morning sunlight would pass through him.

"I bet that milk smells awful. Only you would feel sorry for a dirty ghoul," he said.

Leona wiped down the counter in front of him and kept her voice low. "He can't help what he is no more than can the rest of us, Cale."

"Be careful, Lee."

"Dorval wouldn't harm a kitten, let alone me. That's the

problem with being a ghoul. Be a sight easier for him if he was rotten." She wiped off the counter in front of him then crouched and pretended to sort the ketchup bottles.

"It's best to steer clear of monsters."

Leona popped up and smiled at him. "Well, if I did that, I'd steer clear of everyone." She left him there and went back to Ed.

"Why are you so surly today, Ed?" Leona put a slice of apple pie in front of him and a fresh cup of coffee.

"I didn't order that," Ed said, glaring at the pie as if it had called him a dirty name.

"Well, no, but you need it." Leona put a clean fork down.

Ed sighed and picked up the fork, then sliced a hunk of pie off and crammed it into his mouth. "Got a lot of work, is all."

"Around here?" Leona scowled. Ames was the seat of Denton County, and it was quiet. Leona reckoned Ed did little more than wrangle old Flip Thomas, the town drunk, a few nights a week and nab speeders down on the state route.

Ed finished the pie in three bites then slurped his coffee. "Looking for Mary Silvus. Her mama can't find her."

Leona furrowed her brow. "You ask Tommy Watkins?"

Ed looked at Leona and frowned. "How would you know anything about Tommy Watkins?"

Leona rolled her eyes. "I ain't even gonna dignify that with an answer. If she ain't at Tommy's, then something is wrong."

Leona worked at the only restaurant in town. She also worked nights at Marv's Tavern, both of which put her in position to know everything about everyone in Ames. But even if she didn't work those two jobs, people came to Leona and her family for help, help with things that others couldn't remedy.

Mary Silvus had been to see Leona several times. She bought love sachets, and when the love sachets worked, she needed herbs to help with other problems. Mary and her current boyfriend, Tommy Watkins, fought and made up in equal parts, and Leona had been involved in much of it, whether or not she wanted to be. If Mary was missing and she wasn't with Tommy, Leona could almost guarantee something terrible had happened to her.

"I know all that. I went out there. He ain't seen her in three days." Ed finished his coffee and tapped on the countertop for his check.

Leona wrote it up and handed it to him. He gave her a five-dollar bill, and she changed him out. "And her mama ain't seen her in three days neither?"

Ed shook his head. "Nope."

The hair on Leona's arms all stood all on end, and she got a familiar, far away feeling, then her stomach lurched. She held back her bile and swallowed. The air in the room grew colder, and Cale stood up from his stool. He looked at Leona with a worried intensity. He was suddenly gone then appeared right next to her behind the counter.

"Lee?"

"Miss Leona?" Dorval Ring's quiet baritone rumbled with concern. He stood up from his stool and shook.

"Leona?" Ed Wagner got up and started behind the counter.

Leona held her hand up for all to stop. "I'm all right. Probably a little low sugar is all. I didn't eat much this morning."

Ed stopped and put his hat on then nodded at Leona. He left her a whole dollar for a tip. "You best go on and eat something, Leona. The Sugar ain't something to mess around about. Donna gets it. Has to eat her a Clark bar from time to time."

Leona nodded. "I-I may just do that, Ed."

"Thanks for the pie, Leona. Take care of yourself. See you tomorrow."

"See you tomorrow, Ed." Leona gave a little wave and

managed a smile, then she straightened up and walked in the back near the big cooler.

Cale appeared beside her.

"You see her?" he asked.

Leona shook her head. "No, I don't think she's close to here, but I know wherever she is, she ain't alive no more."

"You sure? Wouldn't she come to you?" Cale asked. "If you ain't seen her, could be she just run off."

"Not everyone who dies calls on me directly." Leona closed her eyes and thought of Mary Silvus as she had last seen her, with bright pink lipstick and red-rimmed eyes. She'd sat in Leona's kitchen, desperate for a difficult remedy. Leona focused on that version of Mary and that last powerful emotion. When she reached out, she felt nothing. She tried to steel herself, but that desperate feeling bounced back to her, knocking the breath out of her. Leona doubled over, absorbing the invisible blow. As she met Cale's eyes, she shook her head and straightened up. "No."

Cale nodded. He reached out and looked like he was going to stroke Leona's hair, but the touch never met her head. All she felt was a gentle wisp of cold motion.

"Me and Jewel are gonna have to find her. I don't believe Ed can. He ain't ever been much of a detective, even if he's a kind soul. Besides that, I feel something else."

"What?" Cale asked.

"I ain't sure, but it's like something bad's coming." Her hands shook as a dread washed over her. She let it come and did her best to absorb it. The bile rose in her throat, and she coughed then spit the burn into the sink. Leona drank a glass of water to calm her nerves, then she straightened her apron and went back out front to finish her shift.

L eona rushed about the kitchen, finishing up some hamburger gravy and a few biscuits for supper. Her five-year-old daughter, Peggy, tromped around the kitchen, making annoying clacking noises with her hard-soled shoes and hitting everything with the fly swatter.

"Peggy, quit that clacking or your daddy is likely to lose his mind," Leona said.

Peggy did not quit the clacking but rather clacked louder and swatted the Formica of the kitchen table while singing "Daddy's gonna lose his mind" over and over. Leona sighed and ignored her, but when Peggy whacked her in the back with the fly swatter, she turned and grabbed it from her. She went to swat Peggy but stopped herself. That kind of punishment on Peggy usually only led to more violence.

Leona held out the fly swatter and threatened Peggy instead. "I catch you with this again and you'll go cut your own switch," she said.

"I'll go cut my own switch," Peggy parroted as she stuck her tongue out and made a face. The little girl giggled and smiled a sly, mean smile, one that always worried Leona, then ran off to clack her shoes elsewhere.

Leona put the fly swatter up high, on top of the icebox, then turned back to her gravy. She stirred it more, tasted it, then added a little more pepper. She turned the heat off and dealt with her biscuits. Leona had just slid the pan into the hot oven and closed the door when a familiar cold feeling washed over her. Leona stood up and turned around slowly. She wasn't alone.

A tall young man stood in the middle of her kitchen. He had dark brown hair and bright blue eyes. The boy was dressed in a dirty miner's uniform—coveralls coated in black coal dust and equally coated black boots, with worn out soles and holes in the toe. The lamp on his miner's hat flashed a couple of times then went out. He reached up and removed his hat, looked it over, then held it out to Leona.

"I don't think it works no more. They're gonna take it out of my pay."

As he spoke, the temperature in the room dropped even more, and Leona shivered. She knew the boy. His name was Elvin Taylor, and he had been killed in a cave-in up in the Little Pine Bluff mine three weeks ago.

"No, Elvin, it sure don't work no more, but that's all right. You don't need it no more anyways," Leona said. She smiled at him and stepped closer.

"I-I don't? But how am I gonna see in the dark now?"

Elvin's voice sounded frightened, like a little child at bedtime right before you turned out the light.

"Why, you don't need to see in the dark. You don't have to go back down in that old mine no more."

"I don't? But I got to. I still owe ten dollars at the store, and I got to pay that back first thing."

"Elvin. Think. What's the last thing you remember?"

Elvin looked around. His eyes widened, and he seemed to realize he was standing in a strange kitchen. He looked to Leona and started to cry.

"I went down the B shaft with Foster and Gene. They'd just opened it back up and said it was good. Miss Leona?"

"Yes, Elvin, it's me. What else do you recall?"

"Foster and Gene was cutting up about Gene's wife and then . . ." He looked to Leona, and tears streamed down his face. "Miss Leona, I'm dead, ain't I?"

"Yes, Elvin. You died a few weeks ago."

"But . . . that can't be. I-I-I'd known or be someplace else. Why am I in your kitchen?"

"Some folks come and find me when they pass," Leona said. "Sometimes they get confused, like you just was." Leona smiled at him. "But you're all right now, ain't you?"

Elvin stopped crying and looked around. "I-I guess, but where do I go now?"

"To tell you the honest truth, Elvin, I don't know. Some stay around a little bit. Some come back and say hey. And some just go somewhere else, and I don't see them again. But no matter what, I don't think you need to be afraid, nor worry no more."

Elvin looked around the whole room, then he looked at Leona. "I don't guess I am afraid, not if I really think on it."

Leona gave him a smile. "That's real good, Elvin. I'm glad

of it. You can stay around here if you like, until you decide where you want to go."

"Thank you, Miss Leona, but I know where I'ma gonna go now." He put his hat back on his head and tipped it at her.

Leona waved at him and smiled as he faded away. Sometimes the dead folks just needed a kind person to hear them out and remind them before they could move on. Leona was happy to do it and to ease their passing. Not all of them took it so well as Elvin had—sometimes they raised a ruckus and broke things before they calmed down, but Leona had never failed to calm one of them down, not in twenty years of seeing, hearing, and speaking with the dead. It gave her just as much peace as it did them, and as she heard her husband, Bob, yelling at Peggy to shut up her clacking and threaten to beat her black and blue, she sighed and wished that the living could be handled as easily as the dead.

"I ain't got time for this, Bob." Leona finished up the supper dishes and left them to dry on the rack. She used the wet dishtowel to wipe off Peggy's face. Peggy thrashed around and tried to bite her. Leona grabbed her face and held it. "That ain't nice. Now you stop that biting, or somebody's gonna bite you back."

"I'm telling you, Leona, I ain't gonna stand for this no more. A man can't have his wife out all hours doing whatever with strange men at a honky-tonk. I won't have it."

"Well, then you best get you a job, 'cause right now the two I got don't hardly keep ends met." Leona kissed Peggy on the forehead then swatted her bottom and let her run away back to her room.

Bob's face got black and mean from her comment, and he slapped Leona hard. Leona's hand flew to her cheek, and she bit back a curse as rage bubbled inside her. Heat in her guts spread throughout her body, and as it flowed into her hand, she felt a prickle of magic. It pulsed and tingled in her fingertips. Something inside her, not a clear voice, but a raspy whisper, urged her to let go, to squeeze her hand and let the magic free to make Bob pay.

It was a familiar whisper, one she'd been at odds with for her whole life, and even though it was tempting to make Bob scream, that raspy whisper frightened her. She took a deep breath and fought it. She willed the magic back and controlled it as it receded into her guts and abated.

The temperature in the kitchen dropped as if someone had opened the door on a frosty December night rather than the cool September evening, and Leona looked over to see Cale fuming beside her. She shook her head at him but addressed Bob.

"Hit me again and see how you like it," Leona said. The slap hadn't hurt much. But he'd been increasing the frequency and this one had a little oomph behind it. It would leave a mark.

"By God, Leona, I'll do whatever I want and like it just fine." He moved to slap her again, but Leona stared at him and didn't flinch. Her eyes narrowed, and she said two words in her mind: *Ut Assis*

Bob stopped mid-motion as his stomach gurgled. His face contorted in pain and panic, and he clutched at his belt. His gut rumbled louder, and the hot wave of smell that hit Leona's nose indicated Bob had shit himself.

"Son of a bitch!" Bob yelled as he waddled off toward the bathroom.

Leona smiled to herself. That magic was satisfying, and no real harm done, except maybe to Bob's drawers. She found the keys to the rusty old truck then gathered her purse and sweater. Bob usually yelled about her taking the vehicle—and sometimes she didn't—but she didn't feel like walking home that night. Her stomach was in knots about the missing girl, and she didn't want to walk home alone. Bob was too busy shitting himself to protest further.

She was halfway to Marv's Tavern, her night job, when Cale appeared in the seat beside her. A little popping sound preceded his appearance, but Leona didn't need that clue. She'd been expecting him.

"I wish you'd stayed to watch Peggy," Leona said.

"I'll kill him."

"No, you won't," Leona said. She kept her eyes on the road and thought about Mary Silvus. "You can't."

"I'll find a way," Cale said.

The temperature in the truck cab dropped, and Leona shivered and scowled. "You gotta stop all this, Cale. You know you can't do nothing about it, and it just makes it harder for me."

"He's gonna hurt you, Lee. You think that's easy for me to watch? He lays around all day while you work yourself to death and have to deal with Peggy. He just . . . he just . . ." Cale screwed up his face. The air whooshed by Leona's face, chilling her more. "He just needs to go."

Leona sighed. "Well, maybe he will and maybe he won't. That's my cross to bear."

She'd met Bob Monroe right before he shipped out to England in '42. He looked good in his uniform, and he'd seemed so worldly and confident to Leona. He'd sent postcards and letters from England and promised to take her to Paris someday, but in the years they'd been married, they hadn't made it past the Denton county line.

Once he got home, his ambitions waned. He had trouble keeping a job and drank up all their money. She'd been about to leave him, but then Peggy had come. And Leona couldn't be a divorcee with a baby in Ames. That just wasn't done. So, she took all the work she could get and hoped maybe Bob would leave of his own accord if she showed the least amount of interest possible. Instead, he got meaner and drank more. Her lack of interest in him did not translate to him lacking interest in her, much to her disgust.

"I just want you to be . . ." Cale sighed and leaned his head back as he paused. He looked over at Leona, and she felt a little swoosh of cold air as he tried to touch her cheek. "Happy. For once."

Leona leaned her face toward his hand. "Nobody is happy all the time. I got my moments. That's all I can do."

"I'd make all your moments happy if I could," he said.

"I know. I know you would. But can't nobody do that. We just got to bear what we got to bear."

She reached her hand out and put it near his, wishing she could feel him. But there was danger in that too.

He nodded, and the temperature in the truck warmed. They drove the rest of the way in their comfortable silence.

Marv's Tavern was the most happening bar in Ames, mainly because it was the only bar in Ames. To Marv's credit, he had good food and served more than beer, which was a novel thing. When Leona came in, the bar patrons all turned, smiled at her, and erupted into a friendly greeting. She smiled back and slid behind the bar, picking up the empty Stroh's can from in front of Dale Wetzel and wiping down the bar in one motion. In just a few minutes, she had greeted everyone, refreshed their drinks, and cleaned up the untidy bar.

Marv burst through the door from the kitchen, yelling at Annie, the young girl he had hired to cook a few months ago. "I told you, you gotta weigh that meat every time." He threw up his hands and shook his head at Leona. "You're gonna have to talk to her, Leona. She don't weigh that meat right, and I'm gonna go broke."

Leona plopped an Alka-Seltzer tablet into a glass of water and handed it to him. "She only just started, Marv. You gotta be patient."

"I can't be so patient as to land in the poorhouse," he said as he gulped down the Alka-Seltzer. He looked at her face where the red mark was, and his own face got red. He took another swig of the antacid. "Bob hold you up tonight?"

Leona busied herself cleaning. "No, something was wrong with the truck. Couldn't get it to start right off."

"I'll take a look at it for you, Miss Leona," Minky Barkus said. He was a tall, awkward kid, only just eighteen. He worked down at Doyle's gas station, and he was in love with Leona. She'd had to speak to him about bringing her flowers and walking her to her vehicle.

Leona smiled and set a Coke down in front of him. "Thanks, Minky, but it's all right."

"It wouldn't be no trouble at all," Minky said as he slurped the soda. "If you want, you can bring it by the garage tomorrow, and I'll have me a look. Won't charge you nothin'."

She smiled at him and moved down the bar. "If it acts up again, I just might, Mink, thanks."

Cale sat in his normal spot. Everyone just sort of knew to leave the three stools at the end unoccupied. If you sat there, it was cold and smelled funny and sometimes the hair on the back of the neck stood on end. It amused Cale and annoyed Leona. But she knew he needed the space, so she let it be.

"There goes another one," Cale said, laughing.

"Another what?" Leona asked.

"Another one over the moon for you."

Leona rolled her eyes. "Don't start that again."

Cale shrugged. "All of them love you. Not that it's a mystery why.

"Well, I can't help it."

Cale nodded in agreement and smiled at her. "No, you can't help it," he said.

Leona saw in his face a joyful radiance and, knowing that was for her, she felt her cheeks grow hot. They stared at one another a bit, and then the bar erupted in chaos when Leona's younger sister, Jewel, walked in.

Jewel was perfectly done up in a white and red polka dot dress with matching red pumps. Her fire-red hair was styled high, and she wore scandalous red lipstick to match her shoes. Jewel turned every head in the bar, and, while they all might be in love with Leona, they were all in lust with Jewel. Unfortunately for all of them, Jewel knew it.

"What a sorry bunch in here tonight!" Jewel laughed as she waved at them all then sat down on the bar stool next to Cale.

They all yelled at Leona at once, and she rolled her eyes and nodded as she mixed up a pink lady and set it in front of Jewel.

"Who's it from?" Jewel asked, grinning as she sipped the drink in her most lady-like imitation of propriety.

"Does it matter?" Cale asked.

"Nope, it don't. I'll get 'em all." Jewel looked in his direction and winked at the space. She couldn't see him. Jewel didn't have the gift that Leona had where ghosts were concerned, but she had been around Cale enough throughout the years that she could hear him. Since they usually picked at each other until one or both of them erupted into an annoyed fury, Leona often wished she couldn't.

"Where's George at tonight, Jewel?" Cale asked.

"At home in bed, where I left him."

"And he didn't say nothing to you about getting all dressed up to come here?"

Jewel shook her head and smiled in Cale's direction. "Why no, Cale, he did not. He did not because I drugged his surly ass to keep him from ruining another fine evening." Jewel batted her eyelashes toward Cale and smiled even sweeter.

"Jewel, we got work to do," Leona said.

"When don't we?" Jewel replied. She turned her gaze toward Henry McNabb and smiled as she sipped her drink. "Henry, did you send this here drink to me?" Jewel's voice oozed with sex and sweetness.

Leona and Cale both rolled their eyes at the same time. "For Pete's sake, Jewel," Leona said.

"What?" Jewel asked, turning her attention back to her sister. "Leona, you're like an old lady. Audine acts younger than you, and she was old when she got squirted out forty years ago."

"Listen, we got work to do later," Leona said.

"Not tonight, we don't. Tonight is for dancing. And besides, I just done up a whole mess of them wards like you was fussing about."

"Not that work." Leona stared at Jewel. After a few seconds, Jewel stopped smiling.

"Somebody come to you?"

"Yes, but that ain't the work that I'm talking about. I think we're gonna have to go find her."

"Who?"

Leona held up a finger. She made a trip down the bar, took care of everyone, then mixed up another pink lady and set it in front of Jewel, this time from Dalvin McKinney. "Mary Silvus has been missing three days."

Jewel rolled her eyes. "Well, that ain't no mystery. She's laid up with Tommy Watkins."

Leona shook her head. "She ain't. And Tommy don't know where she is."

"I bet you he does," Jewel said. "I reckon we can get it out of him."

"You can't just go slinging curses to get information," Cale said.

"The hell if I can't," Jewel replied. "That's a pretty good way to get information."

"You all stop your picking. Look, we may need to go talk to Tommy, but I just don't think he done it. You know how he is about her."

"Yeah," Jewel said as she downed her drink. "He's like how they all are. Sweet when things are going their way, sour when they ain't."

"You just described every human on this earth." Cale scoffed.

"That ain't true at all, Cale," Jewel said. "Some people is sour no matter what." She smiled and winked at him. "Take you, for example. Hanging around my sister, fussy and fitful like a little old lady."

The water droplets on Jewel's glass froze, and Leona shook as a chill came over the area.

Jewel grinned at the ice and plucked a little drop off the side of the glass. "Thanks, my drink was getting warm. Looks like you are good for something."

The glass cracked and the pink, milky liquid spilled on the bar. Leona looked at Cale. "Cale. Calm down." She turned to Jewel. "You ain't helping. Stop poking at him."

"Get rid of him, Leona. It ain't difficult to shake a ghost." Jewel scowled.

"Ain't nobody going nowhere," Leona said. She picked up the glass and cleaned off the bar. "I ain't working tomorrow night. We need to go see about it after I get off at the diner."

Jewel shrugged. She looked non-committal, but Leona knew that neither Jewel nor Cale would leave her to find Mary

Silvus alone, no matter how much either of them grumped about it.

"Well, looks like I ain't got a drink," Jewel yelled as she got up and sauntered over to the jukebox.

Four men began yelling for Leona and waving dollars at her to make them a drink for Jewel. Leona and Cale rolled their eyes at the same time, then Leona sighed and grabbed a dollar from Jim Stengal and made another pink lady. Jim strutted over to hand it to Jewel, who was dancing with Eldon Murphy. Jewel took the drink and, in a few minutes, was holding court with every man in the place. They all jockeyed for position around her, asking for a dance, pumping a nickel into the juke so she could hear her favorite song, buying her drinks. Jewel loved attention, and one man was never enough. She got what she needed, but she certainly didn't need one all the time, at least not the same one.

Leona was the opposite. She only needed one, just not the one she had. She wiped down the bar and looked at Cale. Jewel's antics annoyed him, as always, but he was a good man, or at least he had been. Kind, steady, loving. They'd just missed each other in life was all, and now neither could let go.

"This will get her in trouble one day," Cale said, shaking his head.

Just then, George Smith, who was technically Jewel's husband, barreled through the door. He was an enormous man, loud, beefy, and red. George was a fast talker with a quick temper, which did not pair well with Jewel. Normally careful about his appearance, his hair stood all on end in places and flat and greasy in others. He swayed as he looked about the bar, unsteady on his feet and woozy from whatever Jewel had drugged him with.

"I knowed it! I knowed you'd come on over here, Jewel." George pointed at her and shook his finger, over-exaggerating the motion as he struggled to remain standing. "You get your ass in the car right now."

Leona came from behind the bar. "Listen, George, you don't look like you feel too well. Let's get you home and see about you."

George looked at her and squinted his eyes. "Leave me be, Leona. All I come to do was collect my whore wife. It ain't none of your affair."

"No dirty talk in here, George," Leona said. She nodded to Cale, who slumped his shoulders.

"Really? Do I gotta?"

Leona nodded. "Please?"

"Say please all you like, Leona. I ain't going no place without Jewel." George pushed his way through the crowd and grabbed Jewel's arm. "Girl, when I get you home, I'm gonna give you something to be sorry about."

"Oh, I'm for sure sorry about it already," Jewel yelled. She jerked her arm away from him.

George hauled back to slap her and, just as he did, Cale rushed forward and disappeared into George's bulk. George shook and dropped his hand.

"Come on, Jewel, we better get home," he said. His shoulders slumped, and he walked out the door, calm and quiet.

Jewel and Leona followed him out, ignoring the protests of the other patrons, and watched him walk over to his truck. He climbed up in the back and flopped over, face down, and the truck groaned under his weight. Cale appeared beside Leona, and they all looked down at the sleeping George.

Jewel shook her head. "I should have drugged him more. I reckon I'm gonna have to shoot him tomorrow and get me a divorce." She climbed in the truck and started the engine. "I'll pick you up about two, Leona. You want me to bring you something to drug Bob?"

"No, Jewel, that won't be necessary," Leona said.

Jewel shrugged. "Suit yourself. Men's a sight easier to handle when you drug 'em good." She took off into the night with George snoring in the truck bed.

"You think she'll really shoot him?" Cale asked as they stood there together and watched the taillights fade into the dark.

Leona nodded. "It wouldn't faze Jewel none."

Cale doubled over and groaned. His face scrunched up, and he panted. Leona went to pat him, and her face fell in frustration. "I'm sorry. I wish there had been another way."

He held up a hand as he continued to fade. "Get somebody to walk you to your truck tonight. I'm not going to—" His words cut out, and he faded.

Leona felt the air move, a vague feeling of emptiness come over her, and she sensed he was gone. She reached out and thought of him, of them, connected by an invisible string. In her mind, she plucked the string and waited as the energy traveled away on it. It faded, and her heart seemed to stop in her chest at the stillness. When the wave traveled back to her on that string, she smiled and sighed in relief. He'd be back as soon as he was able, she knew, but the periods he was gone got longer every time.

Leona finished out the night pouring beers, refusing to give out Jewel's phone number, and wondering where to look for the ghost of Mary Silvus.

L eona had to admit that, while Jewel was known to be fickle, she was never known to be unpunctual. She often remarked that it was an odd virtue for Jewel to possess, and that thought flickered through her mind as she stood outside her house and waited for Jewel to show up. It was exactly two in the afternoon when Jewel pulled into the driveway, with Bill Haley and the Comets blasting from the truck. From the neck up, Jewel looked like a movie star. She'd bought the fashionable sunglasses from a department store in the big city, and her red curls were pinned up under a silk scarf. From the neck down, she was country. She wore a pair of overalls rolled up to her calves and well-worn work boots.

Leona wore the same clothes, minus the sunglasses and

make-up. They were both dressed in their root grubbing outfits, which wouldn't surprise anyone should they be inclined to ask where the two of them were headed that afternoon.

After Jewel stopped and honked the horn, she used the rearview mirror to reapply her bright red lipstick.

Leona slid into the seat and immediately turned down the radio.

"Don't blast that noise so loud."

"Did you drug Bob like I said to?"

"No, I didn't drug Bob. Jewel, you can't just go around drugging husbands."

Jewel laughed and threw the truck into gear, spinning the gravel merrily as she hit the gas. "Sure you can. I never met a man who deserved a drugging more than Bob Monroe." She said the last sentence with a vehemence that almost made it seem like she'd spit after saying it to clear her mouth of the hate. "Besides, you put the whammy on him easy enough so he shits himself. Drugging is cleaner. You're the one what has to deal with his drawers."

"Jewel Elizabeth Spencer. You stop that dirty talk, or I will hold you down and wash your mouth out with soap."

Jewel shrugged, and they sat in silence for a bit as Jewel drove them out to Tommy Watkins's trailer. Tommy worked shift work at the power plant up in Dixon. It paid well, so he had the nicest trailer in the park. All silver, the rounded chrome of the bullet-shaped Airliner shone in the early afternoon sun. Tommy sat outside under the awning. He looked as if he had just woken up, with his hair askew and greasy looking and his eyes red-rimmed and groggy. He was shirtless and smoked an unfiltered Camel all the way down before he carefully stubbed it out and lit another.

"Mary ain't here," he said.

Leona heard the crack in his voice and watched as his hands shook, trying to hold the cigarette. She didn't need a spell to know he was telling the truth. She looked over at Jewel, who was scowling with her hands on her hips. "Jewel, don't—"

Jewel paid her no mind. She spat the spell and waved her hand. Tommy dropped his cigarette and keeled over on the ground like somebody had kicked him in the crotch. His face strained, and the veins popped out on the side of his head as he coughed and moaned.

Jewel knelt beside him. "Where is she?"

"I-I don't know. Jesus, somebody's squeezin' my balls."

"Jewel!" Leona yelled.

"He knows something." Jewel tightened her fist, and Tommy screamed louder.

"Well, he can't tell you if he's screaming in pain." Leona put a hand on Jewel's shoulder. "Stop it right now."

Jewel rolled her eyes. "Fine. But if it looks like he's lyin', then I'm gonna—"

"Yeah, yeah. If he's lyin', you can have at it." Leona pushed Jewel back and helped Tommy sit up. "Tommy, it's okay. We just wanna help Mary. When did you see her last?"

Tommy sucked in a few big breaths of air and his face relaxed a little, but he still grimaced in pain. "A week ago."

Leona helped him to sit in the lawn chair. "Her mama ain't seen her in three days."

"I know that. Ed Wagner come out here," Tommy said.

"What happened the last time you seen her?" Leona asked.

"She broke up with me."

Leona didn't dare look over at Jewel. She didn't want to see the triumphant, smug look that would be plastered on her sister's face. "Well, I doubt she meant it permanent." Leona sat down in the chair next to him. "We want to help, Tommy."

Tommy looked at her skeptically then shot Jewel a hate-filled look. "That's all there is to tell."

"Oh, that ain't all there is," Jewel said. She pointed at Tommy. "Why did she bust up with you?"

"She said we just wasn't going the same way no more. She was real involved with church and always on me to go, but that just ain't my thing."

"And?" Jewel tapped her foot impatiently.

Tommy shrugged and lit another cigarette. "She wanted me to drive her and her mama over to Shadyside for some big tent revival. Her mama hates me, and I wasn't gonna go to no Bible thump."

"And she broke things off because you wouldn't carry her over there?" Leona asked.

"That's what done it, but she said it was just because I wasn't never gonna accept Jesus. That's true, I guess, but Jesus never played no part in it before."

"When did all this churchy business start?" Jewel asked.

"About a month ago. She started helping out with the youth ministry and got all worked up about it. Been yammering about that revival for two weeks solid. When I finally said *no*, that's when she left."

Leona nodded. She reached in her pocket and pulled out a handful of blue powder and blew it into Tommy's face. He coughed, then his eyes went white, and he relaxed in the chair. "You don't remember us being out here or asking you anything."

Tommy nodded. When his gaze met Leona's, he wrinkled his brow and looked confused. His eyes clouded over again, and he sat back in his chair and ignored them.

"He knows more," Jewel said as they got back in the truck.

"It don't seem like he does to me," Leona replied. "You wanna believe the worst."

"That's because the worst is almost always true." Jewel started up the truck. "What are we gonna do now?"

"Let's go see Shirley."

"Shirley hates me," Jewel said.

Shirley Silvus was Mary's mother and did indeed hate Jewel. Shirley got Jewel fired from the five and dime for wearing too much make-up and red shoes. She was the busiest of busybodies and the head bitty at the church. Jewel and Leona had never been good at regular church attendance, and it scandalized Shirley and her bitty circle. Leona kept peace with them. Jewel told Shirley to shove a hymnal where the sun don't shine.

"She won't care nothing about you. She'll be upset about Mary. I'll do the talking."

Jewel shrugged and nodded. "All right, but if she gives me any lip, I'm gonna curse her."

"Maybe it's best you stay in the truck," Leona said.

Jewel didn't argue and stayed in the truck, which pleasantly surprised Leona. Dealing with Shirley was going to be tricky, and she didn't need Jewel getting offended and slinging more curses around. Leona knocked on the door to the orderly, little white house. When Shirley answered, Leona was shocked by her appearance. Her hair, normally carefully curled in conservative finger waves, was a greasy mess, flat in places and askew in others. Her house dress was stained and wrinkled. Shirley's eyes were red, and she wrung a handkerchief in her hands.

"Hello, Shirley. I come to see if there was anything I could do to help out."

Shirley looked past Leona to Jewel in the truck. "I doubt that very much."

"Well, it's true. Ed told me about Mary. I came to see what you needed."

"I been prayin' on it, but God ain't told me yet what to do."

"You wanna tell me what happened?"

"Now why would I tell a witch anything?"

"Shirley, please."

"I know what you are, Leona Monroe. I know what you tried to do to my girl. She was a good girl. You and that Tommy Watkins tried to get your Devil's hooks in her, but I got her back."

Leona shook her head and held up her hands. "All I want to do is help you find Mary."

"Like I'd let a Bride of Satan help me. Everyone knows all about you and what you do. You filled Mary's head with notions of spells and gave her dirty potions. Well, we're wise to you now and we are not gonna—"

Shirley's mouth continued to move, but no sound came out. She seemed oblivious to this and kept on even as Leona stepped around her into the house. Shirley stood at the doorway pointing and yammering as if Leona were still there.

Leona made her way through the entryway and down the hallway. The first bedroom she poked her head in was Mary's. Leona had known Mary Silvus nearly all her life. She had always been comparable to Jewel in temperament, and her relationship with Tommy had been passionate and volatile. Mary was quick to joke and laugh, and she liked pretty dresses and bright, cheerful colors.

Had Leona not known Mary, had her first exposure been Mary's room that day, she would have been dead wrong about the person who slept there. The room was stark and uncomfortable looking. The walls were bright white, and the bed was neatly made up with a worn, muted quilt. Her desk was devoid of any cards or letters. Only a Bible remained. The only decoration was a large cross hanging on one wall. There was a pillow on the floor at the foot, a place to kneel and pray. It wasn't what she expected out of Mary, who had done a good many things forbidden in that Bible with Tommy Watkins.

Leona looked around the room and noticed spaces on the walls that were lighter—square shapes with places at the corners where the paint wasn't as shiny. She looked closer and touched the places. A sticky film remained where tape had once been, likely holding up posters and decorations that had been removed. She scowled and wondered how long ago the redecoration had occurred. Had it been Mary's idea or Shirley's?

She picked up the Bible. Leona wasn't a non-believer so much as she was a selective skeptic. She had seen many things that told her some of the things in the book were possible, but a great deal more that told her most of that supposed *good book* was written by men with agendas, and those agendas weren't really all that good. As she hefted it, she noted that its pebbled, red faux-leather cover was unblemished. She examined the spine. It was stiff and unmarred, a clear indication of newness or at least of minimal use. When she flipped it open and thumbed through the pages, she smelled the scent of new ink and paper.

The pages were crisp and unbent by dog-ears—no signs of frequent reading or favorite verses. Mary hadn't gotten around to that much devotion yet. Still, the pages eventually fell open to the place where the little satin ribbon kept a place, and there, underlined in red ink, was a verse, Ezekiel 16:30. *And I will judge thee, as women that break wedlock and shed blood are judged; I will give thee blood in fury and jealousy.*

The word *fury* was underlined twice. Leona wasn't an

expert in scripture, but she knew enough about it to know that beginners at Bible study didn't often start at Ezekiel, and she knew Mary well enough to know that a book about prophecy and judgement wouldn't be up her alley. Whatever it meant, she felt it was important, and her instinct told her to take the book. But then she remembered Ed Wagner. The Bible in Mary's room was a clue, and it was important to Ed's investigation, the only one that would matter in the long run, so she left it on the desk, centered carefully in the exact spot she had found it.

The desk had one drawer—a long one underneath the writing surface. When Leona opened it, she found a few notes, a birthday card from Tommy with a red rose pressed in it, and a small, black leather pouch that closed with a drawstring. Leona recognized it immediately as a charm bag. She had made plenty of them in her life. It was one of the first magics she and Jewel had learned—simple, yet incredibly powerful in capable hands.

But this one wasn't hers. She didn't dare touch it directly; strange charms weren't to be trifled with, but this one especially was not to be trusted. The dark, angry magic coming from it hit Leona in waves that raised the goose pimples on her arms and made her nauseous. This was even more important than the Bible verse and, unlike the book, Ed Wagner wouldn't have any clue as to its meaning. She and Jewel might though, so she decided to take it with her.

Leona went to the kitchen and found a piece of brown wrapping paper and a spoon. The first one she picked up was a normal, everyday old spoon, made of plain metal. That wouldn't work. The metal was no protection against the magic. But Leona knew Shirley well enough to know there had to be silver cutlery around somewhere.

She found it in the sideboard in the dining room. Leona

borrowed a spoon from the velvet-lined case that held Shirley's good silverware. She found a pencil in the desk drawer and drew a rune of protection, a diamond with a line down the center and three forks on each end. Carefully, she used the silver spoon to pick up the charm bag and deposited it in the brown paper square. She wrapped it up tightly.

In spite of the rune and paper, she felt the menace from the bag radiate and pulse. Dark whispers came from the thing, and even though the spoon was silver, Leona could feel the energy traveling from the charm bag into her hand. The silver got warm but not hot, so she dealt with the thing as quick as she could without being reckless. She placed it in her satchel and took a deep breath to clear her mind. She moved to close the drawer, but before she did, she noticed a small flyer printed in green ink. It was for a tent revival in Shadyside, perhaps the one Tommy had refused to attend. Leona grabbed it and shoved it in her bag.

She needed one last thing. Leona spotted the vanity and smiled. She picked up the hairbrush that Mary had left and looked closely. There was plenty of hair there. She took the whole brush and put it in her bag then made her way back out to the door, where Shirley was still going.

Leona blew a handful of the blue dust in Shirley's face and waited for her eyes to go milky.

"You never seen me or Jewel."

Shirley nodded and parroted Leona in a flat monotone. "I never seen you or Jewel."

When Leona got into the truck, Jewel was laughing.

"Oh, you can't just go slinging curses, huh?" Jewel slapped her knee and guffawed. "What was all that?"

Leona rolled her eyes and held up the hairbrush. "Shut up, Jewel, and drive. We're gonna have to do a locator spell."

Jewel sniffed the air, and her laughter stopped. She

grimaced and pointed to Leona's bag. "What nasty thing did you find in there?"

"A charm bag."

"Well, you didn't touch it, did you?" Jewel yelled.

"Of course not! I ain't stupid, Jewel. I put a rune on it. It can't hurt nobody for a bit. We ain't really got time to lose though, so step on it. We got two spells to do."

"It's gonna take some doing to get rid of that filth," Jewel said. She spat out the window in disgust. "Yuck. Tastes like rotten fish."

Leona nodded. "It's nasty business for sure, and it ain't something Mary or Shirley could handle."

"It ain't even something we would handle," Jewel said as she stepped on the gas.

"No. No, it ain't," Leona shook her head and stared out the window as Jewel drove home, thinking of revivals and prophets, and the fury outlined in the book of Ezekiel.

T don't want that thing in my house. Take it out back and I'll get something to clear it." Jewel parked the truck and headed inside while Leona took the bag out back of the house to Jewel's garden.

She walked a little way beyond the neat rows of herbs and flowers to the tree line. Just inside it was a cleared circle, about five feet in diameter. There was no grass or leaf litter. The ground appeared burnt, which it was. Red brick dust ringed the scorched circle, and in the center was a flat stone. Leona pulled the parcel from her satchel and unwrapped it. She shivered when the bag was exposed as the hatred pulsed out from it. After placing it on the flat stone, she stepped backward out of the circle.

"Shew. That thing is like a nasty man-fart intent on murder." Jewel waved her hand in front of her nose and spat again. "I'm gonna be tasting it for days." She handed Leona a red candle and a box of matches then ringed the bag with a mixture of coarse salt and dried herbs.

Leona set the candle on the corner of the stone. She lit it and blew out the match. The flame sputtered and nearly went out, but eventually the wick caught, and it burned bright. She and Jewel linked hands and chanted.

The flame enlarged and turned a brilliant blue. Something in the bag screeched, and the force of the shrill sound grated down Leona's back as if someone had raked metal against a chalkboard. She flinched and felt Jewel's hand clench hers a bit tighter. She concentrated harder and kept up the chanting. The blue flame flared, and the ring of salt and herbs caught fire. It sizzled and burned, and they choked as a burning, rotten stench overwhelmed them. Leona pushed out with her magic and lent more energy to the candle flame. It flared again then extinguished, along with the burning ring of salt. She let go of Jewel's hand and spat to get the burnt fish taste from her mouth.

"Lord have mercy."

"I'd wager He ain't had nothing to do with that bag." Jewel spat, too, and sniffed. "Let's see what was in it."

"You think it's safe?" Leona concentrated on it, wary.

"It gave a good fight, but there ain't no power in it now. I reckon it's safe enough." Jewel stepped inside the circle and examined the pouch. "Leona. That ain't normal leather."

Leona looked closer. The brown material sort of looked like leather, but it was light and strangely tanned.

"Looks kind of like pig skin," Leona said.

"It ain't pig," Jewel said as she grimaced in disgust.

Leona dumped the contents of the bag out on the stone,

then threw the pouch down and shook her hand. The bag contained a wad of curly hair, a good amount of thick, yellow fingernail shavings, and rust-colored dried flakes.

Leona frowned. "Blood."

"What in the hell was Mary doing with that thing?" Jewel yelled. "I ain't sure what that is. We need Kay."

"Sometimes, Jewel, you do make sense," Leona said.

L eona leaned back against Dill as they rode the mule up the hill. He was a gentle beast, and he picked his way carefully up the rocky trail. Mules were smarter than horses, surer of foot, and more suited for the life of the hill folk than a horse. Leona loved him, and she reached down and patted his neck. In truth, she was in heaven, riding old Jack with her favorite person, Dill. Jewel, who squirmed annoyingly between them, kicking Leona in the back of her legs and pointing at stupid things along the trail, was incidental.

"Where are we a going, Dill?" Jewel asked. She shifted around impatiently in her seat, nearly unseating Leona.

"Don't wiggle around, Jewel," Leona said, annoyed that her little sister was invited at all.

"I can't help it. I'm in a bad spot," Jewel complained.

Dill laughed. "You all would squall over anything, I do believe."

"Where are we a going?" Jewel repeated, her little voice shaky yet obstinate.

"To visit a friend," Dill said. "I'm going away soon, and she's gonna help you two out."

Dill and Will, their older twin brothers, were both shipping out for the Marines. They'd joined up as soon as they could, right after the Japanese had bombed that place off in the ocean. Leona had sat straight up in bed and cried the whole day before they had found out about the bombs. She had dreamt of an island, far off in a clear, blue sea, then she'd seen Dill, covered in blood. She refused to tell why she was so upset, and she'd cried until Ida Mae had gotten mad at her for it and whacked her good with the hairbrush.

"You ought not to go away, Dill. Ida Mae will whack us more," Jewel said.

Dill laughed. "Well, Jewel, thump her back, and she'll quit. That's all you have to do with a bully. They don't expect you to whack 'em back."

"Good. I will." Jewel laughed, happy at the prospect of giving it back to Ida Mae as good as she got.

"You ought not have told her that, Dill. She'll wail on Ida Mae," Leona said.

"She'll try," Dill said. "Eventually she'll win, and Ida Mae will quit."

"Well, that might not be for a while," Leona said. "Ida Mae is bigger than us."

"True, but you're growing like a poke weed." He tickled her, and she giggled. "Won't be long and you'll both learn quick enough."

Dill sang one of their favorite songs, and both girls joined in as they crested the hill and descended into a holler. Leona had a funny feeling wash over her, like she'd been there before, only she knew she hadn't. A little brook ran along the edge of the woods, its music dreamy and sweet, and the mule splashed through it then into a green, open field full of blooming flowers and plants. Bright sunlight streamed in and illuminated the holler in warmth and happiness. It differed from all the dark, wet hollers Leona had wandered through before. A little cottage covered in vines and flowers stood in the middle, and goats and sheep and a donkey roamed around, cropping the grass close and keeping it neat.

A woman emerged from the cottage, accompanied by two huge black dogs. She was tall, and her bright white hair sparkled in the sunshine. She smiled and waved at them. Dill steered the mule over, dismounted, then set the girls down. The dogs ran up and sniffed them. One sat next to each girl and leaned against them, inviting ear scratches. The donkey cantered over and brayed at the mule, who pinned his ears back. The donkey brayed at him once more then walked over and sniffed the girls. He gave a cheeky shake of his head to Jewel, who backed away, but he softened and rubbed his head against Leona. She cooed to him and scratched behind his ears.

"He likes you," the woman said. Her blue eyes twinkled, as if she knew something was funny.

"What's his name?" Leona asked. She gave him a kiss on his forehead. The donkey nudged her affectionately then sauntered off to harass the mule.

"I don't know. Why don't you ask him?" the woman said.

Jewel laughed. "Why, a donkey can't talk," she said.

"Surely they can," the woman said. "Maybe you don't know how to listen." She looked over her glasses at Jewel and quirked an eyebrow.

"Girls, this is Granny Kay. Granny, Leona and Jewel." Dill gestured between the girls, an amused smile on his face.

Leona nodded respectfully and smiled up at the old woman. Jewel gave a little curtsy.

"Well, why don't you all come in, and we'll have some tea," Granny Kay said. She motioned them inside. The cottage was warm,

and the wide front widow let plenty of natural light in. It was one big room with a twin bed in the corner and a roomy kitchen work-space. Herbs and flowers hung from the rafters, and the worktable was full of interesting jars and bundles. Leona breathed in deep and felt at peace with the earthy smell of the plants and the pleasant crackle of the little fire in the hearth.

Granny Kay made them some tea. She motioned for Leona and Jewel to sit at the worktable. Once they all had cups, she handed them each a fluffy chocolate chip cookie. She settled into a chair between them.

"Now, you two. You're going to come out here and study up with me from now on."

"Study up on what, ma'am?" Leona asked.

"Lore. Remedies. Magic," Granny Kay said. "Your mama studied with me when she was little."

"Magic? That ain't real," Jewel said.

Granny Kay laughed, then she waved her hand. The cookie Jewel held flew away and landed on the other side of the worktable.

Both girls gasped. Jewel cried for her cookie. Leona stared up at Granny Kay. "Will we learn to do that?"

"Perhaps," Granny Kay said. She winked at Leona. "It might be one of your gifts and then again, it might not be. Everyone is differ-ent." She tipped Leona's face up and looked at her hard for a few seconds. "You got something to tell, girl?"

Leona's face flushed, and she ducked away.

Dill cleared his throat. "It's all right to tell her, Lee. Go on ahead."

Leona watched him for a second, and he smiled at her. She trusted Dill above anyone else. If he said it was safe to tell, then it was. Leona set her little jaw and met Granny Kay's blue eyes. "Yes, ma'am. Sometimes . . . well, sometimes I can see dead people, and they talk to me."

"She says she seen a whole bunch over at the First Church of the

Repentant, over by the river. Delmie Schneider says it's haunted. We went to see. I didn't see nothing, but Leona says she did," Jewel said.

"Some folks can, and some folks can't," Granny Kay said. "And sometimes, certain ghosts will talk to you too. It depends on the ghost."

"Ghosts are scary," Jewel said.

"Some can be," Granny Kay said. "Most of 'em just want to talk. They can't move on. You help them, and they won't hurt you." She regarded Leona. "You see them and hear them. You ever dream funny dreams?"

"Sometimes," Leona said, nodding.

"Do the funny dreams come true?"

Leona nodded again. "Yes. Sometimes. Even though I wished they wouldn't."

Granny Kay gave her a one-armed hug. "I know, girl. But whatever comes will come. Ain't much you can do but bear witness."

"What if I say and tell the person?" She looked over at Dill then back at Granny Kay.

"Mostly they don't believe you. Things happen for a reason. Just because you know what's coming, don't make it your affair to change what will be."

Leona felt a sob well up in her throat as she thought of the image of Dill covered in blood and lying in the rain and mud. Granny Kay squeezed her hand. She got up and looked at a shelf of books. She pulled down a wide volume and turned it to a page. There was a pressed yellow flower there. "This here is a calendula, a marigold. See it? I want you girls to go outside and find me one. You understand?"

They both nodded.

"Alrighty. Go!" Granny Kay said.

Leona and Jewel scrambled out of their chairs and ran outside into the garden. They searched around and found a large patch. Jewel grabbed a flower and plucked it off at the head. Leona winced at that. She knelt down and carefully dug one up, preserving the roots. She took it back inside, and they showed the flowers to Granny Kay. She nodded at them both then quirked an eyebrow at Leona.

"Leona, why did you bring the whole plant and not just the flower?"

"Seems like that would have killed it. I didn't know what you wanted, and I figured I could put it back and it would live a while longer."

"See?" Dill said, smiling.

Kay nodded at him and then turned her full attention to Leona. "You can only use the flower, but you were right to bring the whole thing. We don't waste things, and we don't kill less we have to," the old woman said. "Now hurry and go put him back."

Leona scurried outside, joyful at her intuitive triumph. She hated killing anything. She understood the necessity of it, but it made her sad deep down inside. Here in this bright, pleasant glade, she felt at home, at peace, and connected to everything—the plants, the little creatures buzzing and flitting about the flowers, even the stalwart trees that stood sentry around the place. It was like she could hear them talking in the wind. The whole place teamed with life and conversation, and just being there fostered in Leona a little buzz of something deep down in her belly.

"It's the magic. When you just start out, you feel it most out here, in nature, in your garden. You keep a good garden and you'll always be able to come out and sit amongst the plants and trees and little things of the world and connect." Granny Kay had followed her out, and she waved around at all the life.

"I feel something out here," Leona said. She pointed to her belly button.

"Yes. Doesn't it feel good?"

Leona concentrated and thought for a moment. It did, but she had to admit, sometimes it didn't, when she got angry. "Yes. Right now it does."

"*That's right,*" Granny Kay said. "*The magic does how you do. You feel hateful, it will be hateful. You feel calm and kind, and you can use it for good.*"

"*I don't like it when it feels hateful,*" Leona said. *Once she'd gotten angry at Ida Mae for a vicious pinch, and she'd thought about pinching her back. Instead, she'd shattered a glass, and it had scared her.*

"*Well, feeling hateful sometimes is part of it. That's just being a human. When you feel that way, stop and think about it before you go slinging a curse.*"

"*I don't think I want to curse nobody,*" Leona said. *She knelt down and replanted the marigold then smiled at it as she patted the rich, dark soil down. It smelled heady and earthy and good.*

"*It ain't exactly a good thing to do, but sometimes it has to be done,*" Granny Kay said. "*Now come on inside and let's learn about how we use the calendula flower.*"

"*Can you use it to make people better?*" Leona asked.

Granny Kay smiled and wrapped an arm around Leona as they walked back inside. "*Indeed you can,*" she said.

Leona and Jewel hiked up and over the hill, then descended into the familiar holler that evoked comfort and safety as soon as they stepped off the trail and into the green wonderland, just as it had from the first day they'd seen it so many years ago. Granny Kay kept spectacular herb and magic gardens. Even in the late fall weather, things grew all around, wild looking but controlled by Granny Kay's expert hand. Birds were plentiful and chirped happy little birdsongs as a pleasant fall breeze riffled the orange and gold leaves around. The grass was soft underfoot and well-tended by the goats and the donkey. He trotted over when he saw the girls emerge from the woods. He snorted and brayed at Jewel then nickered at Leona and lowered his head for his customary ear scratching.

"That thing is a menace," Jewel said. She eyed him warily and kept her distance. Jewel had had more than a few bites from the donkey over the years.

"Well, he's a useful menace," Granny Kay said. The old woman knelt in her garden, planting some fall bulbs. Her bright white hair shimmered and shone in the crisp fall sunshine, and her blue eyes sparkled. She smiled at them and raised her ancient body up from the ground. "He keeps bears away and any other unsavory types that would like to wander in here." She hugged Leona then looked over her glasses at Jewel. "Someday you might find yourself needing a menacing donkey. You've always been one to cultivate incivility, Jewel." She hugged Jewel, too, then rapped her on the head. "You best stop poisoning your husband. That ain't the way to manage a man."

"How do you know about that?" Jewel asked.

"I got my ways," Granny Kay said. "There's ways of looking out that you ain't bothered to know yet. You keep drugging people like that, and sooner or later you'll make a mistake and kill 'em dead," she said.

"Well, that might not be a mistake," Jewel said.

"Jewel Elizabeth Spencer. That better just be your smart mouth and not how you really see it. Magic can come and magic can go if you don't act right. Maybe it goes when you need it the most, so you best be careful about how you treat it. You don't use it so you can go dancing the jitterbug out at the honky-tonk and ignore your home duties."

"Well, what if I don't want them home duties?" Jewel asked. She crossed her arms and pouted.

Granny Kay elbowed Leona and cackled. "Lookee there. Jewel, you best pull that lip back in before a birdie comes along and poops right on it." She pointed a gnarled finger at Jewel. "You don't want them home duties, then ditch that man properly."

"He ain't so easy to shake," Jewel said.

"That's why you have to be cautious about them." She turned her attention to Leona. The old woman felt around Leona's bruised eye and cheek. "You as well, Leona Mae."

Leona nodded. "Yes, ma'am."

"Well, come on inside then and have some tea. We'll sort both you girls out, I expect."

Inside, the little cottage was warm and cozy. Every manner of herb hung drying in the rafters. Granny Kay's work bench was full of jars and projects, and the whole place smelled earthy and herbaceous with a tinge of magic prickling at the nose. A little fire crackled in the hearth, and Granny Kay had a kettle going in no time. She moved around her space deftly.

Jewel and Leona sat at the table in their own spots, the ones they'd sat in for years as Granny Kay tutored them in Lore and magic, Jewel on her left, Leona on her right. Granny Kay put the tea down for them and gave them each a cookie, then she sat in the middle.

"Now, tell me what trouble you girls have gotten up to."

Leona pulled the little bag from her satchel and set it on the table.

Kay stopped what she was doing and stared at it.

"Where did you get that?" Kay's voice was quiet and calm, but there was a deadly seriousness about it that immediately alarmed both Leona and Jewel. Leona felt her stomach churn, and when she looked over at her sister, Jewel's face had gone pale and her lips pinched at the corners.

"I found it. There's a missing girl, and me and Jewel set out to find her. I found it in her desk drawer at her house."

"Did you touch it? Either one of you?" Kay asked.

"No, ma'am. I used silver to pick it up and wrapped it up with a rune on the paper," Leona said.

"Well that's something then," Kay said. She seemed to breathe easier, but the tension and worry was still there.

"Well I didn't touch it neither," Jewel said. She gave Leona a dirty look. "I told her she shouldn't have even used the rune because we couldn't be sure."

"You never said that, Jewel," Leona scoffed.

"I did, too, Leona, and I wouldn't let it in my house. We cleansed it outside."

"Quit that picking. This ain't no time for it. What do you mean you cleansed it?" Kay asked.

"We used a salt and herb circle," Leona replied.

"And what did it do when you burned it?" Kay asked.

"Stunk. Screamed. Burned bright blue, but you can see it didn't char or do nothing to it," Jewel went to pick it up, but Kay reached out lightning quick and smacked her hand away.

"If you ain't touched it, don't."

"But we cleared it out. You can feel the energy gone from it," Leona said. "Is it still dangerous?"

"It may very well be. It's best not to get complacent," Kay said. She sat down at the table and relaxed a bit, but she didn't take her eyes off the bag. Leona could see the possibilities and next steps whirling through Kay's mind as she consulted lifetimes of spells and Lore, looking for the answer she needed.

"You want me to show you what's in it?" Leona asked.

Granny Kay shook her head. "I already know. Hair, fingernails, and blood."

Leona and Jewel looked at one another. Both girl's face looked relaxed. If Kay already knew all about it, then they were less worried. Kay always knew.

"I figured the hair was Mary's, the missing girl, and probably the blood, too, but the nails don't look human. They was thick and yellow. Like they had a fungus, but . . . something worse. Who do they belong to?" Leona asked.

"Nobody you're ever going to care to meet," Kay said. "You're partial right. The hair belongs to the girl. The blood belongs to whoever made up that curse bag, and the nails—" Kay paused. "I ain't gonna say his name. Not here."

Leona's stomach flipped and churned. Kay wasn't afraid of anything or anybody. Her magic was safe and loving, but powerful, you could feel it. You just naturally understood not to try her, so if Kay were suddenly cautious and not repeating a name like this, Leona was worried.

"Can't be that bad," Jewel said.

"It can be, and it is," Kay said.

"I thought you said not to be afraid of names?" Jewel had a defiant set to her jaw.

"I believe what I said was to respect names but to know when to keep your mouth shut," Kay said. "A lesson you ain't mastered yet, Jewel Elizabeth."

Jewel backed down but pouted. Leona ignored her.

"Ma'am. What was that thing?"

"It's a curse. It's cursed that missing girl, and it's cursed whoever found it." Kay sipped her tea. "You didn't touch it outright, so that's good, but I fear it won't be enough to keep it off you."

"What's the curse gonna do?" Jewel asked. Her curiosity trumped her surliness at being called out. Jewel did love a curse.

"I don't know. It'll take me a while to figure that out. You best leave it here and let me study it. We can't work up a counter if we don't know its intent, not for sure anyways," Kay said.

"Maybe we can just try a bunch of counters and one will catch it," Leona suggested.

"Let's see what we see first," Kay said. "One thing I do know is that you won't find that missing girl alive."

Leona nodded. "I think so too. I reached out for her and didn't get no bounce back."

"I think we ought to do a locator spell," Jewel said.

"Yes. Do that. Jewel's proficient at that. You got something of hers then?" Kay asked.

Jewel gave Leona a smug look at Kay's compliment. She enjoyed being better at things than Leona and knew that those locator spells and Leona's struggle with them was a source of annoyance, one she loved to exploit regularly. "Yes, we got Mary's hair."

Leona narrowed her eyes at her sister but otherwise didn't antagonize her. She looked back to Kay. The old woman ignored the picking too.

"You girls need to be cautious. There's something nasty at work here, and this mean little pouch is just the start. Don't take no chances, keep up your wards, and don't do any frivolous magic." She cast a stern look at Jewel. "You may need that energy. You girls listening to me?"

Both Leona and Jewel nodded. "Yes, ma'am," they answered in unison.

"Good. And another thing, don't be traipsing through the woods after dark if you can help it."

"What is it? What's out there?" Leona asked.

"Many things and of late, some of them ain't been real friendly," Kay said. "From the look of this bag, I'd say they're about to get real unfriendly." She sipped her tea then looked at Leona and Jewel. "Go on and finish your tea. Get on home before dark. I said my piece, and I counted to three."

Both Leona and Jewel nodded. That was the end of it for now, they knew.

It was late in the afternoon when Leona and Jewel pulled into Jewel's driveway. September brought shorter days, so Granny Kay's directive about no gallivanting at night was not convenient.

"I don't know how she thinks we can stay shut up indoors at night," Jewel said as she killed the truck's engine and got out. "You work all hours, and I ain't trying to sit at home and knit."

"It's not possible, no, but we need to be ready for anything," Leona said. "I've never seen Kay stumped."

"No, nor afraid of a fight," Jewel said. "But I reckon there's a first time for everything."

Leona nodded, and they went inside to Jewel's kitchen.

Leona handed Jewel the hairbrush, then busied herself making a pot of tea.

Jewel looked it over. "Should be good enough." She began to rummage around in her chifforobe, and by the time Leona had made up two cups of tea, Jewel had everything laid out to do her location spell.

She sat down and sipped her tea. "I never tried it on a dead thing before. You reckon it'll work?"

"Only one way to find out," Leona said. "Double it up. It might could be you need to send out a big blast. Maybe use some herb of grace?"

Jewel shook her head. "No, herb of grace is tricky, and anyway, I added extry strawberry leaves."

"They ain't old or moldy, are they?" Leona asked. She quirked an eyebrow at Jewel.

"Leona, I guess I know enough not to use moldy strawberry leaves." Jewel huffed around and assembled her things. She took a few strands of Mary's hair from the brush and added it to the little bowl of strawberry leaves, then she lit a tall white candle and held out her hands to Leona.

Leona took Jewel's hands and concentrated on the flame. She felt the air move around them and concentrated harder as Jewel began to chant and ask for help to find what they were missing. Leona began to feel lightheaded as the air in the room got hotter and hotter. Sweat dripped from her forehead, but she held tight to Jewel and poured every ounce of energy she had into the spell. Just when she thought she was done in, Jewel yelled, let go of her hands, and they both flopped back in their chairs. The herb and hair mixture burst into a bright pink flame, and the candle popped and burnt out.

Leona wiped the sweat off her face with a tea towel then threw it to Jewel. "Well, did you see?"

Jewel nodded, and the look of terror on her face told Leona exactly where Mary Silvus had ended up. She shook her head.

"Really? There?"

"I ain't goin', Leona."

"They can't hurt you, Jewel, they're just surly is all. Besides, night or day, they'll be there."

"I know that, but I hate not being able to see out there."

The hour was getting late. The sun dipped lower on the horizon, and the cuckoo clock in Jewel's kitchen called out five calls. Leona couldn't stay out much later. She'd have to get supper for Bob and Peggy.

"No, we'll have to go tomorrow. I gotta get on home." Leona rinsed out her teacup and dried it then put it up in the cupboard. "What time's George get home?"

"A quarter 'til never if he knows what's good for him," Jewel said. "He squalled at me this morning and got on my last nerve. I blasted him solid with rock salt and told him not to come back."

"Jewel, he'll get the law on you for that."

Jewel only laughed. "Oh no, he won't. He'd never admit to nobody that I blasted him. I throwed out all his clothes too, so if he comes back, I'll load that shotgun with birdshot and see how he likes it."

"I don't know why you married him. I told you he was volatile," Leona scoffed. She found her purse and headed for the door.

Jewel grabbed her own purse and keys and followed. "Well, he had a good job and that white suit. I did like that white suit."

"That ain't no reason to get married."

Jewel laughed as they got in the truck. "You ain't got no room to talk, Leona Jean. The only thing Bob Monroe ever had going for him was that Army uniform. At least George had a good job."

"Bob had a good job back then."

"And kept it for all of three months," Jewel countered. "Anyway, judge not lest ye be judged."

"Oh, reading the Good Book now, are you?" Leona rolled her eyes. "You keep that up and you'll turn into a pile of salt."

"Oh, I ain't Lot's wife. I ain't one to look backwards."

"You ain't one to look forwards neither," Leona said as Jewel pulled up in front of her house. "I'll pick you up when I get off at the diner tomorrow."

"All right, but I ain't going to the Ave Maria unarmed."

"Jewel. They won't hurt you. What do you propose to do? Sage 'em out of a cemetery?"

"If they come for me again, yes."

Leona pointed a finger at Jewel. "No. We might need their help, and if you go out there and threaten 'em, we could be in for trouble."

"Then get Cale to go with you and leave me out of it." Jewel huffed and crossed her arms as she scowled.

Leona hadn't seen Cale since the night before. Possession took quite a bit out of him, and each time, his absence was a bit longer. Leona knew he wasn't gone for good. She could still feel him. It was a prickle that would get stronger the stronger he got. If it had been absent, she'd have been worried, but it wasn't. He was there, trying to come back to her. It was one of those true things she knew.

"I ain't seen him yet. He'll go if he can come back soon. You just be ready tomorrow. We'll go in the daylight since you're such a chicken, and we'll be quick about it. She's there or she ain't."

"She's there all right. I seen it plain as day," Jewel said.

Leona was a bit jealous. Jewel had a talent for that kind of spell, and Leona, while she had many special gifts herself, was a little peeved that Jewel did something better. "Well, just be ready."

"I will. Don't be so damn bossy."

"Jewel. None of that—"

"Yeah, yeah, yeah." Jewel waved her off and spun her tires out, cranking the radio louder to annoy Leona.

Leona stood in her driveway and sighed as she heard Peggy wailing inside and Bob cursing at the radio. As she thought of the grief she was about to take and the endless chores that awaited her inside, she briefly thought that maybe going out to the Ave Maria tonight wouldn't be so bad after all.

S weat beaded on Leona's brow then ran in rivulets down her beet-red face as she concentrated on keeping the oaken barrel of rainwater steady in the air. The barrel levitated about a foot off the ground. Every so often it would shake and dip an inch or two when Leona control over the magic waivered. She never fully lost it, but it had taken her a while to steady the barrel.

"Good. Keep it there." Granny Kay nodded in approval. "Just a minute or two more."

"I-I can't," Leona said. She bit her lip, and her heart thundered with effort.

"Yes, you can. Don't hold your breath," Kay said. The old woman's voice was calm and kind, but firm. "Breathe . . ."

Leona knew what she was supposed to do. She was supposed to

breathe deep and regular. She was supposed to feel the magic all around her and focus it so it went through her.

"A tree lets its roots do the work. That's what you are, Leona, a tree. Send your roots down for the magic," Kay instructed.

Leona felt like she had done that, but sometimes it felt like her roots were all dried up and too close to the surface. In those times she had to try extra hard to find the energy and bend it to her will. This was one of those times.

"I-I can't no more." The barrel fell out of the air and slammed into the ground. A large wave of water sloshed up and out of it from the force and wetted the ground.

Jewel skipped over to the barrel and looked inside, then she grinned meanly at Leona. "There ain't but half the water in it now. When I done it, I didn't hardly lose none." She skipped around the barrel then back to Leona. She skipped a ring around Leona, whistling a saucy tune.

Leona narrowed her eyes and shoved Jewel hard. Jewel lost her balance and fell backward into the soft, green grass. Jewel wasn't hurt, but she was angry. Her face went from triumphant to livid; her skin flushed and went nearly the shade of her red curls. Jewel popped back up and screeched as she flew at Leona, her fists balled up and swinging to bruise.

"I don't think so, Jewel Elizabeth." Granny Kay grabbed Jewel by the back of her collar and held her. Jewel tussled around a bit, but the old woman had an iron grip, so try as she might, Jewel didn't get any closer to Leona. When she couldn't satisfy her anger with her fists, Jewel turned to something else. She bit her lip and narrowed her eyes. The rain barrel levitated then flew at Leona.

Leona threw her hand up and pushed out with all the magic she could muster. The barrel immediately changed directions. It flew backward and hit the ground. The wood cracked, and all of the rainwater spilled out.

In an instant and entirely too fast for any human to have

moved, Kay had a hold of both Leona and Jewel's ears. The girls yowled as the woman pulled.

"Now that's about enough of that, both of you."

"She pushed me down!" Jewel yelled.

"You got what you deserved," Leona yelled back.

"I'm about to whup both of you-uns." Kay pinched their ears and shook them a little. She pulled at Jewel's ear. "You, stop your lording. What Leona does ain't no concern of yours."

"I didn't lord nothing. I just said—"

"You did so lord," Leona yelled.

"Quiet. Both of you. Jewel, keep on being prideful and that magic is likely to dry up on you. Go on out and pick me a bunch of comfrey leaves. Now. Don't come back until you got a good half peck."

Jewel scowled. She wasn't as good as Leona at foraging. It would take her a while to gather that much. She hesitated and stared daggers at Leona.

"Jewel." Granny Kay didn't raise her voice at all, but the tone was warning just the same. Jewel exhaled loudly, but she didn't make a move toward Leona. Instead she stuck out her lip in a pout and stomped off into the woods.

"And you, Leona Mae." Kay pinched Leona's ear lobe once more before she let go of her. "Jewel's excitable. You're older, and I expect you to do better."

"She ain't always got to rub my nose in things," Leona said. She rubbed her ear.

"As if you don't do her the same way," Kay said. "You're sisters. You're always gonna rub each other's nose in things. But you also gotta take care of each other."

"Fat chance Jewel ever takes care of anybody but her own self," Leona said.

"She's young and hot-headed. But she's your sister, and that will always be. You're stronger together, and the magic feels it too."

"I-I don't know," Leona said. She felt tears well up in her as she thought about her failure with the barrel. She often struggled with spell work. She loved herbs and remedies. She loved being connected to the natural world, and she reveled in her ability to communicate with the dead. Levitation, curses, and charm work took more concentration and practice whereas Jewel made it look easy.

"Well I do know. The magic should flow between you and through you. It's easier for a coven to work than any one person. You and Jewel make the start of one. Trust it." Kay sat down in her rocking chair on the porch. Leona sat in her spot on the step and leaned back against the pillar.

"It's hard. I don't have the energy." Leona closed her eyes and felt a lump stick her throat, like she was going to cry.

"It ain't that you ain't got the energy. You got plenty. But you're blocking it. You gotta relax. Breathe. Let it flow." Kay waved her hand, and the broken rain barrel slowly tipped upright. It levitated a few inches off the ground then slowly moved through the air toward the downspout at the corner of the outbuilding. Kay lowered her hand, and the barrel lowered and came to rest. The cracked wood glowed and knit itself back together.

The whole time, Leona could feel it. She could sense the magic flowing all around Kay and between Kay and the barrel. She could even feel it prickling between Kay and herself.

"Leona, what's holding you back?" Kay asked.

"Nothing. I'm trying as hard as I can," Leona said. She bit her lip. It was a lie. She always held a little back. If she didn't, she got a funny feeling in her guts, not a pain, but like a little twist and then a loopy-droopy feeling. That wasn't the problem. The problem was the whispers that came after. A voice, dark and probing, familiar, and yet strange would whisper to her. Sometimes she could make out full words. The voice would say her name and tell her the same things Granny Kay did—breathe, feel, let go. But it wasn't kind like Granny Kay. It was like Leona knew the voice was telling her to do it *for the wrong reason, like it wanted her to use the magic for meaner things, and she didn't want to do that. And yet sometimes, she did; when Jewel made her mad, which was understandable, but sometimes when something was hard and it was going to take extra effort. That made her feel lazy, which she also didn't like, but failure made her feel useless and small. And somehow, that feeling was worse.*

Leona thought she was doing a good job of hiding all of it. She kept clear of mean curses, unlike Jewel, and she didn't use her magic for frivolous things, also unlike Jewel. But as a result of so much worry and self-regulation so early in her development, it manifested in exactly what Kay described—a block.

And Kay knew it. She took Leona by the hand and sat her down at the worn wooden table in the cottage, the place where many lesson had been given. She poured two lemonades and sat next to Leona. "Are you hearing a voice?"

Leona felt her face flush, and she lowered her eyes and sipped her lemonade. "A voice? No."

Kay reached over and tipped her chin up so that Leona had no choice but to look her in the eye. The old woman's eyes were kind but firm. And in that moment Leona knew that Kay knew the truth.

She nodded her head. "It ain't right is it? I ain't right."

Kay smiled and pulled her up and into a hug. "There ain't nothing at all wrong with you. And it's normal to hear that voice. Everyone who has the magic in them hears it."

"Really?" Leona asked.

"Yes, really," Kay said, nodding. "Even me."

"Who is it?" Leona asked. She knew it had to be someone bad.

"Oh, his name ain't important. And you don't need to be afraid of him." Kay smiled. But Leona detected it wasn't a full smile, and that made her think maybe she at least needed to be a little afraid of him.

"Least ways, you don't need to hold back on his account. He's

just in there, picking, but he don't have no control over you. None at all."

"But it feels like maybe if I let go, I'll do something bad. Do bad spells."

Kay shook her head. "No. You control all of it. And any spell can be bad. It's intent that matters. I've told you girls before. Magic ain't good or bad. The same spell that helps can hurt if you apply it different. It ain't the magic's fault."

"But when he whispers, it's like he wants me to use the magic bad."

"He wants you to doubt yourself. He wants you to come to him for help if you're confused, but he won't help you. He wants you to help him." Kay's face was dark, and her voice sort of flustered and far away.

"Help him do what?" Leona asked. She was more confused now than ever, and for the first time, Granny Kay didn't seem sure either.

"He's shut up in a place he can't get out of. I put him there, a long time ago. But so long as he's there, he can't hurt nobody or make you do bad things. So let him whisper all he wants. You're a smart girl, and you know right from wrong. Don't be afraid."

"But what if I get mad? What if I make a mistake?" Leona asked.

"Both of them things are going to happen. They're gonna happen a lot. If you make a mistake, you own up to it and do your best to make it right. That's all anybody can do, magic or not." Kay got up and patted Leona on the shoulder. "I ain't saying to curse Jewel every time she makes you mad. That ain't right neither."

"Well that's what Jewel does," Leona huffed.

"She'll learn," Kay said. "Using magic thataway has consequences. Like I said, you can't squander the energy. Use for petty, nasty things and you're liable to be short of it when you need it. When it matters."

Leona nodded. "Yes ma'am."

"All right then. Let's try again."

They walked outside, and Kay pointed to the rain barrel. "Go on and move it. Don't spill the water."

"But there ain't none in it," Leona said.

"Hmm . . . well," Kay smiled at her. The old woman conjured a little storm that fell just over the barrel, filling it to the brim quickly, then dissipated, leaving a little rainbow. "There we go."

Leona stared wide-eyed at the magic water. She looked to Kay. "Will you teach me how to do that?"

Kay nodded. "Of course, but first thing's first." She pointed to the barrel and smiled.

Leona nodded. She screwed up her face in concentration, then turned toward the barrel.

The next afternoon, when Leona left, Bob was yelling about his dinner, which Leona had left in the oven for him, while Peggy stood on the stoop and sniffed. Leona bent down and hugged her. "It's all right, baby. You go on in and play with your dolly. I'm just going over to help Aunt Jewel. I promise, I'll only be gone a little while."

Peggy shook her head, and her blonde curls swung hard as she scowled. "No, you won't. You'll go and be gone all night because you don't love me."

"I won't. Only an hour or so. You go time me. If I'm not back by four, I'll take you to get an ice cream at the Woolworth's."

Peggy's face lit up, and then a mean look crossed it. Leona

knew her clocks would all be sped up past four when she got back. Peggy would make it so.

"Okay. I'll time you now." The little girl skipped back in the house, humming to herself as she went in search of all the clocks.

Leona climbed in the truck and took off for Jewel's. When she heard the popping sound, she smiled. Cale appeared beside her, and she beamed at him. "Welcome back."

Cale smiled back at her and nodded. "How long was it?"

"A day and a half."

He shrugged. "Seemed longer, but I guess I don't really know how to judge that anymore."

"Takes longer for you to come back each time. I don't think you better do that anymore. I won't ask you again."

"I would like to avoid it, yes," Cale said. He held his hand up to touch Leona's face. "You figure out where Mary is?"

"The Ave Maria," Leona said.

Cale whistled. "I can't go in with you."

"Yes, I know. We're picking up Jewel."

Cale laughed. "Jewel's terrified of it."

"Yes, but she saw it, and I'll need her."

"I doubt it. They won't talk to her, only you. Her, they'll just shove around."

"They don't mean nothing by it. They're just kids."

"They're shits."

"Well, it's where we gotta go," Leona sighed. She pulled into Jewel's drive and honked. Jewel came out directly. She carried a large bundle of sage and a jar of liquid with a rat head floating in it. "What's that supposed to do?" Leona asked.

Jewel shrugged and held up the jar of amber liquid. "I don't know. But I bet it'll do something if they act up." She scowled. Even if Cale couldn't be seen, the cold air could be felt. "I ain't sitting in the middle of you two. Cale, you ride in back."

"I was here first. You ride in back," Cale said.

"Well, truck cabs are for the living. Get in the back or I'll sage you good." Jewel held up her bundle and a lighter.

"That's an over-reaction, Jewel, for Pete's sake," Cale said. Cale popped off to the truck bed, and Jewel climbed in.

"He just got back," Leona said. "Don't fuss at him. He helped you out."

"Well, whatever. That don't mean I want him pressing his chill on me."

The Ave Maria Cemetery was all the way on top of a hill. The Catholics had stopped coming up the mountain to the little place. Most people, even ones who weren't sensitive, could feel the odd energy of it. The cemetery had been put in when a diphtheria epidemic ripped through Ames and killed a bunch of children. One distraught mother had cursed the heavens for taking her son, and ever since that, the place had taken on a sourness that couldn't be dissipated. The ghost children ran the place, and they accosted anyone unlucky enough to stumble on the little forgotten plot.

Leona didn't like it, but she was firm yet kind to them. She'd tell them a story or sing them a little song. Jewel, they would tease—pull her hair and poke at her until it drove her to cuss them.

Leona's truck barely made it. It sputtered and spun its tires as it tried to get up the last of the hill. She parked it, and they all pushed their way through the overgrown grass to the lich gate. The metal was all rusted, and the gate hung on one hinge as it swayed in the breeze. Leona felt a flash of something, fear maybe, and then she got dizzy and sick to her stomach. She bent over and threw up. All three of them stopped at the gate as Leona calmed herself and spat to get the vomit taste out. She stood up and scanned the area. Normally the children would be waiting at the gate, but they were missing.

"Where are they?" Cale asked.

"Hiding and getting ready to do no good," Jewel said. She held the sage out, and her eyes darted around.

Leona shook her head. "No. They're here but . . . I don't know." She pointed to Cale and Jewel. "You all stay here. Something ain't right, but they won't hurt me."

"Lee, you can't go in there by yourself," Cale said. He took a step forward toward the gate then stopped as if an invisible wall were in his way.

"I'll have to," Leona said. "You can't, and Jewel will just upset them. Jewel, if I ain't back in ten minutes, bring that sage on in."

"Oh, I will, don't you worry," Jewel said. She laid out her supplies, lighter at the ready.

Leona nodded at them both then stepped through the gate. The tall, spindly grass obscured most of the worn grave markers. Normally the children would be singing little songs and yelling for her to play hide and seek with them, but the only sound was the rustle of the dry grass in the afternoon breeze. Leona stopped by a familiar marker and called out.

"William? William Dennison? Where are you?" There was no answer. William was the oldest boy in the cemetery, only fourteen when he died, and the least mischievous one. He always greeted Leona and asked about the baseball scores of the day. When he didn't come, Leona knew there was real trouble.

She kept moving through the plot. All the way in the back was the biggest of the memorials. The Schwendamens, owners of the sawmill in town, had been rich and erected a tall, white marble cross. It was the most expensive grave marker Leona had ever seen in her many trips to various graveyards, and it was equal parts beauty and sadness. This time, when she came upon it, it inspired horror.

Somebody had broken it off at the base and inverted the cross. They'd shoved it securely into the earth. Tied to it, upside down, was the naked, headless body of Mary Silvus. Her chest had been cracked open, and not a drop of blood remained. Her head was nowhere to be found.

Leona held back a scream. She scanned the area and called out, "Mary? Mary Silvus."

At her call, the children started to pop up, one by one, around her. They whimpered and cried, and Leona screamed when she saw that all their mouths were sewn shut with thick black thread. They mumbled and cried, and grabbed for her as she recoiled in horror. She backed away from them, trying to calm her fears and them at the same time.

"Okay, all of you all, just calm down." Leona drew in a deep breath and reminded herself that they were ghost and couldn't harm her, and besides that, they were scared children. "We're gonna sort you all out, but—"

The children screamed frantically against the threads that held their mouths shut. Millie Branch put her hands in her face and sobbed. Henry Lovelady and Noble Church jumped up and down, eyes wide and pointed behind Leona.

She kept a little distance between herself and them when they edged closer, pointing and jumping and yelling. Leona stepped backwards until she backed into something cold and lost her balance. She instinctively darted away from it but teetered, slipped, then hit the ground hard. When she turned around and looked up, she saw that she had run smack in to Mary Silvus's ghost.

Mary's head was there, but like the children, her mouth was sewn shut. Unlike the children, she didn't look afraid. Her face was black with rage and her brown hair disheveled. She yanked at it and screamed impotently through the threads, then she reached out for Leona.

Leona scooted back and scrambled to her feet. Mary grabbed for her again, and Leona took off. Generally ghosts couldn't hurt you, but something was different about Mary. She caught hold of Leona's arm and scratched her, leaving four deep, red gouges. Leona jerked her arm away. "No, Mary, no," she said.

Mary let out another mumbled scream. Leona turned and ran as fast as she could for the lich gate. Mary and all the mumbling, crying children were hot on her heels, screeching and wailing. She thought if she could get to the gate, the barrier might hold them all in. Leona's legs pumped, and she was winded as she sped through the rough ground and tall grass, but she knew she could not stop.

She was in sight of the gate. Jewel and Cale argued and fussed at each other, each with an annoyed, exasperated look on their face; however, both their heads turned in her direction when they realized she was running. Cale's eyes went wide as he saw the otherworldly troop in pursuit.

Leona could sense the cold anger of Mary Silvis behind her, felt those scratching fingers brushing her coat, longing to rip her to shreds. Leona concentrated and made one last effort to sprint across the gate. She tripped as she did and fell into Jewel. They hit the ground in a tangle. Leona scrambled to right herself and see the gate.

Mary and the children were lined up at the lich gate; they could not cross. Cale stared in horror.

"Lee, wha-what happened to them?" he asked.

Leona helped Jewel up and backed away from the gate. "I don't know. They're cursed, maybe."

"Cursed? How do you curse a ghost?" Jewel asked. She moved her head around wildly, unable to see them but able to sense the bad energy. "Jesus, they're all . . . I just feel pain and rage."

Leona nodded. "Mary's in there. Well, most of her anyway."

"You reckon that barrier can hold them?" Cale asked.

Leona paused and watched. Dark waves of energy pulsed from Mary, and she put her hands up to the invisible field at the gate. She looked at Leona and pointed then mumble screamed as she began to throw herself against the barrier. The barrier was invisible, but as Mary tantrumed against it, the massive energy pulses caused the barrier wobble and move, like water.

"Somebody killed Mary. Took out her insides and cut off her head." Leona struggled to get control of herself.

Her heart thundered in her chest, and she shivered and shook as Mary bounced off the barrier and fell backward into the grass. The ghost children all scurried away from her and threw themselves against the barrier, begging Leona to help them escape. She wanted to cry as she watched them claw at the invisible wall separating them.

William Dennison pounded on it, his face red and strained as he screamed against the threads. He looked backward in terror as Mary righted herself and ran to him. She grabbed him and forced him to kneel. Mary laid her hands on his head and pulled at his hair. William screamed, and as he did, he faded.

Mary smiled, straining at the black thread that held her mouth shut. Her eyes glowed red, and Leona felt the energy pulse around her. One by one, Mary grabbed each of the ghost children, forced them to kneel, and absorbed them. Each time, her eyes burned redder, and she throbbed with stolen energy.

"Jewel. She's . . . she's eating them," Leona whispered. She backed away from the gate. "She's getting stronger."

"I know. I can feel her," Jewel said. She approached the gate, sage burning in her hand.

Mary backed away from the barrier as the sage smoke

wafted through. Jewel set the jar with the rat head down in front of the barrier and opened it. Red vapor poured from it and spread out across the ground. The crimson vapors rose up against the barrier, icing it an angry tint. Mary screamed in impotent rage and clenched her fists. She threw herself against the barrier, which appeared stouter with the addition of the red mist, and the ghost bounced back further than before. It only angered her more. She ran and leaped against it over and over, shaking the air in front of them and straining the magic fabric that bound her to the cemetery.

"We need to get the hell out of here. That ain't gonna hold her forever," Jewel said as the scrambled in the truck. This time Cale refused to ride in back. He squeezed in beside Jewel, and she didn't complain.

"Who could have done such a thing as all that?" Jewel asked in a small voice, uncharacteristically worried sounding for Jewel. She examined the scratch wound on Leona's arm. "What in the hell, Leona?" Jewel yelled.

"I don't know," Leona said as she sped toward home, her hands still shaking and the deep wound on her arming burning. "But I have a real ugly feeling we're gonna find out." She gunned the truck and bounced the old, rusted thing down the mountain as fast as she could.

L eona and Jewel were taught to always have some kind of protection ward around their home. Long ago, Granny Kay had explained to them that magic use, even good, responsible magic use tended to attract things that went bump in the night. Not everything that bumped was dangerous or out to cause harm, but she warned the girls to always be prepared. They both had ward circles around their houses but agreed that given Mary's anger and ability to consume the energy of other ghosts, more spells would be necessary.

Leona and Jewel worked together and put up additional wards in concentric circles around their homes. They used a variety of spells, figuring because they didn't know the exact nature of Mary's magic, they may as well cover all the bases.

"Well, if this all don't keep her out, nothing will," Jewel said as she finished up the last circle around Leona's house. She capped the jar of brick dust and put it away in Leona's chifforobe.

"I don't know what it will do if she gets much stronger." Leona washed her hands and dried them on a tea towel. "Jewel, we're gonna have to go back out there."

"I was afraid you was gonna say that," Jewel said.

"Ed needs to find that body. We can't send him out there if she's still there. She'll tear him to pieces."

"So we go out there and sage her out?"

Leona shrugged. "That's about all I know to do. Purify the place."

Jewel thought for a moment. "That ain't the only way to evict her."

"Don't you think the other way is kinda harsh? Something's been done to her. Normal ghosts don't do all that," Leona said.

Jewel shrugged. "I'd say harsh is a ghost scratching up the living and eating up little kid ghosts. I ain't happy about sending her to Perdition, but if that's what I gotta do to be safe, then that's what I'm gonna do."

"I don't like it. First off, it's Mary. She ain't ever been evil, and secondly, whatever is going on with her is telling us something about who done it. I just ain't for sure yet what." Leona bit her lip and thought as her scratched arm throbbed. She applied some salve to it and wrapped it in gauze.

"Well, if we get out there and she comes for me, I'm not taking no chances." Jewel crossed her arms and pouted.

"No, you're right about that. No chances. But maybe we can trap her."

Jewel smiled. "You're thinking a mirror?"

Leona nodded. "Yep. Maybe we get her in one then ring it."

"Yes. That might could hold her until we figure out how to de-hex her. Or at least until she vexes me, and I get rid of her."

Leona rolled her eyes and shook her head at Jewel. "All right then. Look, I'm gonna call in sick tomorrow, and we'll go out soon as it's dawn."

Jewel gathered her things. "I'll make us up some good sage bundles tonight and get the mirror ready."

"Careful on the way home, Jewel. Cale!"

Cale popped in beside Leona. "You want me to go with Jewel?"

Leona nodded. "Sure do. Make sure she gets home safe."

"Oh no. Leona, you might like you a ghost man lurking about, but I prefer mine living."

"You prefer yours unconscious with a fat paycheck," Cale quipped.

"I also prefer 'em—shut the hell up, Cale." Jewel scowled. "I guess I can handle old Mary if she wants to chase, but if she gets Cale, she's likely to be too strong for either of us, so keep his cold butt here where he can't mess me up."

"All right already, stop that cussing, Jewel. Ain't no need for it." Leona huffed and inclined her head to Cale. Jewel was right about the danger Mary posed to Cale. She had sucked those little ghost children right up. Cale had ten times their energy. If she got him, they might really be in for it. "Cale, stay here. Jewel. Be careful."

"I'm always careful, Leona. You ain't got to boss me." Jewel got in her truck and sped off down the road as the dark of the evening rolled in. Leona and Cale went back inside, and the rest of the night was spent dealing with Peggy. Mercifully, Bob passed out on the sofa, so at least Leona had some measure of peace.

When they arrived at the Ave Maria the next morning, dawn was just peeking over the trees. The cemetery was one of the first places to see sunlight every day. High on the hilltop and facing eastern exposure, the sun's first rays warmed the grass and grave markers, lending an artificial cheerfulness and warmth that ran counter to the normal state of the place.

They scanned the area, particularly the lich gate where they had last seen Mary.

"She there? I don't feel nothing," Jewel said. Her eyes darted around, and she had a large bundle of sage at the ready.

Leona couldn't see Mary lurking, but that didn't mean she wasn't there. Ghosts had to work harder to hide themselves from Leona, but it could be done. She shook her head at Jewel. "No, I can't see her."

"You think she busted out?" Jewel held up her hand, palm toward the gate and closed her eyes.

Leona did the same. As she reached out, she felt the shimmer of magic bounce gently back to her and touch her palm.

Jewel said, "It don't feel like she ripped it open. So where is she?"

"Only one way to find out," Leona said. She took a step forward and breached the barrier. She stood still as she could and concentrated, searching for Mary. Leona scanned the graveyard, but nothing lurked. It was quiet except for the gentle rustle of the light September wind. "Maybe she dissap—oof!"

Mary hit her from the right side so suddenly that Leona heard no pop nor felt even a tingle. She did feel the cold ground knock the wind out of her and Mary's nails rake her skin.

Mary's red eyes bored into her, and she grinned, straining the ugly black thread on her mouth as she clawed at Leona's arms.

"Mary Silvus, you sneaking spider!" Jewel yelled.

Mary recoiled as Jewel thrust the burning sage bundle at her and grabbed Leona with her other arm. They scrambled back across the barrier as Mary threw herself against it.

"By God, I'm gonna send your mean ass straight to He—"

"Jewel, no!" Leona put a hand on Jewel's arm and stilled her. "Let's get on with getting her."

"I ain't sure about that no more, Leona." Jewel waved the sage close to the barrier. "She's a sneaking snake, and I say we just get rid of her. She's dangerous."

Mary backed away from it, clearly repulsed, but she paid Jewel no mind. Her eyes never left Leona.

"She's dangerous, but I think maybe only to me." Leona pointed at the barrier. "Cross it and see what she does."

"Leona Jean Spencer, you have done lost your mind if you think I'ma gonna cross that ward and let that hateful cow rip me up."

"I don't think she will. I think it's me she's after." Leona walked back and forth along the gate. Mary prowled and matched her. "Try it. If she grabs for you, I'll sage her." Leona pulled a sage bundle from her bag and lit it.

Mary growled and stepped back from the smoke.

"Leona, if she gets me, I swear I'll haunt you to the end of your days." Jewel held up her sage and screwed up her face. She took a step over the invisible boundary, just inside the gate.

Mary ignored her. She continued to stare at Leona and growl. Leona approached the barrier and stuck her hand through. Mary lunged and scratched her as Leona pulled her arm back and whipped the sage bundle up to ward her off. Mary paid no attention to Jewel at all.

"Huh. Well, I don' know if I'm relieved or offended," Jewel said. She waved the sage at Mary and approached, but Mary made no move to grab her. She only moved away from Jewel's smoke. Jewel crossed the barrier again. "Why would she be fixated on you like that?"

"Don't know. She scratched me. I seen her first. Maybe that's it."

Jewel shook her head. "I bet it was that nasty sack. You touched it."

"I didn't though. I used a silver spoon and the rune."

"Then maybe it was just that you found it. That means it was a trap. Somebody was expecting you." Jewel whistled. "Leona, that's some malicious business."

"Sure is," Leona said. "Well, the good news is she won't be no danger to Ed and anybody else who comes out here, but still, I'd rather trap her."

Jewel nodded. "I'd say send her to Hell, but I know you're dead set on stupid, so let's get her in the mirror. Just don't come crying to me when she busts out, eats your boyfriend, and kills you." Jewel set the mirror down in front of the barrier, facing it.

Leona drew a circle around the mirror with salt and herbs. She left a tiny bit incomplete and stepped inside it. "You better be quick on the closing of it."

"Leona, I know what to do, for Pete's sake." Jewel scowled and faced the barrier. "You better be quick out of that circle if this don't work."

"It'll work. She'll come for me, and we'll get her." Leona picked up the mirror and held it facing Mary. "On three?" Leona nodded at Jewel and braced herself. "One . . . two . . . three!"

Jewel waved her hands and brought the barrier down. As soon as she did, Mary screeched and flew toward Leona. She hit the mirror and disappeared. The force of it knocked Leona backward but she held tight to mirror. Jewel closed up the circle with the salt and saged everything for good measure.

Leona and Jewel looked into the mirror. Mary was there, red eyes flashing in rage as she banged incessantly against the mirror from the other side.

"What in the world is wrong with her eyes? And her mouth? Do they always look like that?" Jewel asked.

Mary would be visible to anyone who looked in the mirror now. "No. They usually just look like folks. It's the curse what done that to her." Leona wrapped the mirror in a gunnysack and put it in the truck.

"I swear. That's a hell of a thing to do to anyone. Even a ghost." Jewel shook herself. "I reckon it's safe enough for Ed Wagner out here now."

"Let's have a look around before we tell him. I didn't get a good look yesterday. And besides, I want to see if any of the children are—" Leona choked up a moment as she considered the way the little ghosts had me their end. She cleared her throat, steeled herself, then took off into the cemetery with Jewel wafting sage behind her.

When they reached Mary's body, Jewel's jaw dropped, and she let go of the sage bundle and stared. "I swear."

The corpse was mottled with the beginnings of rot. It was a chilly morning, but that didn't deter the flies much. They buzzed around slowly and loudly, lazily gorging themselves. Leona blocked out the sweet smell of the rot and tried not to breathe through her nose as she examined the scene. The grass was trampled down all around. Leona wasn't good at hunting or tracking, but she tried to find signs.

Jewel was better at it than her and, in a few seconds, had located two sets of footprints: one barefoot, man-sized, the other enormous and not entirely human. The imprint of the heel was there, but it was light. All the weight was on the ball of the foot, but it was misshapen, more of an animal pad with claw marks where it pressed into the dirt. Both sets led out of the cemetery and into the woods.

"What makes prints like that?" Leona asked. She bent down and got a close look. "A bear?"

Jewel shook her head. "Don't think so, but I don't know. I never seen anything like it."

They finished looking around and found nothing else. Leona called out for each of the children, but none appeared. Leona bent her head and took a moment to think fondly of each of them and wish them peace, wherever they might be.

Mary was still banging against the mirror when they got back to the truck.

Jewel shook her head and growled. "Leona, I ain't gonna be able to stand that damn racket forever." She started the truck and headed down the mountain.

"Won't be forever, Jewel. Just long enough for us to set it right. We'll put her in your shed. If it don't hold her, at least she won't be around Cale."

"Great." Jewel groused but she nodded. "You think she can pop off and find you like he can?"

"I don't know. She don't really act like a regular ghost, but I do think she'll do everything she can to get to me." Leona stared out the window as they headed back to Jewel's place.

After stashing Mary in Jewel's back shed and warding it with invisibility and protections, they contemplated their next move.

"We're gonna have to get Ed out there without telling him," Leona said. "Any ideas?"

"Oh yes. I think I got a pretty good one." Jewel smiled.

Leona exhaled slowly and shook her head. "I doubt I'm gonna like this."

"Well, it might be fun and interesting, so I imagine you will hate it, Leona," Jewel said. "But you just leave it to me."

12

How come only Leona gets to see spooks and I can't? That ain't fair." Jewel pouted and crossed her arms as she kicked at a rock.

"Jewel Elizabeth, you better pull that bottom lip in before a little bird comes along and poops on it," Granny Kay said, giving Leona a nudge and smile as they all walked through the woods, looking for roots and plants to restock the larders. A chilly fall breeze rustled through the dry leaves, pleasantly cooling them and making their light sweaters just the right amount of warm.

"Aww, no bird can do that," Jewel said, but Leona smiled when she saw Jewel pull her lip in and quickly look up to make sure there was nothing flying above. "If I work, can't I see me some ghosts too?"

Granny Kay shook her head. "No, it don't work thataway. It's a gift that some has and some don't."

"Well I want it," Jewel huffed. She kicked another rock.

"Kick all the rocks you like. It won't give you nothing you ain't supposed to have," Kay said. "You're both different. Each of you got gifts and abilities. Be happy with yourself the way you are."

"Well, I'm gonna see about it," Jewel said stubbornly. She wandered off, kicking rocks and muttering about all the ghosts she'd know someday.

"That girl is difficult," Kay sighed.

"You ain't got to tell me, ma'am," Leona said. Leona had grown taller and lankier, yet she hadn't ever gone through a particularly awkward phase common to early teens. At least not physically. Socially she felt awkward and, of late, had been labeled as such by some of the girls in the school. They had noticed her whispering to herself and called her an oddball for it, something no thirteen year old girl cared to be known as.

But even with the label, Leona wouldn't stop talking to herself. Mainly because she wasn't talking to herself. She was talking to a ghost boy, who had taken walking her home from school every day.

"Leona, tell me about this boy," Kay said.

Leona blushed. "Well, I met him in the graveyard when I was waiting for Dell," she said. "He's real nice. He meets me after school every day. Only, ma'am, how can he follow me like that? I didn't think they could, you know, go away from the graveyards."

"Oh, ghosts can go about any place. They just don't." Kay shrugged. "It takes a lot of energy for them do anything, and most of 'em, especially the older ones, don't got much to spare," Kay said.

"Energy. That's how they work?" Leona asked.

"Yes. Like everybody else." Kay bent down and looked at a little plant. "It's a hard year for ginseng." She chuffed.

"So if it's hard for him, how come he can?"

Kay laughed. "I'd say he wants to."

Leona blushed again. "That . . . that . . . can't be."

"Oh, can't it?" Kay raised an eyebrow. "It can. Should it?" her face turned serious. "That's another matter. It's best you be careful, Leona."

"You mean he's . . . he's dangerous?"

Kay shook her head. "No, not dangerous. But he's only got so much energy, and if you go . . . Well, look, be cautious is all. You don't want to drain him before he figures out where he's supposed to go."

"What do you mean?" Leona knitted her brow in confusion. She didn't ever want to hurt Cale. She got a happy feeling every afternoon as she left school, hoping he'd be waiting at for her at the footbridge over the creek. The thought of him not being there sent a little trickle of panic through her.

"Ghosts only stick around until they figure out what's going on and decide where they're off to next. That journey takes some energy, and if they ain't got none to spare, well. They go wherever they can, which ain't necessarily where they want."

"Oh, I don't want that for him," Leona said. "It's . . . it's the bad place?"

"Maybe. Maybe not. I really couldn't say, but it's definitely not heaven," Kay said.

"Can they get more energy if they need it?"

"I suppose there's a way. Energy can always change hands, I reckon. It's just real hard to do, and ghosts are limited. I reckon you'd have to be a real mean spirit to do that, and I have never seen one that hateful." Kay put her arm around Leona and hugged her. "It's good you ain't afraid of ghosts, Leona. You don't need to be, but honey, you gotta remember that he's lived his life, short though it may have been. You just started livin' yours."

Leona blushed a third time, and her face burned as she shied away. "Oh, well, it ain't like that."

Kay stopped walking and tipped Leona's face up to hers.

"Leona. Don't lie. It's all right. Loving is good. But that ain't gonna be steady for you. Try as you both might. It just ain't gonna be."

"It maybe could be. I read about All Hallow's Eve, and if we can—"

Kay's face got serious, and she grasped Leona's chin. "Leona. You listen to me good now. The magic on All Hallow's Eve ain't to be trifled with. Some ghosts become flesh, yes. But that veil is thin, and things can come back and forth too easy, things you ain't going to enjoy being forth, so you do like I have told you and stay home that night, protected by a good, solid ward."

"But, I ain't afraid. I can see them—"

Kay tightened her grip on Leona's jaw. "I know you ain't afraid. But you ain't got to be afraid to understand danger and be cautious and smart. Promise me. Promise me you'll not expose yourself on that night. No matter how much you wanna be with that boy. Promise me."

"Cale would never hurt me," Leona stood defiant. The same streak that ran in Jewel ran in her, too, and asserted itself from time to time.

"I didn't say he would, but he ain't the only thing manifesting that night. Swear to me."

"But—"

"Swear it."

Leona warred with herself. She knew she could trust Cale. She knew he wouldn't hurt her or willingly allow anything else to hurt her either. But she also trusted Granny Kay, and Kay's face and voice were as serious as Leona had ever heard or seen. She sighed, but she nodded. "I swear," she said.

Kay relaxed and nodded. "Good."

Jewel came tromping back to them with an armload full of ginseng, a triumphant look on her face. "Lookee here! I bet Leona and her stupid old ghost boy couldn't find this much roots!"

J ewel and Leona waited at Jewel's place for Donna Wagner, Ed's wife, to arrive. Leona paced the kitchen and busied herself making wards and herb bundles. Jewel made tea. She mixed up Leona's with a dash of cream. She made her own with a shot of whiskey.

Leona took her cup and sipped. "Donna didn't say nothing about you calling her?"

"Nope. She wouldn't. She's always so convinced Ed's looking up somebody else's skirt that if we call her, she'll be here in two shakes," Jewel said. She sipped her own tea, added another bit of whiskey, and held up the bottle to Leona. "You want a slug?"

Leona scowled. "Jewel, it's only eleven in the morning."

"So?" Jewel slurped her drink and smiled. "What does the time matter if I need it?" She eyed Leona. "You could use a slug. What are you so nervous about? Donna ain't smart enough to sense nothing."

"I don't like doing spells like this. It's—it's dishonest."

Jewel laughed. "It's just a suggestion spell. It ain't like we're gonna steal from 'em. It's for Ed's own good, and it helps poor old Mary."

"It's dark magic, Jewel. Granny Kay wouldn't approve."

"Dark? Light? It's the intent that makes it that, not the magic. If we ain't got no ill, the magic don't care," Jewel countered.

"Well, I don't like it," Leona said. She finished her tea and went back to the wards.

Some spells felt heavy and dark, some light as a feather. Leona preferred not to mess with the dark and heavy. It scared her, and when she cast those kinds of spells, she had this feeling like she was moving along a path, farther away from any place she wanted to be.

All magic had a price, and Leona felt the darker spells cost more, more energy, more of herself. Of course, Jewel didn't agree with her on that point. Jewel believed that the end justified the means and that no spell was good or bad; the witch determined the intent when they cast it. Leona guessed that was mostly true, but she felt bad inside when she had to use dark spells, no matter her intent.

Donna Wagner banged on Jewel's backdoor. Jewel rolled her eyes as she got up to let her in. "I don't know why she comes around back. Everyone can see her car in the front." She plastered a smile on her face and opened the door. "Hey, Miz Wagner."

Donna Wagner was a large, dour woman. The leather of her shoes creaked in protest when she walked, and her face was doughy and pinched in a permanent scowl. She was paranoid about her husband's fidelity, and she had been a regular customer of Jewel and Leona for many years. She had rushed right over when Jewel called her and told her they had a new spell for her that would guarantee Ed's virility and loyalty.

"Jewel. Leona. What about this new spell?"

"Will you take some tea, Donna?" Leona asked.

"Cream and sugar." Donna nodded and hefted herself down into one of Jewel's kitchen chairs, which groaned under her bulk.

Leona already had the tea made. She set the cup and a plate of cookies down for Donna, then nodded at Jewel. Jewel was better at lying.

"Oh, we found you a new one. I know that old one only worked about half the time. This one, we guarantee."

Donna raised an eyebrow at Jewel and scrunched up her nose like she smelled something rotten. "How much?" She clutched at her coin purse.

Jewel looked at Leona then smiled at Donna and waved her hand. "No charge. See if you like the results, then when it wears off, we'll talk about price on the next."

Donna narrowed her eyes then looked both girls in the face for a few seconds. "Don't hardly seem like you'd give me nothing for free. You ain't never before."

"Well, first time for everything," Jewel said. "This one is pretty potent, there, Donna. Why"—Jewel paused, and her face got a serious, concerned look and she held up her palms— "supposing you don't like Ed and his carrot coming for you every night? He's liable to bother you with flowers and necking and all sorts of things that maybe you ain't used to. Heck, you might call us up and ask for us to reverse it. He might not leave you be."

Donna's face flushed, and she coughed a bit. "You say it works that good?"

Leona felt her face flush too. Not from any romantic notions, but from embarrassment at Jewel's snake oil sale. She looked down at her teacup and sipped.

Jewel laid it on thick. She scooted closer to Donna and whispered, "I used it half strength on George. I swear, Donna, I didn't walk straight for a week."

Leona nearly spit her tea out. Donna's face went bright red, but she smiled and fanned herself. "My word," she said. "My word."

Jewel grinned and nodded. "You see if it don't make Ed crazy. If it don't, you ain't lost nothing. If it does, well . . ." Jewel smiled sly and winked. "Girl, you'll be set right by Jesus, Mary, Joseph, and the Holy Ghost."

"All right. I'll try it." Donna nodded and fanned herself some more. "My word."

Jewel laughed and nodded at Leona. Leona got up and rummaged around in her chifforobe. She pulled out a medium-sized jar of white powder and a little leather pouch. She wrapped both in a piece of newspaper, then handed them to Donna. "Pour the powder out all around your bed. Make a rectangle all the way around it. Put the pouch under Ed's side of the bed."

"I ain't got to feed him nothing?" Donna asked. "Last time I had to feed him."

"Naw. Not this time," Jewel said. "Just make sure you ring your bed good. Tonight. It'll take a few days, but then, girl, well, don't blame us if you're tuckered out."

"My word," was all Donna could say. She smiled and stood up, her scowl gone and a spring in her heavy step. They waved at her as she waddled back around the house.

"Ed Wagner's a saint," Jewel said.

"You laid it on thick. What's gonna happen when none of what you said happens?" Leona asked. "We need to do something nice for Donna."

Jewel shrugged. "Well, I reckon when we're in his dream, we can tell him to roll on over after we leave and give old Donna a good ride."

"Jewel Elizabeth Spencer. That is dirty talk." Leona slapped Jewel hard across the back of the head.

"Not as dirty as Donna likes apparently," Jewel retorted.

They met at midnight out back of Leona's house. They didn't need to converse, nor did they need a light. The October moon was big and bright in the sky and lit their path just fine. And anyway, they didn't need to go far, just a little way back up in the woods.

Leona kept a sharp eye out for any sign of the trouble that Kay had warned of but saw nothing. Jewel walked normally, unconcerned.

"Do you see anything, Jewel?"

"Nope," Jewel said. "Maybe Kay was just being dramatic."

"That's your way, not hers," Leona said. "We should be safe enough once we get to the circle."

When they reached the little place Leona had cleared out

for spells, they went to work. Jewel poured them a circle of brick dust. Leona placed a handful of millet in four places on the circle. She made up a little fire bundle and sat down on the ground. Jewel finished the circle then sat opposite Leona and nodded.

Leona lit the fire, blew on it to bring it to life, then took a deep breath. She mixed up several herbs. She tossed a handful of the mixture in the flame. Leona used her good sharp knife to cut her palm and squeezed some of her blood into the fire. It flared up, and she felt a rush of magic. It tingled all over, and she smiled. It was such a pleasant, good feeling. How could anything she did with it be bad?

Leona handed the mixture and the knife to Jewel, who repeated Leona's movements, and then they asked the spirits to help them into Ed's dreams.

It took a few minutes, and they had to add a couple more handfuls of blood and herbs. But soon Leona got a funny feeling in her stomach, and the trees and bushes of the forest faded away.

She found herself in Ed and Donna's bedroom. Donna snored as her great mass heaved and sighed under the quilts. Ed tossed and turned, a worried look on his face. Jewel popped in beside her and they linked hands, the ones they'd cut, and both focused on Ed.

After a few seconds, Ed mumbled then sat up in bed and opened his eyes. They had a hazy look, unfocused. Leona nodded, and Jewel squeezed their palms together. They were gone from the bedroom. When Leona looked around, she found herself in the diner. She wasn't behind the counter. She was sitting beside Ed, with Jewel on his other side. The diner was its normal busy morning self, and Leona scowled when she saw a dream version of herself pour Ed his coffee. With a much shorter uniform dress and a bigger bosom that strained at the buttons, the Dream Leona smiled at Ed and winked.

"Coffee's fresh, hon," the buxom, Dream Leona said.

Leona's cheeks burned. She would never speak to Ed that way.

Leona heard Jewel cackle. "Lookee at you, Leona."

"You hush up, Jewel," Leona whispered. She turned to Ed. "Hey, Ed."

Ed never took his eyes off the Dream Leona, but he nodded and opened his mouth to speak. Nothing came out, but Leona could read his lips, saying, *Yep*.

"Listen, Ed. Mary Silvus. Tomorrow, you're gonna get an idea to search graveyards. You'll find Mary at the Ave Maria. You got it?"

Ed nodded and mouthed *Ave Maria*.

"Good," Leona said. She looked over at Jewel. "That should do it, you think?"

Jewel nodded. She elbowed Ed. "Listen here, Ed, about Donna—"

"Jewel!" Leona yelled. The dream space rippled as their concentration broke. Leona breathed in deep and stabilized it, then she scowled at Jewel and snapped her fingers.

They were back in Ed and Donna's bedroom. Ed closed his eyes and flopped back on the bed. Donna's snores never stopped, and the force of Ed falling back into his pillow didn't disturb her in the slightest. The bedroom faded out, and Leona stared into the dying fire. She shook herself awake. Across the fire, Jewel did the same. When they made eye contact, Leona narrowed her eyes and pointed her finger at Jewel. "Not one word, Jewel."

Jewel slapped her knee and laughed for a bit, but she agreed. "Fine."

They set to cleaning up the circle. As Jewel was about to

sweep the brick away, an icy wind whistled through the trees. Off in the distance, Leona heard a wolf howl, and she got a prickly feeling. She remembered Kay's warning and put a worried hand on Jewel's arm. "Wait."

Jewel stopped and looked around the glade. "Somebody here?"

Leona scanned the tree line but couldn't see anyone. Still, she could feel someone watching them. Her skin was all goosebumps, and a strong smell of rot and animal hit her.

"Whoever's out there, we don't mean you no harm," Leona called. "We're leaving. You need help, you find me in the morning."

The underbrush crackled and snapped, and something stalked around the circle. It was big from the noise it made, and Leona's heart jumped up in her throat. She and Jewel put down their bags and prepared for a fight. The thing growled long and low, and Leona saw eyes, big and yellow, glimmer in the dying fire. She rubbed her hands together then inched them apart as a red ball of light formed between them.

"Go on and leave us be. We're not here to do you harm. Go on now," Leona said, her voice calm and even. She concentrated on the ball in her hands, and it crackled with energy.

The thing in the underbrush growled louder, and Leona shook her head. "All right, but it don't gotta be like this." She let loose of the red ball, and it flew into the underbrush. The big thing snarled then yelped as the red ball flew all around, pelting it with shocks.

"Run," Leona said. Jewel took off, and Leona sent another ball at the thing before she followed. She made it to the house and joined an out of breath Jewel. "Kay was right."

Jewel nodded. "What do you reckon that was?"

"Don't know," Leona said, "but it was big, and I think it meant business."

"Smelled funny too. Like when that cur of Daddy's used to roll in dead things. If it comes back, I'll blast it into next week." Jewel's face was grim and determined. She meant it.

"Come on. Let's go inside." Leona put a hand on Jewel's back and guided her inside. She got a familiar feeling of magic and turned, smiling, thinking it was Cale, but when she turned back toward the woods, she saw Mary Silvus standing just at the edge of the trees, glaring at her. Her vision tunneled in on the ghost, and her mouth went dry.

Leona heard a pop, and Cale appeared beside Leona.

"Go. I'll watch her."

Leona put her hand out to him and felt his cold. "No, she can't come in. I got a ward up."

"Then why can I come in?" Cale asked.

"Because I buried a counter in your grave," Leona said.

"She's strong. Strong enough to break the mirror," Jewel said. "But the ward's holding good."

"What makes you think your ward will keep her out?" Cale asked.

"Cause she ain't here right now," Leona said as she motioned to the trees. "It rings the house. Nobody can come in without my say. It's holding. At least for now."

Mary Silvus banged herself against the barrier. She stalked around it, testing the strength. When she couldn't get through, she stopped, and she screamed her silent rage. The force of it strained the heavy black thread that sewed her mouth shut, and Leona was hit with a blast of frigid air. Mary tried to back up, but she met another barrier. She screamed and banged against it. She was trapped between the warding rings Leona and Jewel had cast. Mary stalked back and forth, growling and occasionally clawing at the field of magic.

Cale shook his head. "I swear. Lee, you ever seen a ghost do that?"

Leona shook her head. "Nope."

"Serves her right," Jewel said. "Now she's stuck in between them circles." She pointed in Mary's general direction and laughed.

"Jewel. Really?" Cale huffed at Jewel's taunting.

"I wish I'd thought of this years ago with you, Cale," Jewel said, batting her eyelashes in his general direction.

"Enough. We need to go see about that mirror. I wanna know how she broke it so quick," Leona said.

"Maybe she didn't," Cale said.

Jewel stuck her tongue out at Mary one last time as they headed into the house.

"Cale, you're gonna have to go room up with Jewel for a bit."

Both Jewel and Cale yelled.

"Oh no, I ain't!"

"Oh no, he ain't!"

Leona held up a hand against their mutual protests. "He can't be where she is. If she gets through, she'll absorb him and then . . ." Leona got a funny feeling in her gut as she thought about watching Mary take Cale the way she took William and the other children at the Ave Maria.

Both Cale and Jewel quieted, resigned to the logic.

"Fine. But I'm going home tonight, and if Cale haunts me and annoys me, just know I got plenty of mirrors." Jewel grabbed her things. "Let's go."

Cale held up his palm to Leona. She put hers up, mirroring his and felt the cold air between them that passed for a caress.

"Be careful," he said, smiling at her. "Call me if you need me."

He disappeared, and Leona heard Jewel cuss about the cold air as she started her truck and tore off down the road.

S mells like a great big wet dog mixed up with a dead
possum," Jewel said as she pulled her scarf up over her
nose. "And . . . I swear Leona, piss."

Leona scowled at the language, but she couldn't disagree
with Jewel's assessment. The garden shack had the stank of
urine all about it in addition to a strange funk that reminded
her of several other smells, none of which she had ever smelled
mashed up together.

Jewel held up a shard of the mirror, which had been
smashed to bits. "You reckon she broke it from the other side?"

"I don't know, but don't seem like she could. Never
heard tell of it," Leona said. She knelt and checked the
salt circle. The circle should have held Mary even if the

mirror did not, but somebody had cleared the ward by brushing the salt and herbs aside. "Somebody scuffed the circle."

Jewel looked where Leona pointed. "How would anybody even know it was here to scuff it?"

"Somebody was expecting magic, I'd say." Leona stood up and examined the mirror. The size of the hole and the way it was spider-webbed suggested to Leona that somebody smashed it with a big fist.

"Yeah, but my blind ward is the best they is. Can't nobody see it. Nobody." Jewel was huffy. She didn't like her spells being countered.

"I guess some things maybe don't need to see to know there's magic about. Well, no use crying about it now." Leona held up a bit of the mirror. "We're gonna have to think of something else. I brought a mirror out there today, and Mary popped off to somewhere else. I guess we ain't getting her twice with that trick."

"Leave it to Mary Silvus to be a smart and murderous ghost. Where you reckon she pops off to?" Jewel asked.

"Don't know. I guess I don't know how it works for all of 'em. I just know Cale."

"I highly doubt he's typical," Jewel said.

The air in the shed chilled, and Jewel rolled her eyes. "Cale, if you don't quit doing that to me, I'm gonna sage you into Hell."

Cale appeared next to Leona. "You think I do that just to you? I can't help the chill, Jewel."

"Well then, stay far from me. Not every Spencer woman wants you shoved up their—"

"Jewel! Really." Leona huffed and left the shed.

"Well, they don't!" Jewel huffed in return as she followed. "So what are we gonna do now? Mary has help."

Leona nodded. "Yes, she does. Somebody who knows magic."

"What if Mary can just pop in wherever you are?" Cale asked. "You ain't gonna be safe."

"I don't think she can, otherwise she'd be here right now," Jewel said. "But who knows how long that will last? I say we fry her and be done with it."

"I won't. Not until I have to. And I want to talk to Granny Kay first."

"I agree that Kay may have some answers, but it's too late for that," Jewel said. "What if Mary decides to get crazy at her funeral? People could get hurt."

"We're gonna be there to make sure that don't happen," Leona said.

Jewel sighed and shook her head. "I was afraid you was gonna say that."

16

L eona knew something as soon as she saw Mary Silvus
all torn up on that cross. She knew that when Ed
Wagner saw it, he wouldn't know what to do about it,
and it would eat him alive.

Things like that didn't happen in Ames. Drunks had to be
wrangled. Sometimes people stole. If somebody died, it was
drowning in the river or old age or a car accident. That's what
Ed had to deal with, not women beheaded and torn open.

It showed. When he sat down at her counter, Ed was a
mess. He hadn't shaved. He normally wore a neat mustache,
but it was unkempt, and the dark stubble of his beard showed
in stark contrast to his pasty white skin. His eyes were glassy

and bloodshot. He looked like a man who hadn't slept in a week.

Leona poured him a cup of coffee and set his usual order down in front of him. The diner was eerily quiet. Her normal customers were there, but as soon as Ed walked in and sat down, they all stopped talking, and the only noise was the scrape of utensils against the plates as everyone ate in silence.

"He looks awful," Cale said. "Like he'll never get over finding that girl. Wrong profession for him."

Leona didn't know about that. Ed was patient and smart and caring. He looked out for the people of the county and kept everyone in line, pretty much as much as anyone could. Nobody could be expected to see what had been done to Mary Silvus and go on about their life as if nothing happened. You couldn't fully understand that kind of carnage existed in the world unless you saw it, and most people never did.

"It's gonna be all right, Ed," Leona said as she freshened his coffee.

Ed looked up at her, and his eyes were moist, like he was on the verge of tears. "I don't even know where to start, Lee. How am I gonna find the monster that did that?"

Leona patted his hand. "Start at the end."

His eyes searched hers. "What?"

"You start there. At the end. Thing like that . . . it means something, Ed. A person who does a thing like that, they . . . they're . . . they meant all of it. Start there and see if they left any clues behind."

"We searched the place. Didn't find anything. Not even her blood."

Leona shrugged. "You ever butchered a hog, Ed? My daddy never wasted no blood, but he still couldn't get all of it."

Ed's eyes lit up just a little. "He moved her."

"I ain't the detective, Ed."

"I never seen anything like that," Ed said. "Who can do that? Who can break off concrete like that cross?"

"Well, that's a fair place to start, I'd say. Normal person would need something, I reckon."

Ed's eyes lit up a little more. "Tools."

Leona nodded. "Sounds like you maybe know where to start after all." She watched as Ed slurped his coffee and ate a little of his eggs. She could see the wheels turning in his brain as he chewed. A light had come back to his eyes, and from the set of his jaw, Leona knew that he had some of his confidence back.

She also knew it was not a crime Ed Wagner could solve, at least not on his own. Whoever had killed Mary Silvus wasn't an ordinary person. If they were a person at all. Ed had never dealt with a crime that approached this one, and he had certainly never dealt with anything as malevolent as the thing that had killed Mary and cursed her ghost. Leona wasn't sure anyone had. The bottom line was that Ed was going to need her help, and she was going to need some help as well. At least Leona knew where to start. Ed had no clue.

When he finished his eggs, Leona brought him the check. She noticed him eyeing Dorval as she counted back his change.

Dorval looked even worse than Ed. His cheeks were sunken in, and his skin sallow and thin looking. Leona could see every bone in his face and arms, and his hands shook as he sipped his glass of water.

"He been coming in regular still?" Ed asked.

"Yes. Same as always," Leona said. She finished with Ed's change. "Dorval Ring wouldn't hurt a fly, Ed."

"I don't know that to be a fact, Leona. Don't know that at all."

"Ed, don't go looking for things that ain't there. Focus on the ones that are."

Ed snapped his head up and looked at Leona. His eyes narrowed, and he pouted a bit, which told Leona she had pushed him as far as she dared that day. You could only tell a man he was wrong so many times a day before he became unmanageable.

"I guess I know how to do my job just fine," Ed said. He got up from the counter, jammed his hat on his head, and stared down Dorval.

"I know you do, Ed," Leona said. Leona came around the counter and put a hand on his arm. "We all know you do."

He looked down at her, and his face softened.

Leona smiled at him and patted him before she stepped away. "Mind you take care of yourself, Ed."

He nodded and tipped his hat to her then strode out the door.

Throughout the years, Leona had been to the Powell Funeral home many times. Her mother died when she was five. Her brothers, Layman Jr. and Albert, had both been killed in a mine cave-in when she was seven. Her sister Opal died in a car crash, and her sister Beryl died having a baby. They couldn't even have a funeral for her other brothers, Darcy and Dillard. They'd died in 1941 on Guadalcanal, some island far off in the Pacific. There had been nothing to ship back, so they had just put up a marker in the cemetery.

Leona hadn't cried for anyone else but Dill. She'd looked for him everywhere after that. Stayed by his grave, hoping to catch him and talk to him again. She wasn't sure how it all worked, why she could see some dead people and not others, why some of them lingered for a long time and some faded away right after, so Leona couldn't even wrap her mind around what had happened to Mary Silvus, save that some very powerful person cursed her.

Mary could not break the plane around Leona's house. Leona had not seen the ghost at all, which was concerning. Mary wasn't gone; Leona knew that. How Leona knew it, she couldn't have said other than she felt an emptiness when one of the spirits left her, and it was distinct to that ghost. She could still feel Mary, her rage, her fear, and she knew that the ghost was still out there somewhere, trying to get to her.

Leona went to the McClure Funeral home well prepared to deal with an unruly spirit. She had her special bottle of salt and a sage bundle Jewel had worked up with a little extra oomph, since Mary seemed surly.

"Leona, how are we gonna do anything in this funeral home? We can't just start a fight with a ghost during a eulogy," Jewel said.

"That's why we're going early. I figure we block the main doors and windows and she ain't gonna be able to do anything if she is of a mind."

"Yeah, well, we don't even know if all that's gonna work. This is beyond us, Leona."

"Yes. I know. I'm going out to Granny Kay's. I just need to get through this service, and then we'll go."

"I don't know. Do you think she even knows anything about getting rid of a surly ghost?"

"Well, if Kay don't know, then nobody does," Leona said. She parked the truck a bit down the street from the funeral home. Jewel adjusted her lipstick in the mirror.

"Wipe it off, Jewel," Leona said as she handed Jewel a handkerchief from her purse. "You know that color will set them off in there. We're here to help, not to make Shirley call the Law on us."

Jewel huffed. "Shirley Silvus can . . ." Jewel paused and looked at Leona, who raised an eyebrow and held out the handkerchief. Jewel sighed and took it. "Fine," she said as she wiped most of the lipstick off. "I guess it don't do to antagonize nobody at a funeral, not even her mean ass."

"Watch that mouth, Jewel Elizabeth," Leona growled.

They walked all around the Powell Funeral home. Jewel blocked every door with the salt ward and Leona cast a few extra protection spells and spirit blocks, the same as she had around her house.

They straightened their dresses and hats before they went in.

"What if she's already in here and we just fenced her in?" Jewel whispered as they entered.

"Well, then I reckon it will be an eventful funeral," Leona said.

The lights were dimmed, but even at their brightest, most of the light was natural. And with few windows, the Powell Funeral home was a foreboding place. It had always been that way: dark, unnecessarily so, Leona thought. She understood the need for the muted light, but she also believed there was little need to make it more ominous than it already was.

Somebody was playing the organ. Not even the Church had an organ; all they had was a beat-up piano donated by Martha Joy's husband when she passed. The organ was the fanciest musical instrument in Denton County, and it was the pride of Old Gaffney Powell, who had it transported in pieces at the turn of the century. He wanted a draw to his business, which was laughable because it was the only funeral parlor in three counties.

Jewel and Leona made their way in, and each signed the

guest register: Leona's script neat and precise, Jewel's flashy and swirly. Leona took a funeral card. She went to hand one to Jewel, and Jewel waved her off.

"We don't need but one. They make you pay for them."

Leona shook her head but didn't argue as they filed into the room. They took seats in the back, to go unnoticed, but it was Ames. Shirley's gang of gossip hens were looking out since Shirley was indisposed in her grief. They all turned in their seats, and their scandalized eyes widened as they mouthed, *well-I-never*s.

"Bunch of old biddies," Jewel whispered. She scowled back at them, and Leona elbowed her.

"This ain't about that, Jewel. Don't start nothing."

"I never start it. I just finish it."

Leona shook her head. "Not today." She looked around the room. All the family was there, all the ladies from the Lydia Circle at the Church, the mayor even. Leona figured they were all there for the spectacle. It wasn't every day in Ames there was a funeral for a murdered girl. It was a closed casket, of course. Leona had heard the gossip, and everyone was saying how they had found Mary in pieces and marked all up with Satanic signs. Leona had been the only one to see Mary, and while she knew those rumors were fabrications of a gossip mill, there was no way they could do an open casket funeral. Ed still hadn't found her head.

The organist played on, and when she started a requiem, Shirley Silvus wailed. Her hens flew to her, and they wailed too. There was a solid twenty minutes of crying and screaming, but they all hushed and composed themselves when the Reverend Asa Greenleaf, pastor of the church, took to the little pulpit. He bowed his head for a moment and paused. His lips moved in a silent prayer spoken to nobody but himself. When he raised his head, Leona saw something in Reverend Greenleaf's eyes she had never seen before: fervor. His eyes flashed, angry and wide.

"In these times, we have to listen to our Father. And He speaks through this man like nobody I have ever seen. Brother Levi, please. We need you in this hour." Greenleaf looked heavenward when he called, but nobody came from above. Instead, he came from the back of the room, moving down the aisle and toward the pulpit casually, as if he was out for a Sunday stroll. Greenleaf's face was beatific, and he jittered with excitement as he watched the man. Leona had never seen Asa Greenleaf this excited about anything, and it immediately raised her suspicions.

Levi Walker was one of the best-looking men Leona had ever seen. He had big brown eyes, sad and thoughtful, yet fierce and intense. His sandy blond hair had curls and waves and was unruly and flowing, hitting his collar just right. His face was perfectly smooth and chiseled, like a movie star's, and he was tall and fit. He wore a collar but no jacket. His sleeves were neatly rolled to his elbows, as if he were ready to get to work. And that was exactly what he did. He got to work.

"Now, I know, sisters and brothers . . . I know you're sad. You grieve." He turned and looked at the coffin behind him then nodded as he turned back to the crowd. "You feel that something was taken from you. Mary was sweet and innocent and beautiful."

Jewel gave a little snort beside her, then whispered. "Innocent? Not hardly."

"Shush," Leona said. She couldn't take her eyes off the preacher.

"But I can tell you this, brothers and sisters, nothing was taken from you."

The crowd mumbled and murmured. Levi held up his

hands, then pointed a finger and shook it in the *no-no* gesture at them all.

"Nothing was taken from you because Mary Silvus was never yours. Mary Silvus belonged to the Almighty Father. Mary Silvus belonged to Jesus, our savior. Mary Silvus belonged to the Holy Ghost. She was not yours. No, no, no, indeed she was not! She belonged to the Lord, our God, and He called Mary home."

He waved his hands around and sometimes gripped the edges of the lectern so hard the skin went white. His eyes flashed and danced as he spoke, and they darted about the room, contacting every single person there. Levi was a masterful speaker. He began to rant and rave and quote obscure scripture.

The crowd yelled and screamed "Amen!" after nearly every sentence. They fed off his energy, and the more animated he got, the more riled up they became. The Old Biddies fell to their knees around Shirley and waved their hands in the air. One man began dancing up the aisle, yelling gibberish and crying. More followed suit, and soon, Levi Walker had the room of mourners riled up into screaming, Pentecost-filled jubilants. Leona and Jewel were the only ones not flailing about.

Levi scanned the room, breathing heavily and pleased with himself. Leona could see the glee in his eyes at what he'd done and the power that he wielded so effortlessly. She sensed something else, a dark energy that surrounded him. It was equal parts intoxicating and terrifying.

"He don't preach at the church," Leona whispered.

"No. He's that Revival hack from over at Shadyside," Jewel said. "I heard Shirley and all her biddies is keen for him."

Levi made eye contact with Leona, and Leona shivered. His eyes lasered in on her. For a second she felt connected to him, and she knew she didn't want to be. She grabbed Jewel's hand. "Let's go. Now."

"We ain't gonna stay for all of it? That seems—ow!"

Jewel yelped when Leona pinched her. "All right already, let's go. You ain't got to pinch, Ida Mae."

They got up to leave, and Levi's voice boomed louder.

"The devil is here, among us, and he uses many tricks and deceits. Give yourself up to the Lord! Renounce sinful ways and witchcraft! For if you do not . . . you will surely perish and be consumed by the ever-burning flames of retribution!"

"Is he talking to us?" Jewel whispered.

"I don't know," Leona said. But she did know. Leona suddenly felt sick. She bent over as waves of nausea hit her.

Jewel helped her stand up and supported her. "It's him, Lee."

"Yes," Leona nodded as she clutched her stomach and let Jewel lead her out. From the pulpit, Levi Walker smiled and winked at her as she and Jewel made their way through the maze of folding chairs and out of the funeral chapel.

18

Leona was fixing up the saltshakers and sugar caddies with her back to the door of the diner when the bell tinkled, signaling customers. Her stomach lurched, and a feeling of unease washed over her, leaving her with a queasy feeling and an immediate worry that wrinkled her brow. When she turned around, saw who had entered, she understood why.

Reverend Asa Greenleaf came in, ushering Levi Walker and showing him around as if he was visiting royalty. He puffed out his chest and motioned with his hands all formal-like. Greenleaf was on the wrong side of middle age, dumpy, with a pot belly, beady eyes, and a sparse comb-over. He was the opposite of Levi Walker, who was tall and muscular. His sleeves were rolled up again, as if he had work to do, and Leona saw the corded muscles ripple as he shook hands with a few of her customers before he and Greenleaf sat down in the best booth. Greenleaf continued to explain about Ames, but Levi Walker said nothing. He just smiled and nodded. When he caught Leona's eye, his cocked his head and his flat smile turned into a smirk for a split second, then he changed back to a normal smile without any threat. Leona knew she had just seen him in his true form, and her stomach rolled again.

Everyone in town had heard about Mary's funeral and about the charismatic, handsome preacher. Henry Barker and Dan White clapped Levi on the shoulder. Joseph Biehl offered to pay for their breakfast. Levi Walker fielded every admirer like a Hollywood actor walking the red carpet at a movie premier. He smiled and made everyone feel like he knew them personally. His charm flittered on to everyone in the room, and they all adored him. Everyone except Leona. Leona wanted to vomit.

She took a few breaths and calmed herself then grabbed two glasses of water and her coffee pot. She smiled her best smile as she set the glasses down and poured up the coffee.

"Good morning, Reverend," Leona said.

Asa Greenleaf had no love for Leona. Like all the folks in that church, he distrusted Leona and Jewel and yet, he was usually polite.

He motioned to Walker. "Leona, this is Reverend Levi Walker."

Leona tried to smile at Levi, but it came hard. She had a feeling it didn't look genuine. Levi's eyes seemed to bore right through her, and though he gave her a beaming smile, all perfect teeth, his eyes were cold. And Leona thought that if she stared into them too long, something would come out of them and steal her breath.

Levi stood up from the table, bowed a little, and took Leona's hand in both his as she shook it. His hand was too warm, almost burning warm to her skin, and his grip was strong. It felt like he was searing her flesh. Leona grimaced but kept her smile, and she didn't flinch.

"I'm blessed to meet you, Miss Leona," he said. Levi sat back down and smiled at her as he sipped his coffee.

"Likewise," Leona said. She took their orders. Greenleaf was terse, as usual, his tone barely tolerant of her. Levi Walker was pleasant and gentle, but those dead eyes of his stared daggers into her. Leona's head pounded, and she had a funny whooshing sound in her ears.

"Miss Leona, are you alright?" Levi stood up and put a hand on the small of her back. She jumped and almost dropped the coffee.

"Yes, yes. Fine. Be right back with your breakfast," Leona said. She walked back into the kitchen and bent over as she tried to calm her pounding head and rolling stomach. Cale popped in beside her.

"Something's not right with him," Cale said.

"You're right," Leona said. Levi Walker unnerved her in a way she had never experienced before, and she was shaken. She bent over and breathed deeply to center herself.

Leona righted herself and peeked out. Levi stared at them. He got up and came to the door.

"Miss Leona, you sure you're all right?" His enormous frame blocked the door, and Leona had a slightly panicked feeling that she should run. The air temperature dropped again as Cale got agitated.

"I'm fine. Just tired, I reckon," Leona said. She put the orders up and tried her best to smile.

"You're quite busy, I hear. Three jobs, plus a husband and a child."

Leona's stomach dropped. It was a small town. Everyone knew everyone's business. It wasn't shocking that Greenleaf or one of the old biddies would have told about her. It was the three jobs comment that bothered her.

"Well sir, the Lord helps them what helps themselves," Leona said.

"Indeed, He does, Miss Leona." Levi looked in Cale's direction and smiled, then he looked back to Leona and bowed. "I look forward to helping you any way that I can," he said. He left and went back to his booth.

"Leona?" Cale's voice sounded small and far away and scared.

She swallowed down a bit of bile and took three breaths to calm down before she answered the question he didn't need to ask. "Yes. I know he can see you," she said.

19

W hat do you mean he seen Cale?" Jewel asked. She leaned in the doorframe of Leona's kitchen as Leona stirred her cabbage and potatoes.

"Well, Jewel, I mean, he could see Cale, with his eyeballs, and knew Cale was there. What do you think I mean?" Leona rolled her eyes and wiped the sweat from her forehead. She checked the clock. Bob would be home in a few minutes and having food ready was at least one way to avoid a fight. She sliced off a ham steak and put it in the frying pan to crisp up.

"Well, how is that even possible?" Jewel asked. "We never met nobody else could do it. I can't even do it." It had always been a sore spot with Jewel that she couldn't see the ghosts and communicate like Leona could. Jewel could hear Cale, but she couldn't see him, and she could sometimes hear others if they made their presence known, but the ghosts didn't come to her, they didn't choose her, and it seemed to stem from a magic Jewel did not possess. She had a hard time accepting that.

Leona was the only person they knew of that could see and talk to a ghost like they were regular folks, as if she'd run into them down at the Woolworths and passed the time of day to be polite.

"How should I know the answer to that? He just can, I reckon." She heard the truck pull up in the drive and she nodded at Jewel. "That's Bob."

Jewel rolled her eyes. "So? I ain't a bit afraid of Bob Monroe."

"Jewel," Leona sighed, "I don't need no fights right now."

"If Bob don't start one, there won't be one."

Leona stopped and looked at Jewel, then quirked an eyebrow. Jewel rolled her eyes again and huffed.

"Fine. I gotta go anyway. What do you wanna do next?"

"I don't for sure know. I'll come by tomorrow." Leona put the ham steak on a plate and dished out some cabbage and potatoes. She set them down at Bob's place, then made up some potatoes and cabbage for herself and Peggy. Peggy came bounding into the kitchen with a headless doll. She sniffed at the cabbage and started yowling.

"I don't even like no cabbage!" she screamed.

Bob burst into the kitchen, scowling. By his slightly off-kilter motion, Leona knew he'd been down at the Legion in Middleberg drinking all afternoon. It wouldn't be a peaceful night.

Bob narrowed his eyes and pointed at Jewel. "What's she

doing here? Why do I always gotta come home to shit in this house?"

Leona shook her head when she saw Jewel ball up her fists and start to curse Bob. "Jewel was just dropping off something. She ain't got the time to stay." She inclined her head, begging for Jewel to back off.

"That's right. I ain't got time to stay," Jewel said through clenched teeth. "I'll see you later, Leona."

"See that you don't!" Bob yelled, his mouth full of ham and cabbage. Some of it fell out on the table. "Get me a beer."

Leona shoved Jewel out the door and pulled a beer from the refrigerator for Bob. She sat down next to Peggy and eyed her. "Peggy, stop crying and eat, or you can go to your room."

Peggy knocked the bowl of cabbage off on to the floor and kicked the table.

"By God, I'm getting the belt," Bob yelled. He stood up and went to take off his belt, but he wobbled and sat back down.

"Bob, just eat." Leona grabbed Peggy and hauled her kicking and screaming back to her room. "Missy, you can stay in here and not have any supper if you're gonna act that way."

"I want some ice cream," Peggy screamed, throwing what meager toys she had around the room. She grabbed a teddy bear and ripped its arm off, then pulled the stuffing out as she cried.

"Margaret Elizabeth Monroe, that is enough!" Leona grabbed the teddy bear and yanked it away from Peggy. She put the child facing the corner. Peggy turned around and screamed in her face.

Leona wanted to cry herself. She had never spoiled Peggy. Peggy had just always been . . . Peggy. Obstinate, sneaky, reactive. When she behaved it was under threats, which was not how Leona liked to operate, but she really didn't see as she had much choice. She grabbed Peggy's face and held it firm as she narrowed her eyes and stared into her daughter's. "Now you listen to me, right here and now. You are gonna stand in this corner and be quiet. If you don't, I'm gonna go cut a switch. Do you understand me?"

Peggy grabbed her bottom and big tears welled up in her brown eyes. "I didn't even do anything to get the switch."

"You did too. And if you don't stand here and be quiet, you'll get more than the switch." The air temperature in the room dropped. Cale popped in beside her.

Peggy shivered, but at the cold she nodded and put her nose in the corner, sniffing and giving little *boo hoo*s every once in a while.

"My mother would have whupped the tar out of me," Cale said as they left the room.

Leona shut the door. "I don't like spanking," she said. "And anyway, she feeds off of Bob."

Cale scowled. "He better not—"

Leona held up a hand. "He hasn't done anything."

Cale looked back the hallway to the kitchen. Leona turned her head and sighed as she heard Bob bitching, slurring his words. She turned back to Cale. "Go on back to Jewel's and stop popping over here. It's too dangerous."

Cale sighed himself and nodded. "I hope Bob chokes." He scowled and popped off.

Leona went back to the kitchen. Bob had finished his dinner and two more beers in the time it took her to deal with Peggy.

"That girl needs beat."

Leona sat down and ate a bit. "She's just . . ." Leona paused. She really couldn't defend Peggy, except to say she was too much like Bob to manage. She shrugged and went back to her dinner.

Bob slammed his beer can down. "By God, I'm gonna go

back there and whup her 'til she got some manners." He tried to get up from the table, but Leona waved her hand. His chair wouldn't budge. She continued to eat as he fussed around at the chair and struggled to stand. Finally he yelled and threw his plate against the wall, smashing it just like Peggy had done with hers.

Leona looked upward and closed her eyes as she tried to maintain her calm. After a few seconds, she opened her eyes and went back to her food, ignoring Bob as he yelled. When she finished eating, she got up and set about cleaning the kitchen. She relaxed the hex on Bob's chair, and he stumbled to his feet. Bob looked in the refrigerator and slammed it shut.

"There ain't no more beer!"

"Is that so?" Leona asked as she picked up the shattered dishes. She found herself jerked off the floor and spun around. Bob's fist clocked her on her ear, then he slapped her so hard she fell back down on the linoleum.

"I'm done with your lip tonight." He was breathing hard from the effort, and when he picked up his foot to kick her in the ribs, he teetered, pausing just long enough for Leona to get a hand up and cast a field around herself. Bob's foot stopped six inches from her, and the force of it hitting the field pushed him back. He tottered and fell on his back.

"Sonofabitch. Leona, I'm gonna—"

His words cut off, and he clutched at his throat as Leona's spell choked him. She got to her feet, her ear ringing, as the anger rolled off her in waves. She clenched her fist over and over as he choked. Two voices yelled in her head. One voice screamed that she should stop it, that she was killing him. The other voice laughed and told her to choke him harder. That voice was winning. As her ear throbbed and her face burned, she heard a tiny voice from the hallway.

"Mama?"

Peggy's voice snapped her out of it, and she let go with the magic. Bob sucked in a big breath and coughed. Leona went to help him up.

"Is Daddy dyin'?" Peggy sniffed.

"No, Daddy just had a piece of ham go down the wrong pipe." She got Bob situated in the kitchen chair then went to Peggy. "Everything's all right. It's bedtime though, so you go on back and brush your hair and put on your nightgown. I'll be back in a few minutes."

Peggy looked between them and seemed to understand she wanted nothing to do with it. She nodded and walked back the hallway to her room.

Bob stared at her. The expression on his face was a mixture of fear, hatred, and inadequacy. No combination of things could be more dangerous. Bob's hands twitched. Leona felt grateful he'd sold their shotgun months ago when he had needed beer money. He would have killed her then. Leona pulled a jar of the blue memory charm dust from her herb chifforobe. She scooped out a handful and blew it in Bob's face.

His eyes went cloudy. His face relaxed, and when his eyes cleared, the only emotion Leona read in them was his normal disdain for her. That she could manage.

"Make sure you get some beer tomorrow," he said as he rubbed his neck and stared past her. After a few minutes, he spat on the floor, then got up and left. She heard the old truck cough and whine as he drove off.

Leona cried, disgusted with herself for a variety of reasons as she finished cleaning up the mess. She tucked Peggy in bed then went outside and stared out at the woods.

Since that night they'd done the spell, she hadn't seen or heard anything more from the big thing in the woods. She was more worried about Mary Silvus at the moment. The first few days she had seen Mary prowling, testing the edge of the spell and screaming through her sewn up mouth. When she got close to the tree line, she felt the anger and magic.

Even Peggy could sense something. She'd asked Leona to get her doll she'd left in the back yard. She wouldn't go back there. Leona supposed it was only a matter of time until Mary broke through. Leona's spell was powerful, but it wasn't permanent. She had to keep recasting it, and since that night, she'd come out every day and put up a fresh ward.

It was getting dark early now, and it was cold once the sun went down. Leona could see her breath puff slight white clouds against the blue-black of the late twilight. She shivered and wrapped her arms around herself. Her ear gradually stopped throbbing, and her cheek cooled. She scanned the woods. She saw nothing. She felt him before she saw him, as Cale pooped in beside her.

Leona nodded as she hugged herself against the chill. "The wards are strong. Maybe I ought to put up a few more rings."

"Couldn't hurt," Cale said. "Where do you reckon she goes?"

"Don't know. Where do you go?"

"For me, I always know where you are. I can go there. I can go back to my grave. I can go where you say to."

"Could you go back to where you died?"

Cale shook his head. "Never tried. Wouldn't want to, but even if I did, I ain't sure I could. It's far. That one time I popped to where you was at over at Dephi took it out of me, and that was only fifty miles. If I had to go clear to Kansas, I don't know what would happen."

Leona nodded. "Seems about right." They stood in companionable silence for a while, each just feeling better because the other was there. Still, a heaviness hung between them. "You gonna say something?"

"What's there to say?"

Leona turned to him. Cale's face fell when he saw the enormous bruise that had already welled up on her face. He reached his hand up to touch it, cupping Leona's cheek without contact. She dropped her head and sighed.

"I almost killed him, Cale."

"Good," Cale said. "I'd kill him if I could."

"It was easy. If Peggy hadn't been there, I think I'd have choked him dead."

"It's better than he deserves," Cale said. "Leave him."

"And go where?" Leona threw up her hands. "I barely got enough money put back to pay the bank for the house and buy groceries."

"He don't generate money."

"No, but everything is in his name. I can't even get a bank account. And I sure can't afford no divorce."

"Jewel will help."

"If I wanted to poison him, sure. But to help with all the other things? Jewel ain't steady sometimes."

Cale nodded. "He's gonna push you to do something, Lee. You wanna be pushed or you wanna do the pushing?"

"It ain't really about him, Cale. It scared me tonight. What I did. No matter what, I can't use magic like that again. It's like you lose a bit of yourself you can't never get back."

"If something happens to you . . ." Cale's voice choked and broke.

"That's just it. I think the only real danger to me here is me. Do you understand?"

"No," Cale said as he shook his head. "No, I don't."

Leona threw up her hands. "Well, I don't know. I just know I don't wanna be that kind. You can lose yourself to this thing, and I don't ever want to be that person."

"You could never."

"But I could! I almost was tonight."

"He deserves so much worse."

"Deserve ain't got nothing to do with it. Lots deserve worse than they get, that don't mean I need to be the one to give it to them."

She didn't want him to keep telling her she was good and better. It wasn't true, and it reeked of naivety and falsehoods. It made her sick. She turned back to him and squared her shoulders.

"Best help you can be to me right about now is to go back to Jewel's and stay there."

"Bob?"

"You know not to get in the middle of it."

Leona spat those words with more meanness than she meant to and decided it was a second character failing of the night. Cale's eyes saddened, and his lip quivered just a little, like a child's, But he nodded.

"All right then." He popped off and left Leona shivering in the night.

The rest of the evening she spent cleaning and making up some tinctures that her monthly customers would be coming for soon. It was past eleven when she went to bed, and Bob still wasn't home. The only part of it that worried her any was that Bob was sure to be in a state when he finally came home.

She had just dozed off when she heard Bob come in, banging around the hallway, bouncing off the walls like a cue ball. He threw open the bedroom door and crashed into a few things as he shucked off his clothes. She wrinkled her nose when his weight hit the bed. He smelled of cigarettes and rotgut and something else, like wet dog. Bob rolled around on the bed, bouncing them both around before he finally ended up pressed against her back.

She shut her eyes tight and cursed her luck when she felt his carrot perk up and stiffen against the back of her legs. He grunted a few times, and his breath was hot and vile against the back of her neck as he pressed himself against her and clutched at her backside. He'd keep worrying at her until she let him, so Leona rolled over. Bob fumbled at her nightgown and pushed it up past her waist. He fumbled at himself a bit and huffed around. He poked it at her, but from the feel of him, he wasn't all the way ready. He grunted in frustration and blew stinking alcohol air in her face. To speed up the process, Leona took his carrot in her hand and gave him a few squeezes. He immediately threw his head back and moaned. She rubbed him a bit and tried to avoid his heavy breaths, and he grunted his pleasure. When he was as stiff as she knew he could get, she let go. Bob grabbed himself and shoved it into her, moaning as he pumped against her.

He had given a few thrusts when she felt him go soft, and his grunts turned to frustration as he pulled back. He fumbled at himself more, and Leona tried helping again. But nothing could help this time. Finally Bob grabbed her hand and shoved it away. He flopped over on his back, and they lay there a while. She could sense the hate and anger rolling off him. Half relieved and half afraid of what that failure would make him do next, Leona rolled over to face the opposite direction. He tossed around a bit more, but finally, the liquor won over the carrot, and Bob began to snore.

Leona closed her eyes tight and prayed sleep would come for her too, but it did not. She lay awake all night and thought about all the things lurking around for her in the dark: ghosts, a sadistic murderer, and her hate-filled husband.

20

B ob left out as Leona was cooking up an egg sandwich for him.

"Don't want it," he spat out, not looking her in the eye as he slammed the screen door.

Leona heard the old truck start up and sighed. She'd have to walk to work. She ate the egg sandwich herself and made Peggy eat a few more spoons of oatmeal before she ushered her out the door and on to the school bus.

Her shift at the diner was uneventful, save she had to stay a little later than normal and was running behind in getting home to collect Peggy off the school bus. She just barely made it as the bus rolled up, and as she and Peggy walked up the drive to the house, she noticed the truck parked. The engine still ticked, and the hood was hot. She found him in the kitchen, drinking a beer. He looked right through them when they entered. Leona shoved Peggy down the hall to her room and went to put her tip money in the little tin she kept it in. When she opened it, there was nothing there. Leona had put back fifty dollars to pay the rent. She turned and looked at Bob, holding back tears as the angry magic swirled around her, begging her to let it loose on him.

"Bob, where's the rent money?" Leona asked through clenched teeth.

Bob finished his beer, got up from the table, and smacked Leona across the face. "Don't you question me about money."

The slap had been a solid one, but the pain of the blow barely registered. All Leona could think about was the missing money. That hit harder.

"That was all we had. What did you do with it?" Leona could hear her own voice, but it sounded deeper and with a strange echo that boomed through the kitchen and made Bob's eyes go white with terror. The voice was there, encouraging her to crush him, to rip him apart, and Leona want to do it, badly, but she couldn't. She wouldn't.

Instead she grabbed her pouch of yellow charm dust and blew a handful in Bob's angry face. "Bob, where is that money?"

"I owed it. I paid a debt."

"To who?"

Bob screamed and grabbed his head. He seemed to be fighting the charm. Leona blew another handful of dust in his face. "Who?"

"Galen Nolan!"

"Who is Galen Nolan?" Leona asked.

"He's . . . ah, oww, He's new in town. Runs some games."

"Was that all you owed him?"

"No. I owe him three hundred more."

Leona's heart sank. It would take her months to save up that much money. She thought right then just to let Galen Nolan, whoever he was, have Bob. But Bob had owed money before, plenty of times, and he hadn't been scared enough of anybody in Denton County to pay it back. If he was worried enough to pay this Galen Nolan, then Leona figured Galen Nolan must be a man you didn't not pay when you owed him.

Leona bent down and put a finger in Bob's face. "You lay a hand on me again, and it'll be the last thing you ever do. You understand me?"

Bob nodded.

"I should let him have at you, but something tells me it wouldn't end there. Where's this man stay?"

"He's taken over a holler, out by Covey Ridge."

Leona sighed and stood up. Covey Ridge was a mean place, and the hollers out that way were filled with nasty, dark things. If Galen Nolan pushed them out, he wasn't nobody to take lightly. Leona packed a bag for Peggy and put her in the truck. Bob followed her outside.

"Where do you think you're going?" he yelled.

"I'm going to work, just like every night."

"Where are you taking Peggy?"

"Somewhere you ain't," Leona said. She wasn't fooled by his sudden interest in his child's well-being. He was asking if she was leaving him. "Oh, don't worry, I'll be back. I'm the one what worked for everything we got, and if you think I'm leaving it all to you to lose, think again." She tore off down the drive and to Jewel's, where she dropped off Peggy, then headed to work her shift at Marv's. After Peggy was gone, Cale popped in beside her.

"Who is Galen Nolan?" he asked. She knew he had seen

everything, including Leona's use of dark magic, but said nothing else.

"Likely nobody I'm gonna wanna meet," Leona said as she hit the gas and sped toward Marv's.

She arrived late, but Marv and everyone else were too distracted to give her any guff. The bar was quiet, no music played, and everyone spoke in hushed whispers as they hovered over their beers. Leona went straightaway to cleaning up, and when Marv emerged from the kitchen, he was silent and gray faced.

"What's going on in here tonight?" Leona asked.

"Mikey Donnal came in right before. They found another girl down by the river, over by the softball field. Dead, just like Mary Silvus."

21

Karla Hupp was a big girl, over six feet tall, and built broad and lean like a man, with wide hands and a square jaw that only accentuated the masculinity. She always wore pants, and she worked a hard, physical job in the power plant, shoveling coal on the belt and keeping up with the men in brute strength and in dirty mouth. She came in Marv's some nights. When she did, she was shy, polite, and she tipped Leona well.

Everyone knew what Karla was. "Funny" they said, and they didn't mean comical. Still, nobody really made a big deal of it because Karla was kind and generous and took excellent care of her widowed mother. Karla worked and Karla played softball and Karla went to church with her mama. If she did other things, "funny" things, nobody paid much attention. Karla had no enemies and no close friends. As Ed Wagner had told Leona over his coffee that morning, "No irregularities that might warrant that."

The diner was empty save for Ed. He had lingered after all the other regulars left. His lips were drawn and tight and his eyes red-rimmed as he told Leona about the crime scene. He wrung his hands as he spoke. "I swear, Leona. I don't know who could do such a thing."

Leona had already heard about Karla from Jewel, who had extracted the information from Jim Tupper, one of Ed's deputies, but she pretended not to know the details. He wouldn't like it if she spoke of them, but Ames was small and everyone knew the details by now, whether Ed wanted them to or not.

Somebody had pulled up two poles from the outfield fence of the softball field and bent them into a grotesque metallic cross. They jammed it into the pitcher's mound, upside down, then tied Karla to it. Naked, drained of blood, and chest cracked, Karla was also missing her head. Leona had shuddered when Jewel had told her.

This time, Ed Wagner didn't need Leona to infiltrate a dream and tell him anything. No woman in Ames or Denton County had a body like Karla Hupp. And further to that, there were few who could manhandle Karla, so to subdue her and crack her open like a Maine lobster were feats that only a few could have accomplished.

Ed might have been thinking it, but he wouldn't say it. Whether it was foggy on his brain, or he just couldn't see how a gigantic woman might put up a good fight, Leona didn't know.

"Karla was a big girl, wasn't she, Ed?" Leona said as she set his eggs down in front of him.

"Yep," Ed said. His hand shook as he guided the fork full of scrambled eggs to his lips.

"Well, she worked on Harv Pottmeyer's crew. None of them are weak."

"So?"

"Well, so Karla was strong as a bull. Did it look like she put up a fight at all?"

"Nope. None."

"Don't that seem funny to you, Ed?"

He chewed a bit and looked off past her. When his eyes came back to her, they were tired and confused looking. "How do you mean, funny? Wasn't nothing funny about it, Leona."

"I mean, how many men you know could do what was done to her and there be no marks, no resistance, nothing else tore up around?"

"Somebody bent that pipe up too," Ed said. "But tools can do that."

"Yes, and there are big strong men about, but Karla wasn't just big. She could handle herself."

"So, we're looking for somebody strong. They broke off that cross, bent up the metal, and they waylaid Karla," Ed said, putting things together.

"Exactly," Leona said, nodding and smiling, pretending to be amazed at Ed's acumen.

Ed finished his eggs and left, off to look for a large and burly man, she supposed. At least he had a purpose, Leona thought. She hated seeing that hangdog look in his eyes.

Leona didn't know that she exactly agreed that the murderer was a big man; magic could make a small man big, and whoever had murdered those girls had known magic. But Ed needed to go do something, and he'd be safer looking in the wrong direction.

The bell above the door jingled, and Jewel flounced in. She sat next to Cale at the counter.

Leona set a cup of coffee in front of her. "What did you find out?"

"Galen Nolan is a hood. Come to the County about a month ago. He run them Cunningham boys right out of that holler. Took over all the girls and the gambling."

Leona shook her head. "That don't hardly seem like it could be so. There was ten of them boys, and they was the meanest there was."

"Well, now Galen Nolan is the meanest. If Bob owes him, he's done. I say let Bob lay in the mess. Solves your problem, really," Jewel said.

"You think this Galen Nolan would just stop at killing Bob? He'll want his money, Jewel."

"That's Bob's misfortune," Jewel said. "Let him wiggle off his own hook."

"He can't. He never could." Leona sighed. Bob and Galen Nolan were only one of their problems. "All right, enough about Galen Nolan. I'm gonna have to go see about Karla's ghost after this."

"Why?" Cale asked. "If she ain't shown up, then why tempt fate?"

"Because what if she shows up to somebody who ain't us and she's the same as Mary? And anyways, Cale, it ain't their fault what was done to them, what they've become," Leona said. "I need to find Karla and see if she's the same off as Mary. We gotta help them."

"Leona, helping ghosts that want to rip us apart seems likely to end in us being ghosts ourselves," Jewel countered.

"We'll sage her good if she tries," Leona said. "We're gonna have to go down to the ball field and have a look. First, though, let's go to Karla's." She crossed her arms and stared down at both Cale and Jewel, who were giving her the same disapproving look. "My mind's made up. You can help me or not."

"We're not letting you go alone," Cale said.

"I would, because you're contrary and stubborn about this, Leona. But I reckon we might also see something Ed Wagner missed," Jewel said.

"I'm sure there's plenty Ed Wagner missed," Cale said.

Jewel chuckled.

"You're both hateful today. It ain't Ed's fault he's never had to hunt a murderer before." Leona took off her apron and hung it up.

Marcy Dobbins had come on to take over. Leona smiled at Marcy and checked in. "Everyone is good. Should be quiet 'til your lunch rush hits."

Marcy popped her chewing gum as she tied her apron. "I can't make no money like this. My new boyfriend wants us to go to Wheeling next weekend, and I ain't got no money put back."

"Tell you what, you can have my breakfast shift tomorrow. I got something I need to do," Leona said.

"Really? Thanks, Leona. Frank will sure be happy."

"Don't mention it," Leona said. She grabbed her purse and coat then looked to Jewel. "You can take me to my appointment?"

Jewel scowled then rolled her eyes as she tied her handkerchief on her head and jammed the sunglasses on her face. "I don't reckon I got a choice, since you won't listen to reason."

As the truck rumbled over to Karla's house, Jewel looked thoughtful. "You're looking for the curse bag."

"Yep. And I sure hope nobody found it first." Even though she hadn't touched the curse bag at Mary's house, she'd found it, and maybe that had been the point of the spell. If there was one to find at Karla's, she wanted to be the one to find it. She had defenses against the dead. Not everyone was so fortunate.

"Ain't her mama in a wheelchair?" Jewel asked.

"Yes. Karla was all she had."

Karla shared a neat, but tiny, two-story cracker box house with her mother. Sandwiched in between two larger houses on Second Street, the long, thin house was basically two hallways stacked on top of one another. Small though it was, it was the best maintained house on the street. The siding was new and freshly painted. There wasn't much yard to speak of, but it was tidy. Someone had raked the leaves and left them bagged for the trash crew.

Leona, Cale, and Jewel stood in front of the little house for a moment as they decided on a plan of action.

"I think we ought to block the house before we go in," Jewel said. "I'm gonna ring it good." She pulled a jar of ward out of her bag and began casting her spells.

"I can't go in now," Cale said. The wards would keep any ghosts in and Cale out.

"Yes, and that's good. If Karla is in there and the same off as Mary, she'll attack you. Go on back to Jewel's."

"No way. I'm staying with you." The air around Leona stirred and dropped a few degrees in temperature, too much, too fast to be attributed to the October weather.

"I know that upsets you, but if she gets you, she might be too strong for us, and you'd be . . . gone." The idea of that flashed through Leona's mind and gave her goose pimples.

Cale's head dropped, but he nodded. "All right. I'll wait for you back at Jewel's, but if you ain't there in an hour, I'm coming back." He popped off, leaving Leona with another chill and the slight smell of ozone in her nose, a sure sign he was agitated.

Jewel finished blocking the house, and they ascended the front steps then hesitated.

"You reckon we should knock?" Jewel asked.

"I guess so. It ain't our house." Leona rapped on the door, and they waited. Nobody answered. Leona looked at Jewel, who pulled a sage bundle from her bag and lit it. Leona tried the doorknob, but it was locked.

"Figures," Jewel said. "You want me to do it?"

"No, I reckon I can handle a lock." Leona held her palm to the lock and closed her eyes. She didn't like unlocking spells. They had always felt wrong to her, an invasion of privacy and dark in intent, even when she had no such intent.

She concentrated, and when she did, she got a little flutter in her stomach and heard a quiet whisper, as if something passed her ear. It hissed at her and encouraged her to keep going. The dark whisper frightened her, and Leona lost her concentration for a second. She shook her head, and the voice was gone. She tried again, and this time her palm heated up, and the metal glowed. But the door remained locked.

"For Pete's sake, Leona, move." Jewel elbowed her aside and zapped the lock. It clicked, and the knob turned on its own. "You gotta mean it. It ain't like we're trying to rob the place."

"I did mean it," Leona said as she elbowed Jewel back. In her heart, she knew she hadn't meant it. Not really. "I'm going in first. Give me some sage and don't you touch nothing." She snatched the lit sage from Jewel and opened the door, knocking again as she called out. "Miss June? You in here? It's Leona Spencer. We came to see if we could help you."

Leona got two steps in the house and smelled two things: the ammonia-like smell that told her a ghost was near, and the sweet, metallic smell of death. June Hupp sat in her wheelchair facing the corner of the room, only her head faced the other way, out into the room, her dead eyes wide in fear. Her head had been twisted clear around on her body. Her daughter's ghost paced around the body and growled. Her mouth was sewn shut the same as Mary's, and her bloody-red eyes stared down at the corpse. Every once in a while, Karla would swipe at the dead woman, scratching her. Leona scanned the area around the body. June's hand hung limp beside the wheelchair. On the floor below it, Leona saw the curse bag.

"Damn. Poor Old June found it first," Jewel said. She stepped even with Leona and held the sage bundle up. Karla caught wind of the sage smudge and growled, but she kept going back to June's body. "What are we gonna do now?"

"Well, I reckon we ought to look in Karla's room. Then we'll deal with Karla."

Jewel eyed her. "Leona, you better leave Karla be just how she is. She's cooped up here and even if she ain't, she's stuck on her ma."

"She won't be when Ed finds her and picks up that bag," Leona said. "I don't think she'll follow us, but we best not linger." She pointed toward the staircase. "Come on."

"Leona—"

"Jewel, just hush up and go!" She shoved Jewel toward the back and edged between her sister and Karla. She ignored Jewel's cussing and focused on the ghost. Karla paid her no attention and instead scratched at her mother's chest.

They ascended the staircase and found Karla's room at the back of the hallway. Like everything else in the house, the room was neat and spare. The twin bed was made with military precision, the corners of the plain, olive-drab wool blanket as tight and square as the pyramids of Egypt. They looked around the room, but the bed, a nightstand, and a desk were the only furniture. The bare walls glowed white in the mid-morning sunlight that streamed through the window.

Leona examined the nightstand. It was a simple thing—no fancy woodwork and only a plain varnish. She opened the only drawer and pulled out a Bible. Like the one in Mary's room, this one looked brand new. When Leona found the ribbon page marker, underlined in red, was the first sentence of Ezekiel, chapter 18, verse 20:

The soul that sinneth, it shall die.

Jewel peered over her shoulder. "Guess they figured that violent part was the only one that mattered."

Leona nodded and put the book back in the drawer. "Same as Mary's."

Jewel held up a flyer for the tent revival in Shadyside and a photograph of Karla smiling, standing next to another woman. "That's Ella McKown."

Leona nodded. "Yep. But she died in that house fire a few years ago. Her and her folks."

"You think maybe her and Karla was—"

Leona shrugged. "Could be, but that don't hardly seem like it matters now."

"It don't. Except maybe it did to somebody." Jewel put the picture and the flyer in her pocket. "I don't see much else up here, do you?"

"Nope," Leona said. "You go out the back way, check out there for sign. I'll deal with Karla."

"Leona, let's just get rid of her and be done. She tore up her mama, and she'll do it again to somebody else if she gets the chance."

"Yes, she will. That's why the somebody has to be me."

Jewel sighed and shook her head. "Stupid is as stupid does, Leona Jean. If she gets you, I'm gonna exorcise the both of you." She left the room and thumped down the stairs and out the back.

Leona made her way downstairs and found Karla where

they left her, tearing her mother's corpse to pieces. Miss June's eyes were gone. Only bloody holes remained, and Karla scratched deep wounds down the old woman's face. Leona lit her sage bundle. When the smudge hit her, Karla looked over at Leona and growled. Her red eyes glowed, and the black thread that held her mouth closed vibrated.

"Karla, I know you wouldn't have wanted to do any of this, and I'm real sorry," Leona said, keeping her voice quiet and steady, as if she were trying to calm a spooked horse. Leona held out the sage bundle and pinned the ghost in the corner. She kept her eye on Karla and bent down to pick up the gris-gris bag.

As soon as she did, Karla's head snapped to attention, and she stared at Leona. The bag burned in Leona's hand, and she dropped it. Karla growled and lunged. Leona thrust the sage at her, and she recoiled. Leona grabbed the bag and ran for the front door, but Karla was too fast. She grabbed Leona by the hair, jerking her backward. Leona's feet slipped out from under her, and she fell flat on her back, staring up into Karla's blazing red eyes.

As Karla reached for her head, Leona pulled a handful of salt from her bag and blew it at her. Karla screamed as the salt burned her face, leaving raw places and blisters, just as acid would burn the living. Leona got her feet under her and rolled across the doorway. Karla slammed against the invisible barrier and raged. She pounded at it, and the whole house shook from the force of her blows.

The bag sizzled against Leona's skin, and she dropped it on the front porch. The palm of her hand was burnt, the skin red, angry, and seared, as if she'd grabbed a hot coal. Leona directed her other palm at it and willed it to burn. The bag shook and pushed back against her will, but she channeled the searing pain in her other hand and pushed. The curse bag emitted a high-pitched sound and shook, then it burst into bright blue flames. As it did, Karla screamed and dropped to her knees, holding her head. The flames burned out, leaving a black crater on the porch. Karla stood up. She pointed at Leona, and her eyes blazed with hatred.

Leona jumped as Jewel spoke. "I reckon she hates you more than Mary does."

"Great Balls of Fire, Jewel Elizabeth! You scared me half to death." Leona clutched at herself and scowled at Jewel as she tried to calm her racing heart.

She grabbed Leona's hand and examined it. "Leona, you ought not to have touched that nasty thing."

"Couldn't be helped," Leona said. Karla banged against the barrier and growled. "If she gets loose, I'm betting she shows up at the house." Leona grabbed the curse sack and shoved it into her bag. It didn't burn her skin any longer, but she could still feel a bit of magic on it.

"Then you'll have two of them to deal with," Jewel said. She pulled a piece of cloth from her bag and wrapped Leona's hand. "That'll have to do 'til we can clean it good."

"Let's go check out the softball fields." She eyed Karla, who pounded against the ward for all that she was worth. "I doubt we have too long before she busts that ward. She's strong."

"I know. I can feel her. All rage and hatred." Jewel said, as they headed for the truck.

22

T he softball fields were plain grass and dirt, ringed by
a chain-link fence. The local Noon Lions had cleared
out the land near the river, kept the fields up, and
sponsored the summer softball leagues. Karla Hupp had been a
fixture at those softball games. They made her play on the
women's teams, and all the women hated her. She played hard
and hit farther than most men, but the men hated her, too, for
showing them up. Poor Karla didn't fit in anywhere, and now
Leona figured she didn't fit in with the dead either.

They saw where Ed's boys had tromped around and made
a mess of the crime scene. Their big boot prints ringed the
gaping hole where the makeshift metal cross had stood. It
wasn't far from the tree line. Back up into the trees, you could

watch both the ball fields and the river, which meandered by, big and muddy. From the prints, it didn't look like Ed's boys had bothered to go much further back than a few yards into the woods. Leona had a feeling. She got them sometimes, and right then the feeling told her there was something back in the woods.

They walked only a few hundred feet, to a little cleared out space, ringed by three solid-trunked buckeye trees. Leona stepped on a nut and nearly turned her ankle. When she looked down, she saw the familiar yet strange footprint sunken into the riverbank clay. It was huge, larger than the biggest man's shoe. It had a human look to it, barefoot, except the front half looked as if it belonged to a dog, with wide toes and claw marks.

Jewel bent down and looked at it. "Same as at the Ave Maria."

"Something big and only part human," Leona said. She looked around at the trees and pointed to the nearest buckeye. "Look."

A huge claw mark ran across the width of the tree trunk. The gouge marks were deep, and it wasn't a slash; it girded the tree, effectively killing it.

"Maybe a bear done it," Jewel said as they examined the tree.

Leona shook her head. "No, that there is deliberate. They meant to kill this tree. Whoever done it, done it out of pure meanness."

"You think it was the one who killed Karla?" Jewel asked.

"Don't know. Maybe. Maybe not," Leona said. She looked all around the spot. The footprints led off into the woods.

Both Leona and Jewel whirled when they heard a guttural smacking noise behind them. Both had their palms up, ready to blast, but Leona recognized the shape huddled on the riverbank.

Leona had never seen a ghoul in full feed before, and while she was well-used to strange creatures and nasty scenes, this one wasn't one she was likely to forget. Dorval Ring crouched over the bloated body of a dead dog. His shirt was off, and the skin stretched tight, outlining every bone in his chest. It had turned from his normal jaundiced coloring to a mottled black green, the same color as rotting flesh. His face was misshapen and wrinkled up, with a flat muzzle and bright yellow eyes. He clawed at the dog and shoved great hunks of the putrid thing into his mouth, which was lined with wicked jagged teeth. He purred as he chewed, his eyes closed and a blissful look on his face as if he had a mouthful of medium-rare filet mignon and not bits of a rotting dog's guts.

"Have Mercy," Jewel said as she turned and doubled over, about to vomit.

Dorval's eyes snapped open, and he stood up. He reverted back to his normal appearance in a blur, turning from them in embarrassment. "I-I'm sorry, Miss Leona . . . I-I was just . . . so hungry . . . I didn't mean for you to s-s-see," he stammered.

Leona exhaled and approached slowly. "Dorval. You don't need to worry about me, but this wouldn't be a good place for anybody else to see you," she said. She picked up his shirt from a log and handed it to him.

"I didn't kill it. It drowned." Dorval pointed at the dog. "Sometimes things wash up and I-I—"

"I know. I know you wouldn't hurt nobody or nothing. But they found a body over there." Leona pointed at the little knoll that hid the softball field from where they stood. "Clear on out of here. I don't want nobody to bother you." She did her best not to gag at the smell of him or the gore smeared across his face. "Go on now. I'll see you at the diner."

"Thank you, Miss Leona." Dorval put his grungy shirt on and took off down the riverbank in long, loping strides that didn't look human.

Jewel held her sleeve up to her nose and examined his tracks next to the dead dog. She backed away and shook her head. "His prints just look like a barefoot man. He didn't make the other marks."

"Of course he didn't. He's a ghoul. He don't kill things. He just eats them. Poor thing." Leona had a bad feeling again, fear for Dorval and fear of something else to come. "We best get home."

"Peggy is with Ida Mae," Jewel said. "She's gonna stay the night."

"Did she cry when you left her?" Leona asked. Their sister Ida Mae had many opinions about how Leona ought to raise her daughter, although Ida Mae didn't have any children herself. In an odd twist, Peggy was one of the few humans Ida Mae actually got along with, which mystified both Leona and Jewel as they had neither one ever gotten along with Ida Mae or known anyone who did.

"Nope. They went off to make a cherry pie," Jewel said. "It ain't natural to get along with Ida Mae."

"Well, Peggy does what Peggy does, mostly just to go against sense," Leona said. "I won't look a gift horse in the mouth."

When Jewel finally pulled up to the house. The lights were on inside, which meant Bob was home.

"You want me to come in? I'll curse him good, so he leaves you be," Jewel offered.

"If I need to curse him, I can do that myself," Leona said. "Anyways, don't worry. He won't come near me. He's scared to . . ." Leona stopped and stared at the tree line.

"What? What's wrong?" Jewel asked, looking around and scanning the woods.

The ghosts of Mary Silvus and Karla Hupp stood side-by-side at the edge of Leona's protection spell.

"They're both here, ain't they?" Jewel asked.

Leona nodded. Cale popped in beside Leona.

"With two of them now, they might have enough juice to break through," Cale said.

Jewel shivered. "I can't see them, but I can feel the anger rolling out of that one spot over yonder," she said, pointing to the exact location of the ghosts.

Leona nodded. "They're trapped between the circles. It's working just like you figured."

Jewel smirked at the rare concession from Leona about her logic, but for once had the good sense not to make a big deal of it. "Like a crawdad trap. They can't go backward. Only through to the next ward."

"Yes. That's so. But I guess it's only a matter of time before they figure out how to break through," Leona said. "We got to go see Granny Kay."

Jewel nodded. "Yes. Before they figure out how to bust in here and kill us all."

"I'll pick you up tomorrow morning. We'll go see Galen Nolan, then we'll head out to see Kay."

Jewel nodded and left them staring at the fuming ghosts.

"Not one part of this is a good plan, Lee," Cale said.

"Not a one," Leona agreed.

23

L eona decided it was too dangerous to take Jewel with her out to Galen Nolan's holler. Jewel would have been good backup, but Leona was hoping to avoid any violence or curse slinging, and Jewel was quick with a hex. Instead, she took Cale. Cale could serve two purposes. He was a messenger if something should go awry and, in a bind, he could cause some problems for the living if he chose. He was under strict instruction to pop off and bring Jewel back with the big magic, should it be needed.

The truck bounced over the rough gravel road, hitting big washouts that the county didn't bother to fix. When they got near the holler, the road evened out—someone had graded it and laid fresh gravel.

"County didn't do all this. Too much money for way back out here," Cale said.

"Yes, no way Dan Vogel and that Township bunch did it either. They ain't got two nickels to rub together," Leona said.

"So maybe Nolan did it?"

"Could be."

"Who did he run off?"

"Frank Cunningham and his bunch," Leona said.

Cale whistled. "Didn't they drag that man to death for talking to their sister?"

"Yep. The Cunninghams were all mean as snakes and knew a little magic."

"Who's meaner than a Cunningham?" Cale asked.

"Galen Nolan apparently," Leona said as she drove the truck over the plywood bridge that spanned Goose Creek and into Nolan's Holler. There were plenty of other vehicles there. The Holler, even when Frank Cunningham ran it, was a haven for gamblers and men looking for a good time. From the main clearing, paths ran back up the hills that led to various entertainments.

The main path was dotted on either side with shacks and old trailers. Women could be seen on the porches or out in front of the hovels. They craned their necks and peered down at the truck. When they saw Leona get out, they looked disinterested and went back to their shacks.

"He runs girls," Cale said, looking back up the holler at the rough, sad-looking women.

"I imagine that's just the start of it all," Leona said.

Barks and snarls—and the cheering of men—could be heard coming from the other path. From the noise and the stale, rank smell of big dogs in the air, Leona figured Galen Nolan was running a dog fighting ring too.

Before they could start down either path, a tall, skinny, rat-faced man greeted them. His beady eyes looked Leona up and down.

"We's full up on whores right now, gal. You'd be best to get on gone."

Leona shook her head. "I want to see Galen Nolan."

"I doubt that you really do," the man said. He grinned and lit a cigarette, then ogled Leona some more.

"Yes, I'll agree, *want* was a poor word choice on my part. I got business with him. He here or not?"

"He might be, if the price is right, there little gal." He smiled and reached for Leona. "Maybe me and you could—"

He squawked and clutched at his nuts. His face reddened, and he couldn't seem to speak.

Leona's eyes narrowed, and she frowned. The dark whisper was there, in her ear, encouraging her. "No arrangements between me and you. I want to see Galen Nolan now." She released her spell, and he relaxed.

"I reckon you're gonna wish you hadn't done that, witch," he said.

"Please take me to see Galen now," Leona said, ignoring his threats. She pulled a handful of yellow-tinged powder from a little pouch and blew it in his face. His eyes clouded over, and he smiled and became compliant.

"Yes, ma'am. He's out yonder." He pointed to the path with the dog noises and cheering men. Leona's shoes squelched through the thick mud of the path as she followed the man.

The smells of big dog got stronger, and the cheering and snarling got louder. Up ahead, the path was lined with dog boxes. The creatures chained to them could be called dogs, she supposed. They were huge muscular things, misshapen and torn, monstrosities from their miserable lives fighting for the entertainment of nasty men. When they saw her coming, they all growled and snarled and lunged at her as she passed, their jaws snapping, straining their chains to their limit. Leona kept to the path and avoided them. She wished she could set them all free, but they were miserable things so mean as to be beyond a hope of redemption. If she were kind, she'd put a .22 in each of their skulls and give the poor creatures some measure of peace.

When they reached the end of the path, they found a circle of men waving fistfuls of money and yelling. In the middle of the circle, a massive, hulking pit bull had a German shepard dog by the throat. His jaws were clamped so tight Leona could see the big muscles standout, and he snarled then shook the other dog until it went limp.

Money changed hands, with some men happy and some mad that the shepherd dog had lost, Although how anyone in their right could bet against the behemoth pit bull, Leona didn't know. The dog stalked around the ring with his kill, growling at everyone and daring them to take it away. He settled down in the middle of the blood-soaked ring and began eating the other dog. When a man stepped into the ring with a long chain and a muzzle, the thing lunged and caught the man's arm. It shook its head, and the man screamed as the dog ripped his arm. The men all laughed and cheered the creature then fell silent and parted for the enormous man who stepped into the ring.

Leona wouldn't have to be introduced to Galen Nolan to know him. He was the largest man she had ever seen, close to seven feet tall and broad, intensely muscular, but lean instead of bulky in spite of his broadness. His face wasn't young, and it wasn't old. It was unlined as a youth's, but his eyes looked older. They weren't weary looking, but rather held the hard edge of experience and cruelty that Leona had only seen in older men. He wore no shirt or shoes. His broad back was rife with scars of every kind of wound: bullet holes, slashes, stabs, and burns. His face held no emotion at all as he walked over to the screaming man and snarling dog.

In one massive hand, he grabbed the dog, in the other, the arm of the man. The dog clamped down harder. Galen pulled at the man's arm and ripped it off his body. He dropped the screaming man and wrapped the chain around the dog's neck. It bit and lunged for him, but he held the thing swinging in the air until it choked itself quiet. When he let it to the ground, its tongue lolled from its mouth, but it was calm. Galen snapped the chain on its collar and handed it to another man, who led the creature away.

The first man, now missing an arm, screamed as he bled out onto the muddy ground.

Leona's healer instincts screamed at her to help the man, but he was beyond saving. And Leona knew that, in this place, compassion would be a weakness.

Galen walked away, ignoring the screams. When he saw Leona, he stopped and looked her over. "You ain't got no business out here."

"I can judge my own business," Leona said. She wrinkled her nose at the smell of him. He reeked of body odor, cigarettes, and that manky big dog smell. "I come about Bob Monroe."

"What about him?"

"He owes money, and I come to see about it."

"He owes me five hundred dollar."

"He said three."

Galen didn't even blink. "He owes five."

"He ain't got it."

"He better get it."

Leona narrowed her eyes. "That's what I came to see about. We ain't got a whole lot to pay you with."

Galen sniffed the air, and Leona thought she glimpsed something akin to a smile flash over his face.

"You gonna work off his debt?"

The other men standing around sniggered. Leona felt her face grow hot from embarrassment, but she ignored the comment and set her jaw. "I can save you out ten dollars a month 'til you're square."

"Take too long. There's other ways you can square up, witch."

So that was it. He knew. From the smug look on his face, Leona got the feeling he had known all along who she was and what she was.

"How do you figure?"

"I got some whores that need doctoring. We'll start there," he said.

"And that's worth five hundred dollars to you?" Leona asked.

Galen Nolan laughed. "Ten women ain't worth that, but they can't work like how they are."

"Is that all?" she asked. She knew it wouldn't be. She knew what he wanted was the magic. He'd want dark magic spells she wouldn't want to do, but she'd have to cross that bridge when she came to it.

"No, but we'll see where it gets you." Galen stepped closer, and Leona choked at the smell of him. He towered over her and looked her up and down. "You thinking you're gonna hex me, witch, you think again." He smiled and revealed longer canines, then his eyes flashed yellow, and he growled long and low.

A chilly wind swirled round Leona. It raised up the goose pimples on Galen's bare skin and her own. Neither of them backed away as they recognized in one another what they both were. Cale's voice whispered in Leona's ear.

"Lee, you need to go now."

Leona nodded. She spat in her palm and held it out to Galen Nolan in the old way of making the bargain. "The bargain is struck," she said.

Galen smiled. He spit in his palm, then his enormous hand swallowed her tiny one. "It's struck."

Leona nodded and marched back out the way she'd come, past the snarling curs and the greasy men who all stared at her with a predator's hungry grin. Neither she nor Cale said anything until she was out on the road and on the way to Jewel's.

"Leona, what is he?"

Leona wiped at her spit covered hand with her kerchief. "He's a werewolf."

werewolf?" Jewel yelled. "Leona, we can't associate with no werewolves. We'll all get killed!"

Leona shrugged as she drove them deep into the hills of Morgan County. "Well, I'd rather not, myself, but if I don't associate with this one, he's gonna kill us all for sure."

"No wonder he run old Frank Cunningham out. He like as not ate him," Jewel said. "You think that's what's been banging around in them woods?"

"I'd say so," Leona said. She pulled the truck on to a dirt cutoff. She drove it up the hill as far as she could and parked it when the road ended. "He knows what I am, and he didn't care that I knew he was a werewolf. He's bold, and I'd say he laid out for Bob. He don't care about that five hundred dollars. He wants magic."

"Bob Monroe can go straight to Hell," Jewel said. She spat on the ground.

"Jewel!"

"Leona, if this ain't an occasion for a cuss word, then I surely do not know what is!" Jewel yelled. "Bob Monroe is gonna get us all killed by a damn werewolf! Well, Bob don't know jack all about magic or anything you do, so it ain't like he could go brag to that wolf," Jewel said.

"No, that's right. It wasn't Bob that told him. Maybe nobody did. I don't know that we're all that stealthy about it, and besides, I think he can smell magic. He gave me a good sniff there this morning. Werewolves can smell all sorts of things," Leona said.

"Well, Granny Kay will know," Jewel said. "She's liable to throw her shoe at you when she finds out you're trucking with a damn werewolf."

"Probably, but it can't be helped," Leona said.

They had barely set a foot inside the cottage when Jewel tattled. "Well, Leona is trucking with werewolves," she said.

Leona scowled. "That ain't the worst of our troubles, Jewel."

"Well, if trucking with werewolves ain't the worst of it, you girls are in hotter water than you know," Granny Kay said.

"There's another girl murdered. Karla Hupp. We found another bag at her place." Leona pulled the curse from her bag and put it on the table. "We also found their ghosts. Something is wrong with them."

Granny Kay eyed the little bag. She ringed it in herb salt then spoke an incantation. The bag burst into flames. Then she turned to Leona and Jewel. "Yes. Something is bad wrong with them girls."

"Looks like their mouths is sewn shut, and they're violent. They're trying to break the ward around my house," Leona said. "And Mary, well, she did something to them little children in the Ave Maria."

"Yes. She absorbed them, all their energy," Kay said. "She'll do it every chance she gets."

"But how? I never seen a ghost act like this. They don't hurt nobody, not really, and if they do, they sure don't mean it."

"But they can," Kay said. "I've warned you about that. Ghosts ain't pets, Leona."

"Or boyfriends," Jewel said under her breath, but not so quiet as to go unnoticed by Leona.

She scowled at Jewel but ignored her otherwise. "I know they ain't pets, but they're not usually aggressive. They do harm when they get confused and upset."

"That's right. And these two girls is about as confused and upset as any ghost can be. And somebody has set them on you, Leona."

"What about Cale?" Jewel asked. "He goes where Leona goes."

Granny Kay sighed, and a sad look crossed her face. "Yes, well, exceptions prove rules," she said. "Cale is attached of his own accord. These ones don't wanna be, and I'd say that's part of why they're angry. They can't move on."

"What kind of spell does that?" Leona asked.

Granny Kay sipped her tea and thought for a moment. "A real mean bind. Done by somebody who made a poor bargain." She got up and looked around in some notebooks, muttering to herself. When she found what she was looking for, she tapped the page with her finger. "Something like this, only stronger. Strengthened by a pledge to a being that the caster won't be able to satisfy, only they won't know that 'til it's too late and they've opened the door. It's a bind you'd use on a demon, but it wouldn't exactly work that way on a human. That explains them sticking around," Kay said.

"So the bags? That's the bind?" Leona asked.

Kay shook her head. "No, the bags are a trap. It's how he set them girls on you. The bind itself is something nastier. Were them girls all tore up?"

"Yes. Split clean up the middle. No blood, no innards left. Hung upside down on crosses and missing their heads," Leona said.

"Excessive, don't you think?" Kay said.

Jewel nodded. "Yes, that's a fact. It don't seem like all that is necessary unless you're trying to prove a point."

"Or get somebody's attention," Leona said.

Kay smiled. "Maybe you girls do listen every once in a while. Yes. You got two problems here. One is that somebody killed them girls and they used the ritual to call up somebody who shouldn't ever be called. They can't keep doing that because, eventually, that somebody will stay, and none of us will survive that."

"Whoever's name you didn't want to say," Jewel said.

"Yes. You girls ain't ready for all that mess, so let's just focus on stopping anymore calls to him.

"Your second problem ain't just that them girls are bound to this plane, they're bound to you, Leona. They won't stop until they've killed you. This is personal," Kay said. "Who's got a beef with you?"

"Why, nobody that I know," Leona said.

Jewel laughed. "Leona, all of them church ladies hate both our guts and livers. Shirley Silvus would shoot us as soon as look at us."

"Maybe, but she don't know exactly what we do, and she surely wouldn't have done nothing to her own daughter just to get at me," Leona said.

"Well, then maybe she ran her mouth off to somebody," Jewel said.

"Jewel may be on the right track," Kay said. She looked around in her notebooks and found another spell. "If I was gonna do it, I'd bind them here, and I'd set them on you with this object of obsession spell. "

"So somebody killed Mary and Karla, bound them here, set them on me. Why?"

"Don't be dumb, Leona. You're the only one I know of what can talk to the dead. If those girls wasn't hateful, you'd have figured out who's doing the killing straight away and put the Law on them," Jewel said.

"She's right," Granny Kay nodded. "That's how it would be done."

"Jewel, who else but you knows I can talk to ghosts?"

"I don't know, Leona, but plenty of people seen you talk to yourself when you're talking to Cale. And plenty of people know we do magic and such."

"They know we do little love potions and home remedies. I don't know as they know we do magic," Leona said.

"Well that dirty werewolf knows," Jewel said. "And it could be him that's killing girls."

"A werewolf doing violence intentional like this? They wasn't killed under a full moon," Leona said. "Besides, since when can they do magic?"

"A werewolf ain't got to be in his change to be strong and deadly. And anyone can do magic if they're inclined to learn," Kay said.

Leona shook her head. "He can't, or he wouldn't have used Bob to get to me. Has to be somebody else. Who knows we do real magic and not just herbs and root work?"

"It wouldn't take much to put all of it together. Anybody

who can figure out how to bind a ghost and set them on you is smart enough to figure out we're magic users," Jewel said.

"Jewel's right. I warned you girls this could happen. You've got to be cautious about using magic."

"Granny, we don't go around doing flashy magic. We stick to domestic wards and remedies," Leona said.

"Well, the werewolf knew you was magic," Jewel said. "You said so."

Granny Kay nodded. "Yes. A werewolf can smell it," she said. Then she scowled and rapped Leona on the head. "You know better than to associate yourself with a werewolf."

"Ow! Can't be helped," Leona said.

"Bob got her indebted to one. Now we got to doctor his women and who knows what all," Jewel said.

"Leona, you best get out from under that debt quick," Granny Kay said. "Any deal you make with a werewolf is a bad one. They ain't known for keeping their word, but they are known for eating people."

"I know, but Bob owes him and that means I owe him," Leona said. She set her jaw and counted to three. "Look, one problem at a time. Right now the werewolf don't want to kill me, or he'd have done it. The ghosts do. How do we deal with them?"

"Easiest way is to do a high-powered cleanse and blast them off you. I can show you the things you need," Kay said.

"When you cleanse them, don't that send them to a bad place?" Leona asked.

Granny Kay nodded. "Yes. They don't go up, that's for sure."

"Granny, it ain't these girls' fault. Somebody done this to them, made them like this. Can't we help them?" Leona asked.

"Leona, I understand, and it's good you want to do right by

these girls, but we don't know for sure what spells were used. We can't undo what we don't know for sure."

"That's what I told her!" Jewel yelled.

Leona rolled her eyes at Jewel, then took up Granny Kay's notebook. "We know mostly what they done. Something binds them here and to me. The gris-gris. Can't we just cleanse that? Won't that undo this?"

"No. Once they set that on you, you can't undo it," Granny Kay said. "Safest thing for you and your family is to exorcise them. Quicklike. I know I ain't got to remind you that All Hallows Eve is coming." Kay looked over her glasses at Leona.

"Yes, I know, but—"

"No but, Leona Jean. I can't say for sure what will happen to them girls on that night. Maybe the bind will keep them from being flesh again, and maybe it won't. There's a lot of energy that night, and if they get enough of it, they break anything holding them, wards I mean."

"Maybe we can suppress their energy, temporary until after the Eve," Leona suggested.

"Leona, that's triple work!" Jewel yelled.

"Well Mary was easy enough to manage when she was in the mirror," Leona said.

"Yes, and somebody busted that mirror and set her loose," Jewel said. "She ain't dumb enough to let us trap her in a mirror again, and Karla won't be either. She'll do whatever Mary does."

"How else can it be done?" Leona looked to Kay.

Kay sighed sadly. "You'd need more power than you have, and it won't last," she said.

"It's only got to last the night," Leona said.

"I know how. We could juice up them rat head jars I figured out. Mary didn't care for that out at the Ave Maria."

Kay walloped Jewel upside her head. "Where'd you learn that kind of bind?"

"I read on it. What? It was useful. I had to use a bit of the herb of grace, but I got it." Jewel rubbed her head.

"Now listen to me, the both of you. The herb of grace is for emergencies, for when you got no other choice. You go chewing it for every whipstitch of a spell. It's poison, and one day you will take it and that'll be it. No amount of calendula will help." She whacked Jewel again.

"Ow! All right, I get it," Jewel yelled.

"Leona Jean?" Kay threatened.

"I understand too." Leona did understand, but she also understood how serious of a problem it would be if Mary and Karla ate up a bunch of spirits coming back and forth between the veil on all Hallows Eve.

"But look, I-I can't. I won't exorcise them. That's selfish, and I-I don't want to work thataway," Leona said. "All we need to do is take that curse off them. You'd need something of theirs, right? Something important. And we know what that something is." She looked at Jewel. Jewel rolled her eyes. Leona smiled, knowing Jewel was following her. "Somebody took their heads."

"They took the heads?" Granny Kay asked.

"Yes, ma'am. Both of 'em. I'd say that's a powerful thing to use in a spell."

Granny Kay nodded. "One of the most powerful," she said. "Well, that's likely what. Your problem now is the who."

"Could be that dirty wolf," Jewel said. "He wanted to get you in his employ."

"By letting a ghost rip me to shreds? I doubt it. Besides, he's done good enough with Bob. No, I think maybe . . . I think maybe it's that preacher."

Jewel nodded. "He could see Cale. And Tommy said Mary

was ate up with that revival nonsense. Plus we found the revival flyer in Karla's things too."

"Exactly," Leona said.

"This preacher seen Cale with you?" Granny Kay asked.

"Yes. I believe he did," Leona said. "Smiled all sly at us and looked right at where Cale was."

"It's possible. He might could sense a lot of things if he's powerful enough to do all this cursing." Granny Kay got up and made more tea. She freshened everyone's cup. "Your problem ain't no easier, girls. You're gonna have to find them heads." She handed them a notebook. "The cleanse is in there. It ain't difficult if you can find the things."

Leona took the notebook. "Thank you."

Granny Kay poked her in the chest with a bony finger. "Now, what about this werewolf?"

"I ain't got no choice but to work with him," Leona said. "I gotta get us clear of that debt."

"Leona, let me just tell you about werewolves," Granny Kay said, her voice testy. "They're violent and tricky. Whatever deal you make with him, he ain't planning to honor it."

"I know," Leona said, "But what choice do I have? You can't hardly kill them."

"Not real easy, no, but you can." Kay pulled out another notebook, then she got up and sorted through one of her books of pressed leaves. When she found the one she was looking for, she pointed it out. The beautiful purple flower was expertly pressed, and the notes beside it detailed how to harvest it and make a potion. "Wolfsbane. You won't mistake it for anything else. Grows in patches up the mountain sides."

"What do we do with it?" Jewel asked.

"Well, Jewel, finally, something you can go along with," Granny Kay said. "It's poisonous to werewolves."

Jewel grinned. "I do like that."

"I doubt I'm gonna trick Galen Nolan into drinking a deadly poison. He ain't one of your dumb boyfriends, Jewel."

"You can do a lot with it, really. It takes some work, but you can refine it into a powder and use it to keep wolves out. They can't cross a line of it, if it's pure. And if you was to blast them with it, the pure stuff, it will knock them out good."

"Will it kill him?" Leona asked. She worried that this was all too easy, this cursing and killing. She felt the urge to do it deep in her heart, in that place the magic retreated to and called out to her from. She didn't trust it.

"Young werewolves, yes. But older, more powerful ones, it's likely just to knock them out. It will keep them from being so powerful during their moons. Makes them real sick," Granny Kay said. She looked hard at Leona, then laid a hand on her arm. "I know how you feel, girl. I know you don't like hurting anyone, but this werewolf, he won't play fair. You got to protect yourself. And if he needs killing, well, there's ways. They heal too quick to shoot 'em. But if you weaken 'em good, there's always fire. Ain't much that survives a burning, save some old demons."

"I don't want to poison nobody or burn nobody to death," Leona said. "I just want him to leave me and my family be."

"I know, but like I said, I doubt very much that a square deal is his game. Eventually, it will come a reckoning. You best be ready." Granny Kay closed her eyes. "I said my piece, and I counted to three."

Both Leona and Jewel nodded. The old woman was resolute. She always had been.

T he doctoring that Galen Nolan had alluded to when Leona agreed to repay the debt was exactly what she had figured on when she spit in her palm and shook his hand. Once she finished her morning shift at the diner, she went back out to the holler where one of Galen's flunky wolves directed her to an old, broken-down woman in the nicest shack in the holler, aside from Galen's house. Her name was Dora Whitling.

If Leona had to hazard a guess, she would have said Dora was about sixty years old, but the woman was so beaten and scarred that she really couldn't tell. Dora's skin was sallow and hung loosely on her. She was rail thin except for her hard belly, which Leona knew was a bad thing. It usually meant the cancer. Dora had likely never seen a doctor in her whole life, so recommending one now would not help anything.

Dora was hunched over, and her face was littered with scars where somebody had cut her up. Her hair was bleached blonde and patchy in places from whatever chemicals she used on it. But Dora wasn't some dumb whore, which Leona quickly surmised speaking to her. Dora was the head of Galen's prostitution ring. He'd brought her along when he'd cleaned out the Cunninghams and took over all the girls in the holler.

"We got about seventeen girls working here now," Dora said as she walked Leona up the path, pointing out each shack and telling her which girls lived where and what was needed. "I'd say we got four for sure knocked up. A couple more are sick with something, but the biggest problem is Liza. Somebody beat her good and tore her up. She has been fevered and out of her head."

"Let me look at her first," Leona said. "Maybe nothing I can do for her."

"Some advice for you, girl. Don't you never tell Galen Nolan you can't do nothing for him. 'Cause if he ain't got a use for you, you'll end up dead."

Liza's trailer was a broken-down, little camper, but it was clean and neat outside. Somebody planted some marigolds beside the step. Staring at the little golden flowers, Leona had a sad feeling, sad that this girl had tried desperately to bring something beautiful into the filth and depression that was Nolan Holler.

The inside of the trailer was sparse, but it was clean, just like the outside. But right away, Leona knew something was terribly wrong. There was a stale, sickly smell of sweat about the place. Liza lay on the double bed just past the galley kitchen. She was red with fever, and Leona smelled the sweet smell of rot. She placed a hand on Liza's forehead, and the girl thrashed and moaned. Leona turned to Dora. "Can you get me a wet towel?" Dora nodded and went in search of the compress. "Shh . . . Liza, it's gonna be all right. I'm gonna fix you right up." She pulled some willow bark tea from her bag and set to work making up a potion. While the water boiled, she had a look at what was causing the fever.

Dora applied the cool washrag to Liza's forehead then gestured to the girl's legs.

"It ain't good. Down there."

Leona pulled back the bed covers and gagged at the smell. Liza's nightgown was crusted black with blood. Leona steeled herself to look and had to hold back tears of anger and disgust. Somebody had bitten a huge chunk out of the girl's inner thigh. Everything was torn and infected. Leona looked up at Dora. She felt the hot rage boil within her, and she fought to control the magic. "This is too far gone."

"Most likely," Dora said, "but you best try something."

Leona called back the rage and held her tears. She pulled out a smock from her bag and put it on. She tied her hair under a kerchief and made up a bath of herbs and salts. Leona cleaned the infection and black pus out as best she could then made up a poultice to draw out more. She decided not to give Liza the fever reducer but to let the fever do its work. Instead, she got Liza to drink a tea that would keep her quiet and knocked out.

"I'll be back tomorrow to change that poultice. I ain't for sure it's gonna work. Her blood's likely poisoned."

Dora shrugged. "Well, we'll just have to see."

"I reckon we will," Leona said. "Who done that?"

"That don't matter. Won't change that it got done."

"I'd like to know," Leona said. She shook with rage. "Those were bites down there. All over her."

"Men pay to do all sorts of terrible things. Girls like Liza do 'em and take their chances."

Leona lost control for just a second, and an empty Mason jar shattered in the galley kitchen. She closed her eyes and calmed herself. She pushed the anger back and flexed her hands, then she packed up. "All right. Nothing more to be done for her today. Who's next?"

Leona saw ten more women. Two had broken bones, which she set and splinted for them. The two that Dora said were sick seemed like they just had colds. Six of the women were for certain pregnant. Leona mixed up the herbs that would get rid of the babies. "These girls ought to all be taking these teas," she said.

Dora nodded. "Some knows how to find their own. Most don't. These girls is mostly green."

They were all young but hard looking, with bad complexions and haunted eyes. They all quietly thanked Leona, and she knew she would have a difficult time leaving these girls to anyone else's care.

"I'd bet some of them have the social disease too. I'm gonna mix up some packets for that," Leona said.

She briefly wondered if Bob had been to see any of these girls. She doubted it because he was much more apt to drink and gamble than to bother anybody else with his carrot. Not that he loved her, she was sure. It was more that he wouldn't pay for something he thought he already had.

As she was getting in her truck, the tall rat-faced wolf stopped her. "Galen wants to see you before you go."

"Best go on, girl," Dora said. "Don't make him wait."

Leona rolled her eyes, but she followed the rat-faced man around the back of the house. Galen sat at a worn wooden picnic table, skinning things. He had a pile of animals: rabbits, a possum, a few coons, and a cat. He worked on the possum, flicking his skinning knife expertly as he pulled the pelt off in one whole piece. He didn't seem to care about the meat. He tossed it in a pile. The pile was covered in flies that buzzed away when he disturbed them with the possum. They returned in number and attacked the new addition. Galen picked up another animal and moved on.

"You know how to find somebody, witch?"

"I reckon so," Leona said, assuming he meant a locator spell. "I ain't got the kit to do it now though."

"Tomorrow then," he said. He pulled the skin off a raccoon and tossed the carcass on the fly pile.

"You got something personal of theirs?" Leona asked.

"Dora will show you," Galen said. "Her trailer's over that way."

He wanted a girl found then. She should refuse. If somebody lit out of this holler, it was better for them. But like always, Galen seemed to know what she was thinking.

"It don't work out, it'll be your ass and our deal's off, so don't get any notions."

"I ain't got none," Leona said. "But if I do this, we need to be square."

"We'll see," was all he said, then he went back to his work.

Leona waited a second, but he didn't speak. He simply flicked his knife and pulled the creatures apart. The smell made her feel sick, and the buzz of the flies made her anxious. So she made for her truck. The rat-faced man followed.

"Hey, you got anything for headaches?" he asked.

"Ain't you got no aspirin?" Leona asked.

"You're supposed to be the new doc," he said, holding her door open.

She climbed in, rummaged in her bag, and tossed him two

pills. She didn't want to be the one doctoring the werewolves. They could all burn after what she'd seen that day. "It ain't a miracle drug. Get you some at the five and dime." She yanked the door handle and slammed it, then started her engine.

"Lookee, gal, we own you. I want you to give me some aspirin, you'll give it to me with no lip."

Leona felt the dark magic push its way to the surface again, and she let it come. She pushed her hand out, and the rat-face flew backward and hit a tree trunk. He slid down and sputtered, dazed and confused. Leona got out of her truck.

"I only take orders from one man out here, and you ain't him." She grabbed his chin and squeezed her other palm. He doubled over in pain as the magic squeezed his privates. "You ever try that mess with me again and you'll find out if you fellas can grow something back after a moon. You understand?"

He nodded and growled. "Galen ain't gonna—" he screamed again as she squeezed.

"I don't care what you tell him. But what you best understand is that I ain't here to be bossed by you. Keep vexing me and see how you like it," she said.

He nodded and cried when she finally released him.

"All right, good," she said. "We have an understanding. Make sure all them other boys have the same understanding."

Leona stalked to her truck with more confidence than she thought she possessed. She started the old truck and fishtailed out before righting herself and gunning the engine. She didn't realize she'd been holding her breath until she was out on the gravel road.

The deal with Galen Nolan would never be square. She'd do his locator spell, and she'd help those girls as best she could, but she knew she needed Jewel to find and refine some wolfsbane because there was only one thing that Galen would understand. Only one thing that would get him to leave her and her folks be, and that was to be as ruthless as he was.

Finally she and Jewel agreed as to how to handle a man.

26

I f Kay finds out we did up these rat jars anyway, she will beat us for sure," Jewel said. She plopped the last of the rat heads in a canning jar and closed it tight. She waved her hand and spoke an incantation. The liquid in the jar shimmered and glowed then bubbled and turned bright red.

"Well, she best not find out then," Leona said. "You're the one that's always got to tell what you done. You'd get away with more if you just learned to keep quiet and not brag on yourself."

"Don't tell me what's what, Leona Mae. We wouldn't even be doing all this if you'd just get rid of them ghosts properly." Jewel picked up one of the jars and shook it at her. The rat head sloshed around inside. "Stuffing rat heads in a jar ain't exactly my idea of a good time."

"The rats was already dead," Leona said. Something itched down deep inside her. She attributed it the being so stressed and close to All Hallow's Eve, but really it was something else.

She felt a little bad about disobeying Granny Kay, but once she and Jewel had taken a little bit of the herb of grace to boost their power and make the binding jars and she'd gotten over the initial nausea, she had felt energized and enjoyed the spells. It was dark magic, Leona knew, but the herb of grace clouded that feeling that said it was bad and let the voice that always laughed and urged her forward have its day. She only had to do three jars and was sorry when her last one was completed.

Jewel on the other hand, had complained even though she had been the one to perfect the binding jars in the first place.

"I don't care if the rats was already dead. I hate rats. They could all be dead for all I care. My point is, this ain't necessary."

They carried the jars out back of Leona's house. Mary and Karla growled as Leona approached. She didn't feel afraid of them at all. She had the urge to blast them, actually, but knew that was likely the herb of grace talking. Leona tamped the surly down, and they got on with the trap.

Leona handed Jewel a sack of coarse salt. "I'll keep them focused on me. You ring them."

"And what if they come for me?" Jewel asked.

"I'll be ready." Leona held up a bundle of sage. When Mary and Karla saw it, they hissed and growled.

"For Pete's sake, Leona, don't antagonize them until I'm done," Jewel said. She began to pour out a thick circle of salt all the way around the ghosts. "How far behind?"

Mary and Karla stayed focused on Leona. "That's good.

They're about ten feet in front of you. They can't go backward toward you."

"You'd better hope not, Leona," Jewel said, keeping a wary eye in the ghost's direction as she laid down the salt.

When Jewel completed the circle, Leona bent down and put her hand on the salt. Jewel did the same, and they blessed it. The salt glowed green, and the ghosts screamed against their mouth stitches. When the glowing abated, the ghosts' eyes glowed bright red. They slammed against the circle, enraged.

"I don't know about this, Leona. They're real riled up now. I can feel them."

"There's still seven circles of solid warding up. If they bust out of this, they still gotta come through that," Leona said. "Get on with the second circle. I'll hold them."

Jewel walked behind Leona and laid down a second circle, making a double salt ring around Mary and Karla. When it was complete, the girls blessed it and watched as Mary and Karla got mad again. They beat on each other and the ward, screaming and hissing as their eyes glowed even brighter.

"We better get these rat jars going," Leona said as she watched the ghosts rage. "Maybe seven wards won't be enough."

"I don't think seven hundred wards would be enough," Jewel said.

They set the jars equidistant around the circle. When they opened them up, they had to jump out of the way as the spell took immediate effect. The red vapor spilled out of the jars and coated the circle, then it rose up and made a dome over Mary and Karla. Their thrashing stopped and their eyes dulled so that there was only a glint of red in them, like the light of a faraway star.

"I can't hear them at all, can you?" Jewel whispered.

"I can, but they're muffled."

"I guess it's working then," Jewel said.

"How long do you think it will last?" Leona asked. Mary and Karla were still inside the red dome, except every once in a while they would twitch.

"When we used the one jar it lasted overnight, but it also had the power of the Ave Maria behind it. Six jars? Longer, but how much longer, I don't know. Tomorrow's the Eve, so you best hope at least two days," Jewel said.

Leona continued to stare at the ghosts. She timed their twitches and noticed that each time they twitched, it was just a little bit sooner than the last movement. They'd break the bind eventually. The power of the herb of grace left her. In its absence, doubt crept in. She always had reason to be nervous on All Hallows Eve.

As soon as the thought crossed her mind, Cale appeared beside them. He stared at Mary and Karla, his face awash with deep worry and fear.

"I hope the two of you know what you're doing," he said.

"Yeah, us too," Leona and Jewel said in unison.

27

L eona, you ain't no account at locator spells. It's best I
go on out there and do it." Jewel crossed her arms and
pursed her lips. She didn't get up to gather the
supplies.

"No way, Jewel. You need to keep as far away from Galen
Nolan as possible. He won't put up with no lip."

"I guess he'll put up with whatever I say so long as whatever he wants found gets found."

"He won't. He'll rip your tongue clean out of your mouth."
Leona got up from the table and began to rummage around in
the magic stores.

"Ha. I'd like to see him try," Jewel said. "I'd curse a dirty werewolf as soon as I'd look at him. In fact, maybe that's what we ought to do."

"Ain't you got no fresh strawberry leaves?" Leona asked. She pulled out a jar of moldy leaves and shook it.

Jewel got up and took the jar. "Them ain't strawberry leaves. It's ague wort. Don't you know nothing?" Jewel pulled down a bundle of leaves from her drying rack and handed them to her sister. "Leona, this spell might not work if whatever you aim to find is far off, and you most likely can't do it on your own."

"No, Jewel. You ain't coming. We can't group up at that holler. I got a bad feeling about it."

"Well, what do you think is gonna happen if the spell's a bust? That dirty werewolf ain't gonna like it none."

"It's dangerous. If I run into any difficulty, you'll know."

"How? And don't say Cale because I know what day it is, and I know he ain't going to be handy."

Leona's face got hot, and she stuffed the bundle of strawberry leaves in a flour sack. "I-I need the right candles." She busied herself looking.

Jewel laughed, then picked up the white candle that was on the shelf right in front of Leona's face. "Leona, you know what your problem is?"

"Jewel. Don't."

Jewel was undeterred. "Your problem is you think you gotta be above the fray. Like all this"—she made a motion to the magic stores—"somehow means you gotta be better than what you are."

"That ain't even remotely my problem."

Jewel laughed again. She took out a fifth of whiskey and poured it into her teacup. Leona went to purse her lips in protest at the early hour, but stopped when Jewel winked at her and toasted her.

"It's precisely your problem. What we can do don't make us better. It don't make me no better at being a human than if I was a great cook like Audine, or a whiz at fixing engines like Albert was. It's just a thing we do."

"I don't believe that, and neither do you." Leona shook her head and finished gathering the supplies for the spell. "We can do good, or we can do bad. We ought to do good if we can."

"That ain't what I mean. I mean, we're humans with a talent and skill. Sure, we do good. But we're still human. And that means I ain't good all the time, and I sure ain't gonna beat myself up if I got human feelings."

"I don't know what you're talking about," Leona said.

Jewel rolled her eyes. "It's Halloween. Everyone knows, Leona."

"Knows what?" Leona's heart skipped a few beats, and her face burned again. She knew that Jewel knew, but they didn't discuss it. Even Jewel, with her brash nature, knew better.

"I know you're gonna send Cale away tonight. You do every Halloween."

"I don't do anything to him. If he goes, he goes of his own account."

"Uh huh. Sure. You ain't got to be embarrassed about it. You're a grown woman. Bob is a piece of shit. Nobody in their right mind would begrudge you Cale on the one night you can have hi—"

"Jewel! You hush up. I don't . . . I don't do—"

Jewel smacked the chifforobe with the flat of her hand and sent jars tipping and tinkling as the force of it knocked them over. Her eyes flashed, and she pointed at Leona. "See? That's it right there! It ain't healthy for you, nor any of us, to pretend and lie. You love Cale. You always have. He loves you. He always has. Tonight, you're both human, even if you'd just as soon pretend you ain't. And anyways, I know you done it before."

Leona sat down in the chair. She dropped her head in her hands and cried. "That was a long time ago. It wasn't right. I can't Jewel."

Jewel sat next to her and stroked her hair. "You could. But you won't. That's your business, only don't beat yourself up because you want him. He wants you too. Love ain't no sin." She handed Leona a dishtowel.

"I made a vow. I broke it once before. I said I wouldn't again." Leona dried her eyes with the towel. "It hurts him to go, but we got no choice."

"That ain't true. You do. You're just making the painful one."

"They're both the painful one," Leona said.

"Maybe, but at least one of them gives you some comfort and love for once." Jewel patted her on the back then kissed the top of her head as she stood up and grabbed another bunch of dried strawberry. She tucked it in Leona's bag. "If you double it up, it might help you. Double up the personal item too." Then Jewel smiled, unable to resist the dig. "Of course, I wouldn't need it myself, but I don't see as it will do you any harm, Leona."

L eona had to run home after picking up the supplies from Jewel. She was missing a few precautions and her medical bag, which she thought she might need should she have time to sneak up to the women's shacks and check on a few patients. Peggy was at Ida Mae's place until she could suss out what to do about the ghosts, and Bob had made himself scarce of late. He wasn't out at Nolan Holler so much that she would have seen him, but Leona doubted very much that he was abstaining from the filthy delights of the place. At least he was smart enough not to let her see him.

Leona looked through her medical bag and decided she was low on willow bark and comfrey root, so she replenished the stores. She added some more bandages and a plain old bottle of aspirin. She looked up at the cuckoo clock on the wall. He was just shy of signaling two in the afternoon. It was barely enough time to go do the locator spell and be back by dark. On Halloween, Leona always liked to be home and in a ward of protection by sundown. If she wasn't, she was more likely than most people to run into something she'd just as soon not.

The bird clucked two, and as it did, the temperature in the room dropped. The mass of cold air was directly behind her, and she didn't turn around as she finished packing her bag.

"You don't have enough time." Cale's voice was close.

"I do. I just have to get it done," Leona said. "No choice."

"There's always a choice."

Leona turned around and stared into Cale's big brown eyes. "Well, my other choice is to get a werewolf after me even worse than I got now, and that ain't no choice."

"If you're not back in time, what if those girls . . . What if they bust through and take form?"

Ghosts were flesh that night, and she'd already considered what would happen if Mary and Karla were able to be physical. She had ringed more wards, and so far the red binding dome held. But in just twenty-four hours, Mary and Karla had gotten louder and had begun to move slowly inside the dome. They were nowhere near full strength, but it was clear it was only a matter of time. Leona could only pray that the binding suppression spell would hold until the next morning when all of the spirits were safely behind their veil again.

Still, she puffed up and did her best to project cocky bravado, like Jewel would have done. "Nobody is getting through my wards. If them girls are flesh tonight, they won't even be able to see this place, let alone cross through and come for me."

"What do you mean?" Cale asked. He had a funny look on his face, confused and hurt.

"I always put up an undetectable ward on Halloween. Anyone comes looking for me will just see an empty lot."

"But what if you know the house is here, anyway?"

"Well, I guess you ain't never attempted it because I do it every year. Any human that comes out here is gonna see an empty field and get addled from trying to work out what's off. Saves me a lot of problems on Halloween."

Cale's face reddened. "Of course I ain't ever tried. I go away." He stared at her a moment, then sighed. "Maybe I better not this year. Maybe I better stick close."

"Cale. You know we can't."

"I don't know that, Lee. I don't. This ain't a normal Halloween. I could help. I could watch out."

"You'll just make it harder and . . . you know we can't."

"That was a long time ago. We were kids. Things are different now."

Leona stared hard at him for a long beat. His face was beautiful. Smooth, but with a hint at stubble that she longed to reach up and run her palm over. She still remembered how it felt, his cheek up next to hers, the slight prickle of his beard stubble rubbing pleasantly against her skin. She remembered how his lips felt, how they tasted, sweet and salty. How he smelled. Clean, yet earthy, all man, but not sour, like Bob. She remembered the feel of his hands all over her body and remembered wanting to touch him and be so close to him that not even a sheet of paper could fit between them. Her face flushed with the memory of the last time they'd made the mistake of being together on Halloween. It was agony to remember and worse to consider forgetting.

Cale was wrong. Things weren't different. They might be older, but her passion for him hadn't waned over the years. Even as she stood looking at him in this form, she wanted to touch him, wanted him to touch her. Her face grew hotter still at the thought of it.

"Things are not different. Not for me. Not ever," she whispered.

He nodded. "We're stronger together. We'll just have to—"

Leona shook her head. "I can handle whatever comes for me. What I can't handle is having you here and not being able to touch you."

"Lee, I love you. If something happens, I'll—"

"You'll die? You're a might late on that." She gave a little laugh then stopped because it felt mean, and she hadn't meant it that way.

Cale wasn't laughing. "Dying was preferable to knowing I'd be here forever without you."

Leona put her hand up to his cheek. Even now, in the afternoon, she could feel a slight warmth there that wasn't normal. The feeling and need stirred inside her again, and she shook her head.

"I have to go do that spell. And you have to go. Please don't be here when I get back."

A dark shadow of frustration and pain flashed across his face, but he nodded. "If that's how you want it."

Leona gathered up her bag and went to the door. She paused but didn't look back at him. She couldn't. "How I want it got nothing to do with it. That's just how it has to be."

After she parked, Leona went directly to Liza's trailer, ignoring the rat-faced man who told her Galen was waiting.

"I reckon he can wait a bit longer," Leona said. Her head hurt, and the sun was sinking lower in the afternoon sky. She didn't have much time, but she couldn't come all the way out there without checking in on patients.

Dora sat by Liza, wiping off her forehead. Liza was awake, and while she looked pallid and weak, her eyes shone brighter. Leona smiled and sat on the edge of the bed.

"You look a sight better, I'd say."

Liza nodded. "I feel better."

"I'm gonna take a look, alright?"

"Yes, ma'am," Liza said.

Leona lifted up the blanket. The poultices had done their job. They were black and awful, but they had drawn the poison out, and the flesh around the bites was less swollen and angry.

"They look better," Leona said. She mixed up fresh medicine, cleaned the bites again, and applied the paste.

"I think you're well enough for this tea." Leona brewed up the willow bark tea and added something to kick up Liza's healing. "I left some of this out. Have as much as you can stand and drink plenty of water."

"Thank you, ma'am. I-I think maybe you saved my life," Liza said.

"I don't know, but them bites wasn't nothing to mess with. Liza, you ain't got to tell me, but I'm gonna ask. Who done that to you?"

Liza's face scrunched up, confused, like she was trying to remember. Leona watched her eyes cloud over. It was so fast, if she hadn't been looking for it, she would have missed it. The magic of the memory spell came and went, preventing Liza from relaying any information about her assailant. She went from confused to angry, then upset, and cried.

"I-I don't know. I feel like I know, then, all of a sudden, I don't," Liza said.

"Don't be troubled over it. I might could help, but not now. You rest easy." She patted Liza's hand and gave it a squeeze. "They'll be plenty of time for remembering."

The rat-faced man burst through the door. "Look here, Galen is awful mad. He says you best not make him come and get you."

Dora nodded. "All right, Billy. She's a coming." She nodded at Leona. "Best go do whatever he wants."

"Yes, we wouldn't want him waiting none," Leona said. She patted Liza one last time and followed the rat-faced man out of the trailer and back down the hill. Dora accompanied them. Billy Rat-Face led them around back of Galen's house, to the skinning pile. Galen pointed his knife at Leona.

"I don't like waiting, witch."

"Well, you told me to fix up that girl that was in a bad way. I was just doing what you told me to," Leona said.

"Next time, don't think. Just do what you're told."

Leona looked around. "The spell won't work back here."

"Why not?" Galen asked.

"Because it's disgusting. Too much bad energy with all these dead critters."

Galen eyeballed her for a second like he was going to hit her, but he didn't. He flicked his knife, so it stuck into the wood of the picnic table and tossed the squirrel in the pile. He didn't bother to wipe his hands off as he stood up. He led them around the other side of the house, to a little cleared out place that had patchy grass and a bit of fading afternoon sun.

"Hurry up about it," he said.

Leona wasn't Jewel. She didn't need to retort, but she did right then wish she had a shotgun to blast Galen Nolan. She ignored him and set to work laying out her spell. She eyed the herb of grace, pausing for a second. She thought of Granny Kay's warning, and she recalled using it just two days prior. But the voice whispered, and she looked at Galen, whose hateful impatience poured off of him in waves. It was late, and she really needed to get home. Delay and failure were not options.

Leona shoved a handful of the leaves in her mouth and chewed. It tasted awful, bitter and burnt, but she swallowed it down and waited. She felt the magic run through her and got a little jolt of energy, like a big slug of coffee hit her.

Once she was ready, she looked up at Dora. "You got something of hers?"

Dora nodded and handed her a scarf. Leona cut a bit of the fabric off with her knife and added it to her mix, then she closed her eyes and centered herself.

Jewel was better at locations. She hardly needed anything of the person's, and she almost always got the location right away. Leona had to use a good deal of the personal item, and it took her a while to see the location. She burned more of the scarf and chanted faster, concentrating on the swirling mist in her mind, willing it to clear and show her the girl.

A wave of nausea hit her, and she held back the bile in her mouth. The force of the sick made her lose her concentration for a second, and the mist thickened rather than abated. Leona swallowed down the sick in her mouth. She began to feel hot, like she was baking in front of a roaring fire, and her headache pinched and made her head throb.

Her eyeballs even felt hot and big, like her eyelids wouldn't cover them. Another round of nausea hit her, and this time she leaned over and vomited. She heard Galen scoff behind her. He sort of tsked and then growled low. Leona shut all of it out. The pain, the sickness, the impatient werewolf lurking. She balled up her fists and set her jaw, then she concentrated.

Gradually the mist cleared, and she saw a girl sitting in a living room. The view panned out as the vision centered on a street. Leona felt dizzy and sucked in a big breath, then the white candle burned out, and the herb and scarf mixture flared, turning to ash. Leona opened her eyes.

"She's at 505 Montgomery Street, in Marietta. Little yellow house."

"You sure?" Galen asked.

"That's what the spell showed," Leona said. The holler spun, and her vision blurred. Leona didn't dare try to stand up or move. The world was a whirl, a dizzying, terrible ride, and she couldn't make it stop. She felt a cold prickle and a rush as her adrenaline kicked in, and she let loose with a torrent of vomit. When she was done, she spat a few times, wiped her mouth, and got to her feet.

Galen watched her, his gaze intense, then he nodded at Billy Rat-Face. "Go to Marietta and bring her back." He looked at Leona. "You're staying here 'til they get back."

"Marietta is an hour away. I can't stay here no two hours." Leona packed up her things.

"Well, you're gonna. And if she ain't there, you're gonna do it again. Maybe I'll have them go get that mouthy sister of yours. She'll do it right."

Leona stopped and cocked her head at him. The rage bubbled below the surface, and she closed her fist, trying hard not to grab him. She'd thought she'd done a good enough job of keeping Jewel out of it. Clearly, Galen had better information than she thought.

"I done it right. She's in Marietta. If she ain't, you won't need no locator spell to find me. You know where I live. You can't find her, well come on then. I'll be waiting." Leona closed her fist and concentrated on a tree. There was a loud crack, and a big branch fell down. It barely missed Galen. He never flinched.

Leona picked up her bag and gave him her back as she walked to her truck. Nobody stopped her, but Galen followed her all the way out to the road. He stood there in his bare feet, watching her. She could hear him growling even over the rumble of the old truck engine. Her head pounded, and when she looked at the sky, the sun was setting. She had to get home —and fast.

30

Leona puked twice more on the ride home, and she was in such a rush that she didn't stop the vehicle and vomit outside. Frothy green sick splattered all over the truck cab, but she didn't bother with it. The sun just barely peeked out over the ridge behind the house, and Leona could feel it, the shift in the veil. It was like a muffled world suddenly sounded clear, and a detectable energy crackled all around.

She had minutes to get inside her wards, but when she opened the truck door, everything went spinning. She fell flat on her face in the sparse gravel of the driveway. Leona scrambled around, panicked as the world spun faster, and she found herself unable to tell up from down. She managed to flip over on to her back and sucked in a big gulp of air as she tried to calm herself.

The surrounding air pulsed and thumped in her head in time with her breathing. Leona closed her eyes and took a big breath and held it, then expelled it as her racing heart slowed. It had to have been the herb of grace. She'd used too much of it. It was poisonous in a large enough dose, and while she didn't think she'd used that much; she had apparently added enough to make her sick. Leona had a curative if she could just get inside, but at the moment, she was like a turtle caught on its back.

She heard muffled voices that got louder and more distinct until they were a throbbing din, and when she opened her eyes, she caught shimmers and shapes as the dead manifested. Some might not make it all the way to full physical form, but she'd be able to see and hear the ones who couldn't the same as the ones who could, She'd go insane from the noise if she didn't get behind her wards soon.

Leona managed to roll over on her side and tried to push herself up onto her elbow in the hopes of standing. But another wave of dizziness and nausea enveloped her, and she vomited again. She could feel them getting more solid and closer to her, and their chatter got louder and more frantic as they all struggled to speak at once. Leona clapped her hands over her ears and curled up into a miserable ball as the noise thundered in her head. Hands clawed and poked at her, and she felt a rush of cold air then heat, hot as a puff from an oven as the dead manifested around her. Leona screamed.

Then someone scooped her up. Strong arms held her to a chest, and Leona sobbed into it as she recognized the familiar scent.

"I-I can't see the house, Lee. Where is it?" Cale's voice rumbled in his chest against her ear.

"Walk straight ahead," Leona said.

Cale extracted them from the throng of half-manifested ghosts then lurched forward. After ten big steps, the noises ceased, and Leona knew they were inside her wards. Cale carried her inside the house and set her down on the couch. When Leona looked into his eyes, she saw fear.

"Lee, what's wrong? What happened?"

"Go into my stores. Get me the bottle marked *calendula*."

"Okay, but—"

"I'll explain later. Just get it."

Cale nodded and raced to the kitchen. Sounds of crashing glass and thuds came from the room. He returned a few minutes later with the bottle and a glass of water. Leona took both. Her hand shook as she emptied the calendula into her hand, then shoved it in her mouth. She chased it with the water. Her nausea got worse, and she had to fight to keep from vomiting the herb before it could work. She curled up tightly on the couch as she let the antidote work.

After a few minutes, the nausea subsided and then another rush of heat hit her, hot as a bonfire. She sat straight up on the couch and gasped for air as sweat poured down her face. There was one final rush of terrible fire, then it was over. Leona collapsed back against the couch and closed her eyes.

"What the hell happened, Lee?"

"I overdid it with the herb of grace. I think. I'm all right now." Her stomach had stopped heaving, and the world was stable.

There was worry in Cale's eyes as they searched Leona's face. She jumped a little as his hands ran up and down her arms. She was so used to the feeling of cold that she associated with him that the warmth of him now unsettled her for a moment. But then her heart raced faster, and her breath caught in her chest. He inched closer and closer to her, and she found herself doing the same, unable to stand any space between them. When she realized what she was about to do, she jumped up from the couch and backed away.

"You should have stayed gone, Cale."

"I got a bad feeling about an hour ago. I tried to put it out of my mind, but I just couldn't. Good thing."

"I'm gonna go clean up." Leona pointed at him. "You stay put."

He didn't object and sat on the couch, awkward and suddenly shy.

Leona wiped her face with a cool washcloth and rinsed her mouth to rid it of the taste of vomit. She stared at herself in the mirror.

"Girl, you best keep clear of him." She shook her finger at her reflection, warning herself as she might Jewel. It was about as effective on her as it would have been on Jewel. Instead of locking herself in the bedroom, she headed back out to the parlor.

Cale stood up from the couch when she entered. He fidgeted and turned red then sat back down.

Leona fought the urge to go to him. She let the wave pass and collected herself. "You want some tea?"

He looked confused then nodded. "S-sure. I guess so."

Leona busied herself in the kitchen making a pot of tea. The silent, empty house both calmed her and made her nervous. The familiar act of it calmed her nerves a bit, and she felt calm and in control when she carried the tray out to the parlor. She passed Cale a cup of tea. Both of their hands shook as they drank.

"Been a long time since I had anything to drink," Cale said.

"I guess that's so," Leona tried to sound casual. But this kind of small talk was foreign to them, and it sounded idiotic to her. "You don't normally have nothing on Halloween?"

"No. I usually just, umm . . . Well, I walk around the woods."

"Huh. Why? You could do all sorts of things this night. Seems like you'd—" she stopped and stuttered. "I-I don't know what."

"There's only one thing I ever want to do," Cale said. His eyes darkened and bored into Leona.

She stared back as she felt a force between them. She fought against the pull, but it was like trying to avoid gravity. An impossibility. Leona closed her eyes and begged someone, anyone, for the strength to stay exactly where she was on the sofa, but nobody was listening. She set the teacup down and moved closer.

Leona reached up and ran her fingers through his sandy blond hair. His scent was so distinctive to her, slightly spicy and earthy, with undertones of leather and sandalwood. The combination was intoxicating. She found herself closer to him still, and she grabbed handfuls of his shirt, leaned in, and breathed in deeply before she pressed her forehead against his chest.

All restraint was gone as he wrapped his arms around her and crushed her to him, his lips in her hair and hands everywhere. When he kissed her, she didn't pull back or try to reason with him that they shouldn't. Their clothes ended up slung across the room, and they moved together on the couch, warm skin to warm skin for once.

She let go and, for at least one night, she put everything else out of her mind—Bob, the two dead girls, werewolves, and ghosts—and let herself be loved and happy.

The first time was over quickly, but he didn't stop touching her and she clutched at him, breathless and desperate for more. She kissed his chest and licked at the sweat that beaded up all over him. He grabbed her head and pulled her to him, crushing her lips with his mouth as she straddled him and gave in to the bliss.

Time ceased to mean anything, and by the time it did, she was drowsy and content as they lay tangled up in each other. She pushed down the guilt and fear that nagged at her and snuggled closer. She let the slow, steady thump of his temporary heartbeat lull her to sleep as she clutched him to her, safe, if only for one night.

When she woke up the next morning, he was gone. She closed her eyes and tried to find him. The energy was slight, almost imperceptible, but it was still there, and she knew he would eventually come back to her. The bed was cold beside her, but the smell of him lingered on the pillow. She buried her face in it. She lay there and cried for a good long while until the sun streamed in through the little window. Then she dried her eyes, got up, and got on with business.

L eona watered the pansies she'd planted on Dill's grave, next
to his headstone. Dill wasn't buried there in the church plot
on the hilltop. He had died on some island, Guadalcanal,
the army man told them. Jewel had been excited when the shiny
black car pulled up, but Leona had known. She dreamt of it for a
month. She hadn't cried at all about him. She was determined not
to, not until she'd seen him.

Leona wasn't sure about the rules for the dead. Sometimes she
saw them and sometimes she didn't. The ones in the old family plot
had long since gone off to wherever ghosts went when they finished
their business or grew tired of the living world. Sometimes though,
you'd find them by their headstones, so she would wait and see if Dill
would find her by his.

At any rate, graveyards were peaceful. Every once in a while, a ghost would wander by and wave a polite hello. Mostly it was old people, ghosts in fancy dresses and hats. Leona would smile at them and wave. She'd talk to them if they wanted her to, but none stayed. They sashayed off, talking and laughing. They had ghost business elsewhere.

So, she was surprised when a young man wandered by and stared at her. He had sandy blond hair and dark brown eyes, the color of chocolate. His face was unlined, and he wore a brown sweater vest and khaki trousers. He stopped and stared at her. His face reddened when she gave him a wave and said, "Hello there."

"You can see me?"

Leona nodded. "Yes."

"How is that possible?" the young man asked.

"I-I don't rightly know," Leona said. "I've been able to see ghosts and talk to them since I was little."

"How old are you now?" he asked.

"I'm fifteen," Leona answered. "How old are you?"

"I'm twenty. I mean . . . I was twenty. I-I don't know how long . . . it's confusing."

Leona nodded. She stood up. "Lots of you get confused about time. I imagine time don't make much sense after you die."

"Why are you hanging out in a graveyard?"

Leona pointed to Dill's headstone. "I come to see if my brother shows up."

"You miss him?"

"Terrible bad," Leona said. "Except I don't think he's coming back."

"How did he die?"

"In the war. Over in the Pacific Ocean."

The young man looked confused. "What war? Is the Great War still going on?"

"The Great War? Oh, you mean the first one with Germany. We

got into a second one, only this time with Germany and Japan. My brothers went off to fight Japan. Both of them. Will died first, and Dill died last August."

"I'm sorry to hear that. He died in Japan?"

"No, some other island. Guadalcanal. They couldn't give him back to us, but they paid to set up a nice marker." Leona gestured to the headstone. It was made of a smooth white stone.

"Ah, well, maybe that's why he ain't here," the young man said. "If he ain't really buried here, then he might not be able to stay here."

"That's true," Leona said. "I guess I can ask Granny Kay about it, but she doesn't like answering questions about ghosts so much."

"Why not?"

"I don't know. She says not to dwell on the dead."

"Seems like you can't help it." The young man smoothed his hair down and shrugged.

"Well, I don't really have a choice in seeing them, that's true enough," Leona said. "Say, what's your name?"

"It's Cale. Cale Murphy."

"I'm Leona Spencer."

"Nice to meet you, Leona."

"So do you know how you died?" Leona asked him.

He scoffed at her. "Sure. I got sick and just died."

"You look hardy. It don't seem like you'd get sick. Where's your grave?"

"Over there," Cale said, pointed a few rows over. They strolled over, and Leona had a look.

"You died in 1918. Musta had the flu."

Cale nodded. "Yes, that sounds right. I was supposed to go to France, to fight the Krauts, but . . . I-I don't think I made it. I think I was in Kansas. Sometimes it gets confusing."

"To remember?" Leona asked.

Cale nodded. "Yes. I know things, about my life, who I am, then sometimes I don't."

"I think maybe it's like that when you're dead a while." She did the math. "It's 1943. You been dead twenty-five years. That's a good long while."

"It ain't that long," Cale said.

Leona sat down and ran her hand over his headstone. She traced his name with her finger, and a little jolt of electric went through her. Cale plopped down beside her. "Well, it's longer than you was alive, so I imagine it's a long while."

"It doesn't feel long, and yet it does."

"How come you stick around?"

"I don't know. Sometimes, it feels like I'm supposed to do something. Like today, that feeling is strong, and everything is bright and colorful. Most days everything is kinda washed out looking and gray."

Leona thought for a moment. She talked to many ghosts, and she'd never heard one have a purpose. Most were just sort of stuck in a habit or genuinely confused. Cale didn't seem like he fell into either category.

"Well, I bet you'll know what you mean to do when you mean to do it," she said.

"Maybe," he said. He smoothed his hair back and smiled at her.

Leona smiled back. He was handsome. She'd been writing to Bob Monroe, and he was handsome in his uniform but dull.

"What did you like to do, before you died?" she asked him.

He thought for a moment. "I liked to read, and I liked dogs. I was going to go to college and be a veterinarian, I think," he said. He knitted his brow and thought hard then smiled. "Yes. That was what I was going to do."

"That's very nice. I love animals," Leona said. "You seem like you'd have made a fine veterinarian."

"You just met me. How do you know?"

"*You're thoughtful and seem kind and gentle. And besides, I'm a psychic.*"

"*Ha, that's funny.*"

"*Well, I am. I see things sometimes. Not all the time, but big things. And anyways, I can talk to ghosts, so that maybe makes me special.*" Leona gave a little laugh.

"*I doubt that's the only thing that makes you special,*" Cale said.

Leona blushed and ducked her head for a minute. She cleared her throat. "*So what's your favorite book?*" she asked, smiling at the way he smoothed his hair back and the thoughtful pause he took as he answered her.

32

T en days had passed, yet Cale had not reappeared. Leona wasn't worried at first when he was gone; he always was on the first of November and for a few days after, but as the last of the leaves fell and the pleasant chill of October gave way to the more persistent cold of November, she worried that their night together had cost them more dearly than they knew.

When Leona closed her eyes and thought of him, she could feel him and hear his voice calling to her, only it was like he was far away, his voice muffled like a child's spoken through tin can walkie-talkies. She didn't have the opportunity to dwell on it.

The rat head binding spell had held for a total of four days.

Mary and Karla had broken free on November second. They didn't seem to be any stronger, but they had broken through the next level of Leona's wards, leaving six in place. So far, the fifth level held, but as she stood in her garden, they clawed at the air and threw themselves against the barrier, which vibrated with the violence of Mary and Karla's joint assault.

Leona had only enough time for a quick cup of tea between her shift at the diner and her evening work at Marv's. She stood amongst the remains of her herb garden, all trimmed and tucked in for the winter as she sipped her tea and watched the ghosts. They thrashed and strained against the thread holding their mouths shut, silently screaming in agony and hatred.

"I'm sorry. For both of you. I truly am," Leona said as she finished her cup and walked inside.

Both Bob and Peggy were gone. She hadn't seen Bob in a few days, which was fine by her. She'd hidden her money in a different spot, and thankfully, Bob had not found it. Peggy felt the ghosts more keenly than Leona would have thought. Thus far, the child hadn't shown any magical ability, but she would stand at the back door and stare out toward the ghosts.

Peggy's behavior had been much worse—with violent tantrums and fits of terror. So, she rotated Peggy back and forth between Jewel and Ida Mae to keep her away from the bad energy, and it seemed to help. Ida Mae made snide comments about Leona's mothering. But she enjoyed dressing up Peggy, so it was easy enough to ignore. And Peggy liked staying there and getting attention. Staying with Jewel was a different matter. Jewel and Peggy had never seen eye-to-eye, and the days when Jewel kept her were fairly volatile, with Peggy spending quite a lot of time standing in the corner.

"Leona, there ain't enough switches in the woods to deal with this child," Jewel would say.

Jewel wasn't wrong. Peggy was obstinate, not unlike Jewel herself, but Leona had the good sense to refrain from the comparison. Jewel advocated sending Peggy straight out to deal with the ghosts.

"She's meaner than they could ever hope to be, curse or not."

Peggy wasn't always a pleasant child, but Leona refused to believe it couldn't be dealt with when she got rid of the ghosts, so until that could be accomplished, she kept Peggy clear of the house as much as she could.

Leona rinsed out her cup and straightened herself up a bit. She had just grabbed her coat and bag when there was a knock at the door.

Reverend Greenleaf stood on her stoop with Levi Walker beside him. He shifted from side to side, and his face reddened as he spoke. "Why, hello Leona, how are you today?"

"Uh, hello, Reverend. What brings you out this way?" Leona asked.

"Well, Brother Levi and I are just paying calls, letting everyone know that we're planning a special revival event."

"Oh, is that so?" Leona asked. She tried to keep her voice casual, but her heart thundered in her chest as her hackles raised. Both Mary and Karla had been to a revival. In her heart, Leona knew Levi Walker had something to do with their murders, but she needed more evidence. Whether or not a revival in town was going to be a boon or a bane, Leona wasn't sure. They needed to be able to snoop around, but if their theory about Levi was correct, the revival coming to Ames could result in more dead bodies and vengeful ghosts.

"We're so excited to bring the Word to Ames," Levi Walker said. He looked past Leona and then smiled his movie star smile at her. "Could we trouble you for a cup of coffee?"

"Well, sir, I was just about to leave for work," Leona said.

She didn't care for the way Levi's eyes searched around her home. He was up to something.

Reverend Greenleaf couldn't have cared less if Leona attended a regular church service, let alone a revival.

"Oh? Well, that's too bad. I was looking forward to getting to know you," Levi said. "Rev here has told me all about you."

"I'll bet," Leona said. "Well, tell you what, come on by the diner some time," she said. "I'll treat you to a slice of pie."

"I will surely hold you to that promise," Levi said.

"I expect you to," Leona countered. "Now, I'm sure sorry, but I have to finish up and run."

"Of course. Well, the revival starts Sunday night and we'll keep the Praise through Tuesday evening," Greenleaf said. He handed Leona a flyer. "We'd be pleased if you'd join us."

Leona took the flyer and nodded. "Yes, sir."

"Oh, and bring your sister, Jewel, as well," Levi said. "I'd love to get to know her."

"I'll let her know all about it," Leona said.

Anyone who knew Jewel for half a minute knew she belonged at a tent revival about as much as an elephant belonged in a China shop. Nobody would really want her there, which meant Levi Walker was taunting her.

"Bye now, Miss Leona. You have a blessed day," Levi said, bowing graciously.

"Yes, have a nice day, Leona," Reverend Greenleaf said.

Leona nodded and shut the door on them. She watched them go back out to the Reverend's big black Chevrolet. Levi kept glancing back at the house and smiling that smile of his, like the cat that ate the canary.

33

When Leona got to Marv's, she felt out of sorts. She snapped at Annie and was quiet with the customers. Marvel looked as if he wanted to say something to her, but he kept quiet and let her brood.

Later, Jewel came in, and Leona showed her the flyer.

Jewel rolled her eyes at it and crumpled it on the bar as she sipped a Coke.

"I'd say he was testing your wards."

Leona nodded. "Yes. I couldn't feel any magic moving on him, but that don't mean that he wasn't. Could be he's good at cloaking it."

"Or he was scrambling you. He's probably got old Green-leaf charmed up to do whatever too. Did he look befuddled?"

"Not no more than he normally does," Leona replied.

"I sure wish I had been there. I'd have flung something at him just to see what he lobbed back."

"I don't think he's dumb enough to fall for that," Leona said. "But we're gonna have to go see about this revival."

"Leona, I would just as soon lick a shaved raccoon's back-side as go to that revival."

"Well, you're going," Leona said. She uncrumpled the flyer and smoothed it out. "This is our shot to see what they're about and maybe have a look around."

Jewel sucked back the last of her Coca-Cola and pursed her lips. "Fine. But I doubt this ends well."

Leona nodded. "Of that, I have no doubt." She looked toward the door when she heard a commotion. Raised voices, whoops, and cheers accompanied Travis Evans and Danny Newsome, two of Ed Wagner's deputies, as they entered. As they sat down, Bill Davis clapped them on the back and yelled at Leona. "These boys don't pay tonight! They caught the monster!"

Leona gave Jewel a look as she poured beers for the deputies. She set them in front of them and gave them a prac-ticed smile. "Fellas. What happened?"

"We picked up Dorval Ring." Travis sipped his beer. His face was pale.

"Dorval Ring?" Leona's heart sank. "How did you . . . How did you figure he done it?"

"We found him with a girl. A dead one," Travis said. "Her neck was snapped clean in two."

"Who was it?" Leona asked.

"Nobody knows who she is. We found her down by the

river, like she'd washed up, only there he was, just standing there looking at her. Like he was gonna eat her."

Danny had the same pale, upset look as Travis. He pushed the beer away and looked up at Leona. "Miz Monroe, it really ain't a nice story for ladies."

Leona patted his hand. She switched his beer for a cup of coffee then went to Jewel. "Ed don't have no evidence against Dorval. That girl had her neck snapped. Not the same as Mary and Karla. Something ain't right."

"Maybe, maybe not. What if he does though?" Jewel asked.

"Jewel, Dorval wouldn't kill anyone. If found a dead girl on the riverbank, well, he can't help what he is."

"Leona, we told him."

"You ever starved, Jewel?"

"Leona, you ain't got to defend Dorval to me. I don't matter. But they found him with that dead girl. What do you expect Ed to do?"

"Jewel, that girl wasn't like the others. Not hung up on no cross, not all split open, had her head. It ain't the same. And nobody knows her? I bet I do, and I bet she come out of that holler."

"Yes, that's likely. Or she coulda come from anywhere. Maybe Dorval interrupted something."

Leona shook her head. "No. We know something was there when Mary and Karla died. Something big and strong and not entirely human."

"A werewolf," Jewel nodded in agreement. "You think that dirty werewolf killed one of them girls and left her? But why?"

"He would know what Dorval is, easy. I'll wager they set him up."

"Why? Ed ain't exactly closing in on them. They can kill all they want."

"I don't know. All I know is Dorval Ring didn't kill anybody, and I ain't gonna let him hang. I don't care who set him up or even if he just stumbled on a dead girl washed up on the bank."

"Looks like we need to go see about Ed." Jewel stood up. "I don't like this Leona, but I ain't gonna let that dirty werewolf win nothing."

Leona nodded. She went into the kitchen and found Marv. "I got an emergency. I gotta leave."

"Leave? In the middle of the shift? Leona?" Marv shut up when he looked at her face. "Okay. I-I'll handle it."

Leona grabbed her things and followed Jewel over to the Sheriff's office. Ed's patrol car was still there. They found him in his office, and as soon as Leona saw his eyes, cloudy and unfocused, she knew he had been bewitched.

"L eona. What are you doing here?" Ed's voice sounded wooden, and his speech was slower than normal. He sat at his desk in the Sheriff's Office, staring blankly at the wall.

"Ed, you arrested Dorval Ring."

Ed nodded slowly. "Dorval Ring is the murderer. Found him with that dead girl."

"What's her name? How do you know Dorval done it and killed Mary and Karla?" Leona gave Jewel a look of knowing, and Jewel tapped her foot impatiently.

"Yeah, Ed. How do you figure Dorval done it?"

"She was some girl from nowhere. Don't know her name. Dorval Ring is the murderer. You girls need to go on home and mind your business. This is a sensitive investigation, and if you interfere, why I might just—"

"Oh, hush up, Ed." Jewel walked up to him and tapped his forehead. He fell to the floor in a heap. "Whoever hexed him didn't care if we knew about it. That's about the laziest spell I ever saw."

Leona checked Ed and rolled him over. He was dead asleep. She pulled up his eyelids, and they were now clear. "He's gonna have a nasty headache when he comes to."

"Serves him right for getting befuddled." Jewel looked around the office. "Well, we're criminals now, I guess."

"We're gonna get Dorval out of here." Leona pulled Ed's key ring off his belt.

The little jail was only three cells, and Dorval was the only inmate. He huddled on the bunk and shook. His skeletal frame made him appear even more fragile than normal, and from the streaks on his face and his red eyes, Leona knew he'd been crying. When he saw Leona, he began crying again.

"Miss Leona, what are you doing here?"

Leona fitted the key into the cell lock and opened the door. "Dorval. You need to get out of here. Now."

He shook his head. "No. No, ma'am. Leave me be. I'm done for here, and I don't want you getting in no trouble."

"Dorval, did you kill that girl?" Jewel asked.

"No ma'am, I did not. I found her on the bank. I thought she had washed up, but she wasn't bloated like how they are once they've floated, but—"

"But nothing. You didn't do it, and you ain't gonna get a fair shake anyways." Jewel whacked the bars. "Now get on up and get on out of here before we go and sling some curses."

"Dorval, Ed's been bewitched. And that girl was left there for you to find." Leona ignored his smell and sat beside him on the bunk. "Somebody is trying to set you up."

"Me? Why me?"

Jewel rolled her eyes. "Dorval, I ain't trying to be mean, but facts is facts. You skulk about and you eat dead things. They caught you standing over a dead girl. What are they gonna think?"

"I didn't kill her. I-I don't kill nothing!"

Leona patted his arm. "We know that, Dorval. Ghouls don't kill. But most folks don't know what we know. You gotta be more careful, and you're gonna have to stay out of sight until we sort out who's behind all this."

"I don't know where I can go . . . I-I can't go to my place." He hung his head.

"Jewel, can you take him to Kay's?" Leona asked. "She'll help, and they can't track him there."

"I guess so, but it won't hurt to ward him good before." Jewel wrinkled her nose as she got closer. "Come on, Dorval. I'll give you a spell and take you out there. But look, you gotta ride in the back of the truck." Jewel backed up and kept her distance.

"You all will get in trouble."

"Oh, we're used to that," Leona said. "We'll straighten all this out, but it might could take a minute, so please, just go with Jewel. And when it's safe, we'll come for you."

Dorval stood up and stared down at Leona. His gaunt frame towered over her, but Leona felt no threat or dishonesty in him. She saw nothing but love and gratitude in his eyes. "I will never forget what you done for me. Not ever."

Leona smiled at him, then she hugged him. He went stiff, but then he hugged her back. She patted him then stepped away. "Why, Dorval, I always help my good friends."

He nodded at her and followed Jewel out.

Leona had no clue as to how to erase all memory of

Dorval's arrest from everyone, but she figured to start with the one who's voice carried the most weight, and that was Ed.

He was still passed out in his office. Leona wrangled him into his desk chair then leaned him back so she could see his face. She rubbed her palms together and concentrated on a little charge to wake him. When she felt the energy in her hands, she touched him with her first two fingers. Ed jumped about a foot and yelped. His eyes flew open, and he looked around, wild-eyed and confused.

Leona blew her powder in his face. He sputtered and recoiled, then his eyes went milky, and he calmed. "Ed, you got new evidence, and you know Dorval didn't kill anybody. It was only right you let him go."

"It was only right I let him go." Ed nodded slowly, then his eyes cleared. He slumped forward in his chair and fell asleep.

Leona maneuvered him to have his head on the desk and patted him gently. She replaced his keys and left him snoring. Unlike the sloppy hex that they had countered, her charm would leave no trace. Whoever had hexed Ed was either a novice or didn't care if anyone recognized the spell.

As Leona drove home, she wasn't sure what ticked her off more: incompetence or disdain.

T he crisp November evening bit at their noses and cheeks as they picked their way through Ed Biehl's front pasture toward the tents and trailers set up for the service.

"Jewel. Wipe that lipstick off right now. Leona. Your hair is a rat's nest. Honestly, the two of you act like you was raised by wolves."

Leona and Jewel's older sister, Ida Mae, scowled at them both. They were too old to pinch, so Ida Mae had to be content doing her bullying with her mean tongue.

Leona pretended to smooth out her hair. It was pulled back into a low bun and not even remotely a rat's nest. Jewel really was wearing red lipstick, which she always did.

"Ida Mae, you ain't the boss of me. If you don't like how I look, you can get your old man to carry you on back home so as not to be seen with me. Otherwise, shut your yap," Jewel said.

Ida Mae huffed, and Leona held back a laugh. Jewel had indeed stopped taking the guff of Ida Mae back when Dill had okayed it so many years ago. She'd told her off that very day and had told her off at every opportunity for the past seventeen years.

"You cannot go into the Lord's House looking like a cheap harlot!" Ida Mae yelled.

"Well, I got some news for you, Ida Mae. This lipstick cost two dollars, so I ain't cheap. Mind your own damn business." Jewel looked at Leona. "Do we really gotta do this?"

"Jewel, you know we talked about it, and this is going to be good for us," Leona said. They needed more information about Levi Walker and thought perhaps they could sneak off and have a look around while the service wailed.

"Nothing is worth this," Jewel said, flipping her hand at Ida Mae.

"Nothing can be done with Jewel," Ida Mae said through pursed lips. "I doubt the Holy Spirit would even try to come into her."

"Well, he sure wouldn't come into you!" Jewel yelled. "The devil himself thinks you're too mean and dried up to bother with,"

"All right, both of you, enough!" Leona yelled. "Jewel, we got too much riding on this. Ida Mae, you invited yourself. If you was gonna be embarrassed to be seen with us, you and Dale can go your own selves."

"You girls is out of control," Ida Mae huffed. She jammed her fat hands into her white gloves and tapped a foot impatiently. "Let's go so as to get a decent seat. Come on, Dale!"

Her husband, Dale, was silent as always. He was hard of

hearing but refused to wear a hearing aid. Leona and Jewel felt his pain. They'd been trying to tune out Ida Mae for a long time too.

"Dale!" Ida Mae stomped her foot and clapped in his face. "I said come on." He nodded then followed Ida Mae toward the tent. For all her guff, she wouldn't pass up the opportunity to be seen at the social event of the year.

The front tent was brightly lit with torches that blazed against the dark of the evening. People of the community gathered around the entrance. Some smiled and nodded at Leona and Jewel, some gave them raised eyebrows and pursed lips. Leona and Jewel were well-used to the mixed reaction and paid it no mind. Leona scanned the tent for signs of magic. She pushed out gently but felt nothing rebound.

She glanced at Jewel, and Jewel's nod and look of concentration communicated that she hadn't felt anything either. There was nothing particularly remarkable about the tent. The plain canvas had a yellow tint and a slight smell of mildew that came from age and repeated use. The air inside was warmer than outside, but they still shivered as they waited.

"What's the hold up?" Jewel asked. She stood on tiptoes to see.

Leona was slightly taller, and she was able to see the crowd moving a bit but stoppered up near the back flap of the tent. "Looks like there's a greeter or something back there."

Ida Mae huffed and would be delayed no longer. She used her bony elbows to maneuver them through the crowd. The crowd parted, and at the back of the tent was another exit. Only one flap was pulled back and bright light streamed through, illuminating Levi Walker, who held court.

All the ladies flocked around him, jockeying for his attention. He smiled and held the hands of each one as he prayed with them. As Leona watched them, she was struck by the sexuality of it all. The prayers were intimate and personal, and when he was done, the women were spent, as if he'd brought them to climax.

Levi's eyes found the Spencer sisters almost as soon as they walked in, like he'd been on the lookout for them. He smiled his fake Hollywood smile and left the group of women. He gave Leona a little bow and took her hand. "Miss Leona, I am so pleased you could come." He looked to Jewel. "And you must be Miss Jewel. I have so looked forward to meeting you."

Jewel gave him a mirthless smile and a wink. "Oh, Preacher, I bet you say that to all the girls."

A brief look of disgust and rage flashed across his beautiful face, and then it was gone, replaced by that trademark smile.

"Exactly how they described you, a pip."

Ida Mae elbowed her way to him and simpered. "Don't judge the rest of us by Jewel, Reverend Walker. We ain't all as brazen as her."

"God loves all his creatures. And who might you be?" Levi asked as he took Ida Mae's hand.

"I'm Ida Mae Roberts, their older and wiser sister."

"Oh, for crying out loud," Jewel muttered.

Leona elbowed her.

Levi went on, oblivious; he only had eyes for Ida Mae. "Miss Ida Mae, will you pray with me?" He pulled her hand close to his heart and squeezed it. Ida Mae's breath hitched, and she nodded.

"Oh yes, Reverend Walker. Yes."

As he prayed, Ida Mae shook. By the time he was done, she was vibrating and rather than her head bowed in supplication, it was back and raised to the heavens, a look of ecstasy on it. When he finished, she moaned and shuddered then choked out, "Amen."

Ida Mae's cheeks were flushed and her breath ragged. He kissed her hand.

"Thank you so much, Sister Ida." Levi looked at Leona and Jewel, then back to Leona. He didn't offer to pray with them. Leona shuddered as a wave of revulsion came over her. "I hope you all find what you're looking for tonight. If you'll excuse me, I have to see if my brother is ready to start our service."

"You got a brother?" Jewel asked.

"Yes, Sister, I do. Joshua. He's a bit frail and needs to rest before a service. I'll say a special prayer for you ladies tonight," Levi said.

He gave them a little bow and ducked through the back flap of the tent. Two ushers took his place. They blocked the exit and stared directly ahead. Leona knew them both, Able Shilling and Frank Wright. They weren't known to her to be particularly religious—Leona saw them at least three nights a week in Marv's—but they were both dressed in their best and taking their sentinel role seriously, with arms crossed on their broad chests and serious faces.

Leona and Jewel looked at each other then at Able and Frank. Jewel gave Frank a smile and wink, but he acted as if he didn't see her. "Well, they're bewitched."

"Just because they won't flirt with you at church?"

"Frank Wright would flirt at his old lady's funeral, so yes, Leona, because of that."

Jewel wasn't wrong. Frank Wright flirted with them both any chance he got, but right then he ignored them. Leona looked closer at the men, particularly their eyes. They were clear, not cloudy, but if a magic user was skilled, it was difficult to tell if someone was charmed.

"That preacher is even worse than you said. He gave old Ida Mae a thrill she ain't likely ever had," Jewel said.

Ida Mae was still flushed and quiet, like she was in a

trance. She ignored them both and fanned herself with her Bible as she stared at the exit.

"Something's wrong with her," Leona said. She looked around the room at everyone else. All the women Levi had prayed with were doing the same thing as Ida Mae, staring and fanning themselves. Every once in a while, they'd give a little gasp or a moan. "Something's wrong with all of them. I didn't feel no spell though. We should have felt it."

"He bewitched them good," Jewel said. "I don't like this, Leona. I got a feeling we need to get out of here quick."

"And leave Ida Mae?"

Jewel nodded. "Yes. Whatever's been done to her is done. We can't undo it here." She looked over at Ida Mae and smirked a Jewel smirk. "Besides, I like her quiet like this."

"Jewel, she's been—"

Jewel held up a hand. "I know, I know, but it's nice to have a minute's peace for once, even if her brains is scrambled."

Leona was loath to admit it, but Jewel was right on all accounts. The whole room, except them, had been bewitched. Even the men sat quiet and stoic, waiting. Something was definitely going to happen, and Leona doubted she and Jewel would like it.

"No, let's stay a bit. We can sneak out once they start the show," Leona said. She opened her purse and pulled out a few wads of cotton, greased up. "Put 'em in your ears. I don't trust him not to try a Siren Song."

Jewel took the ear plugs and nodded as she put them in. "Yes, he's likely to try anything."

Just as they got the ear plugs in, a loud gospel record began to play. It was loud enough the girls could hear it, even through the cotton wads. A gong sounded, and the ushers opened both flaps and went through them and into the next tent. A deep red light glowed from it. Leona and Jewel stood back and let everyone else file past and into the red tent. When it was clear, Leona stepped toward it, but found that she was unable to exit. She pushed at the air, and it vibrated then pushed back at her. Jewel couldn't enter either.

"Well, now that ain't very churchy," she said. "Leona, somebody put up a ward."

"Everyone else got in but us. You reckon he marked us?"

Jewel shook her head. "I ain't never seen him before. He don't know me from Adam. I'm gonna try a glamour." Jewel screwed up her face and shook her head. Her features softened then faded. When they formed again, Jewel looked like Ida Mae. When she tried to advance, her progress was stopped again. She shook and turned back to her own face.

"Seems to me like it's blocking magic," Leona said, holding up a hand. She called up a tiny ball of light and sent it against the barrier. The light bounced back and hit her hard, sending a sharp jolt into her arm, more force than she had sent against it. "I reckon it's not just blocking magic. Seems like it's set to fire back."

"Nifty trick," Jewel said. "I gotta know how. Maybe there's another way in."

"Yeah," Leona nodded, and they exited the way they came in from the front flap.

They crept around the smaller tent, but when they reached the place where it ended and the larger red tent began, they couldn't get within two feet of it. The magic field repulsed them physically, and Leona began to get a rancid taste in her mouth the longer they stayed.

Jewel spat. "Nasty spell. If I wasn't so angry, I'd be impressed."

"Let's see if we can follow it all the way around." Leona motioned toward the tent. It glowed red, but they heard nothing, no music, no preaching, no noise of any kind coming from it.

The field held up and the opposite side backed up against the tree line. The woods behind them were eerie and silent. Leona thought of Cale and wished for him to appear. He might see something they could not, but when she reached out to him, it took a long time for him to pulse a bit of energy back to her. He wasn't gone, but he couldn't help them yet.

Something big moved in the woods behind them and growled long and low. Both girls whirled and held up hands, magic ready to blast.

"Dirty werewolves," Jewel hissed.

Leona glanced up at the sky. The moon waxed but wasn't full yet. She shook her head. "Nope. Not full."

"Well then, what is it?" Jewel asked.

"Don't know, but I don't think we ought to stay and find out." They backed away and began to walk back to the vehicle.

"Of course, Dale took the keys," Jewel scoffed. "And locked it too." She tried the handle. "All right, well, let's just walk home. I'd like a little distance from the tent before we try any other magic."

"Agreed," Leona said. The creature in the trees still growled. It followed beside them as they walked through the field of cars and out to the township road.

The trees lined one side of the dirt road, but the other was open to the river that ambled by. The water shone black in the cold winter night, and the frigid Muskingum would offer no help should the creature attack. It prowled just inside the trees and out of sight. But every so often, it growled, and they heard a loud scratch against tree bark. They got about a mile down the road when Jewel stopped and turned toward the woods. She flung a ball of energy into the trees. It lit up the area, and something large and misshapen snarled and retreated further back into the woods.

Jewel frowned and flung another ball at it, but they couldn't see anything. "Chickenshit!" Jewel yelled.

Leona put a hand on her sister's arm to prevent her from firing more energy. "No. Don't waste no more on it. Let's get on home and figure out how we get inside that tent. We need to see."

Jewel nodded. "All right. I guess if it wanted to come at us, it would, and it knows I'd blast it straight to Hell."

"Watch your language," Leona said as she stared into the woods. The waxing moon came out from behind a cloud, and for a second, Leona caught a yellow eye shine from the woods. The thing growled then gave a long, mocking laugh. Leona set her jaw and held back the urge to blast the thing as they walked the three miles back to Jewel's place, not only because she didn't want to waste a drop of magic, but because she didn't want Jewel to have the satisfaction.

36

I don't like it." Leona wiped the sweat from her face and took a long drink of water. Her breath came in short gasps, and her heart pounded as if she'd run a mile.

A chicken flopped around inside a small salt circle. Jewel poked at it with her toe, and the bird gave a pathetic squawk then went silent. She bent down and checked it then stood up. "It's alive. You need to commit to the spell better. It's harder on 'em when you're scared of it."

"I ain't scared of it! It's a nasty spell." Leona huffed. She bent down and checked the chicken herself. It was asleep, not dead and her relief at that flooded through and calmed her nerves, but in the back of her mind, a shadow lingered.

Jewel assumed she was scared of the magic, but the thing

that really rattled Leona was that she wasn't. Instead of feeling frightened, a part of her had delighted at the control she had over the bird. She'd had to fight that voice that wanted her to keep control of it, the one that whispered to push out, take more control. It felt good and terrible all at the same time.

"It's only nasty if you make the chicken fry itself up for dinner," Jewel said. She was full of herself because she'd controlled the chicken on the first try. It had taken Leona three tries. The chicken was done out, and so was she.

"Consider how you had to dig to find that spell and how many eyeballs it took." Leona held up the charm bag. It caught fire in her hand, and she dropped it to the ground. "And it smells like cow patties."

"Yeah, that's the sulfur." Jewel nodded. "And anyways, they was frog eyeballs. It ain't like we had to kill nothing important."

"That's just the issue, Jewel," Leona said. Her face felt hot as the anger and shame burbled around inside her guts. The dark whisper laughed and said Jewel was right. She shushed it. "You and me ain't the ones to decide what life has value and what don't."

"Horseshit, Leona." Jewel picked up the chicken. It stirred but didn't wake up. She held it up. "We're gonna eat him sooner or later. We make that decision all the time. We say we matter. You said them dead girls matter. We're doing what we gotta do because we say other people matter. So don't go getting high and mighty about some frog eyeballs. Concentrate and do your job so we ain't got to do it but once."

"You watch your language, Jewel Elizabeth Spencer." Leona poked a finger at Jewel. "I'll do my job, and I won't like it one bit. Maybe you like it too much."

Jewel's eyes narrowed. She pursed her lips, then walked over and put the chicken in the coop. She stalked past Leona without saying anything then stopped and turned around. She flung a bolt of yellow energy at Leona.

Rage engulfed her, and Leona's instinct kicked in. She caught the yellow bolt—and in one motion turned it red— then flung it back at Jewel. The dark whisper laughed and cheered in her head. Leona's heart thundered in her chest with two emotions: ecstasy and horror.

Jewel easily sidestepped the bolt, and it landed to her right, leaving a crater in the ground. Jewel looked down at the smoking ruin of the grass then back at Leona and smirked. "Good. Maybe you'll go for the kill when it matters. Hope you improve your aim, though."

Leona dropped to her knees and shook as she cried, horrified that she'd attacked her sister and even more horrified that it had felt so good.

37

The next afternoon, Leona met Jewel at her house. The events of the day before still weighed heavy on her heart. She'd managed to quiet the voice in her head, but the exhilaration of the dark energy coursing through her remained along with the guilt and fear.

In the last twenty-four hours, she'd done the least amount of magic possible, not just to control the urges she felt, but also to conserve. The spell they were about to attempt required a lot of energy, ten times what controlling the chicken had needed. In order to get that much energy, Leona knew she'd have to give the dark whisperer more of herself, and that terrified her.

She had one other option available to her. She'd brought a

bunch of the herb of grace, but taking it promised another problem. When she'd used it on Halloween, it had very nearly poisoned her. She'd tried to tell herself it had just been a bit too much, that it wasn't that deadly, but she knew better. Another overuse and she could end up dead, but in her heart, Leona thought of something worse. When she took the rue, it not only amplified the magic, but the dark voice as well. It was harder to control and tamp back down, and every time, she felt like maybe she didn't want to.

Jewel had prepared the circle. She'd lined it with the salt and herb mixture and brick dust as an added precaution. The candles were ready on the corners, and she had set up a small altar with offerings of fruit and meats. She raised an eyebrow at the bunch of rue in Leona's hand but didn't comment on it as she handed her a small leather pouch on a long string. Jewel sat down in front of the altar and lit the fire.

"Who is it?" Leona asked.

"Hazel McCutcheon. Mine's Betsy Mayle."

Leona nodded. The two women were known to be friends, so it wouldn't look odd if they sat next to one another in the service. She sat on the ground next to Jewel, in the middle of the circle, in front of the altar, and willed her nerves to calm.

Her head pounded, and the blood whooshed in her ears. She flexed her hands over and over and called up the magic. It was there, in that space in her belly it had been since the beginning, straining against the internal rails that held it, like a racehorse bashing itself against a starting gate. That scared her, and she pushed back against it. It diminished, and that scared her more, so she twisted off a small bit of the herb of grace and shoved it in her mouth.

As soon as the bitter herb hit her tongue, she felt the magic amplify, but in a controlled way, as if the jockey had calmed the wild horse and now it was poised and ready to run. She chewed and swallowed then nodded to Jewel.

"Last night of the revival. Last chance for us."

Jewel nodded back. "Something goes sideways, bail. I'll stay in as long as I can." She picked up her silver dagger, cut her hand, then handed it to Leona.

Leona took the knife and cut her palm. She let the magic flow just a little and watched her blood glow, then she squeezed a bit of it into the leather pouch. She spit in it for good measure then closed it up and hung it around her neck. It shifted on her chest as if something was alive in it. Leona closed her eyes and let the magic flow freely as she focused on Hazel McCutcheon. The dark whisper laughed in her ear. Against her chest, the pouch throbbed and burned. Her skin tingled and flushed as the magic connected her with the other woman.

The dark whispered, "*Yes . . .*"

Leona let it have its day. As soon as she did, she opened her eyes to find herself standing in the first tent. She looked around, and when Betsy Mayle came to stand beside her, she nodded. Jewel was in.

Nearly the entire town packed into the tent and waited. Everyone had far away looks in their eyes and hummed a tune that filled the place with an eerie buzz.

"I do not like this. Not one bit," Jewel murmured.

Leona didn't answer. She concentrated on controlling Hazel and drowning out the humming. The dark whisper laughed and begged her to let it free. It would stop all of this, but she held it in check.

"*Okay, not yet . . .*" the dark whispered.

Leona clenched her fists and focused. The gong sounded, and the record played as it had the first night. Everyone cheered and filed through the back flap and into the red tent.

Leona and Jewel looked at one another and moved forward with the crowd. When she approached the flap, her stomach dipped just a bit as she felt a slight pulse of magic push back at her, but the dark whisper laughed and she laughed with it, ignoring the attempt to keep her out. She felt her face smile, and she scoffed at whatever had tried. She stepped forward and into the red tent. To her left, Jewel appeared. At the front of the tent was a dais and an altar. The cross was hewn wood, rough, and blackened by fire. Where the hands and feet of a crucified person would be, there were deep holes that oozed with something black and oily. Leona felt a pang of fear. But she let the dark whisper calm her and she willed herself to move. They found two chairs in the back of the tent and waited as the congregation hummed and swayed, waiting in ecstasy for whatever came next.

A little girl of about eight came out, dressed in a white acolyte robe. She lit the candles all over the dais then banged a gong in the corner. Everyone rose and began to sing along with the record.

"They ain't even got hymnals," Jewel whispered.

Spell, Leona mouthed.

The little girl banged the gong again, and all the men got up and blocked the exits.

"Son of a bitch," Jewel said.

Leona couldn't berate her for the cussing because it was exactly what she said.

Levi Walker wore a purple robe and a starched white vestment. His smile was beatific, and he raised his hands as he sang along with the congregation. They screamed and cheered for him, and he waved at them all. When the hymn finished, they all cheered him more. The thunderous applause made the whole tent vibrate. Levi soaked it up then motioned with both hands, palms down, and the crowd quieted.

He grinned wider. "Brothers and sisters of Ames!"

The crowd screamed again at the mention of the town, and Levi laughed and gave them a few moments to cheer him again then quieted them.

"We're so thankful to be here tonight, in the service of the Lord. You're here because you're missing something in your life. Now you may not know what that something is, but trust me, Brothers and Sisters, the Lord knows what it is. And He will speak through us tonight so that you might find what it is you so desperately seek. Amen."

"Amen!" the crowd roared.

"Now you may have come here tonight thinking you were all alone. You may have come here tonight worried, wearied, troubled that you were the only seeker, but I'm here, standing right here, Brothers and Sisters"—he pounded the pulpit with his fist—"to tell you and to show you that you are not alone, no you are not. For you see, we are all seekers come to look for the Lord, so we can let Him into our hearts."

The crowd chanted more amens, and some of the men began to yell gibberish, like they had at Mary Silvus's funeral.

"But let me tell you something. It's an awful thing. It really is." Levi paused for effect and let fear and curiosity of the crowd build. "There's someone here tonight who doesn't want you to let the Lord into your heart. They do not want you to seek. They don't care if you're missing that spark, that thing that will complete you and bring you into the arms of the Lord. Do you know who that person is?"

The crowd murmured, and some people cried and beat their hands on the chairs. One woman fell to the floor and wept.

Levi Walker stared right at Leona, and he thundered, "Satan! The devil himself does not want you whole. He wants you broken and desperate. He and his agents, oh yes! His agents abound. He and his agents want you to wallow in sin and misery. They want you broken and incomplete. They will do everything in their power to oppose your salvation! We can't let them do that, can we?"

"No!" the crowd thundered. The men shook their fists and spit angrily. The women wailed and cried.

Levi shushed them again and calmed them. "It's all right. You have nothing to fear. You're here tonight among friends. We will lift you up and make you ready to receive the Lord. We will fill you with the promise of eternal salvation, and we will give you a shield and sword to ward off the advances of Satan. You will all be soldiers for the Lord. Let us pray!"

Once Levi finished his prayer, they sang another hymn, and then he shushed them.

"Let's get down to it, what you came here for. I'm going to bring out somebody who has a special gift. Somebody who can look into your heart and know what you need to be complete. Somebody with a direct connection to the Lord. Would you all like to meet him?" The congregation erupted into pleading and begging and righteous affirmations. Levi laughed and smoothed his hair back. His blue eyes sparked, and then he waved a hand at the back curtain. The little girl banged the gong again. "My brother, Joshua Walker. Joshua, come on up here!"

Joshua Walker was the opposite of his brother. His skin was pockmarked and sallow, and he had a gaunt, sickly look about him. His hair was greasy and sparse, and his eyes were too close together. He wore the same purple robes as Levi but couldn't fill them out. It hung on his skeletal frame and seemed to swallow him whole, like a child playing dress up in their father's clothes.

"Something's wrong about him," Jewel said.

Leona nodded. She reached out and tried to push Joshua Walker with a bit of magic. Her push met no resistance, and he didn't flinch or move even a bit. It was like the push went right through him, like he wasn't there at all.

"I want you to come on up here tonight. I want you to come on up here and let my brother have a good look at you. He's the Lord's vessel, and he will know you. He will know what you're missing, what you desperately need, and he will make you whole again."

Levi motioned them to start coming forward. At first, just a few did. Joshua Walker stared at them, put a hand on their foreheads and closed his eyes. When he opened them, his color looked better and the person he touched nearly fell over. A couple of the ushers helped each weak person off, and the next person in line came forward. Joshua repeated it and the music played. Levi danced and sang, keeping the crowd whipped up into a frenzy of ecstatic screams and pledges. And with each supplicant, Joshua Walker grew stronger.

"He's taking their energy," Jewel said.

Leona nodded. He was draining a bit of life from every person who came before him.

It continued until Tammy Doan came forward. Tammy Doan was thirty-seven, single, and lived with her widowed mother. She was dumpy, with big, thick glasses, stringy mouse-brown hair, and a club foot. She wore a special shoe and limped when she walked. Tammy was lonely. She came into the diner sometimes and ate lunch with her mother, but never spoke more than a *please* or *thank you*. She didn't have friends, save her mother, and she certainly had no beau. Tammy was used to being mostly ignored in adulthood, which was likely preferable to the notice she had garnered in childhood.

But that night, Tammy Doan was noticed. When she presented herself in front of Joshua and Levi, they both took up her hands. They laid hands on her and prayed. Tammy threw her head back in ecstasy and moaned as they did. When they finished, they both kissed her cheeks and her forehead. When Tammy went back to her seat, her cheeks were flushed, and she radiated sex and satisfaction.

"Looks like Tammy needs a cigarette," Jewel said.

"Looks like Tammy needs a ward. I'm pretty sure they just marked her for death," Leona said. "This is how they choose the girls."

"Are there any other sveeekers here tonight?" Levi asked. He looked at Leona and Jewel and winked at them. He motioned to his brother, and they jumped off the dais and into the crowd. The congregation screamed and cheered, clapping the brothers on the back and reaching for them, desperate to touch them as they passed. Levi and Joshua stopped in front of Leona and Jewel. Levi looked at his brother and smiled.

"What do you say, Brother?"

Joshua Walker looked at Jewel and Leona. His vigor had faded already. "I say . . . witches burn." His yellow eyes flashed, and he sneered at Jewel and Leona.

Levi grinned and nodded as he looked into Hazel McCutcheon's face. He wasn't confused. He knew exactly who she was. "Soon, Brother. Soon." He laid hands on Leona's shoulder and shoved.

Leona's stomach churned as she stumbled backward through a dark mist. She left her feet and flew through the air, contacted something hard, and had the wind knocked out of her. She found herself flat on her back inside the circle. Jewel choked and coughed beside her. They both fought to catch their breath and sit up. When Leona finally got upright, she gasped and grabbed for her chest as the pouch caught fire.

She ripped it from her neck and flung it to the ground. It burst into flames, and she threw her hand up over her eyes as the fire rose and blinded her. The dark voice raged and begged her to let it free. It wanted to burn the brothers, to rip and twist them, to show them what power really was. Leona tempered it with worry for her friends and neighbors. "We gotta go back!" Leona yelled.

"They won't kill the whole town . . . yet," Jewel said. "We can't do them no good now, anyway." She threw her pouch into the fire and winced as it turned the fire yellow and gave off the smell of rotten eggs. Jewel's face was strained, and she shook. "That took a lot out of me anyways."

It was true. Leona had a sudden rush of nausea and exhaustion that made her limbs feel as if they were made of lead. She was drained, and if Jewel was admitting it, she was tapped out too. Leona nodded and stared into the fire as she attempted to calm her rolling stomach. The dark whisper laughed at the exhaustion.

"*Let me . . . I'll fix it. I'll fix them all. It will feel so good.*"

Leona closed her eyes and nodded. It would. She'd blast them. All of them.

"*Yes . . .*" the voice said. "*So good.*"

Leona clenched her fist and set her jaw as she attempted to get to her feet. She felt a touch and looked down to see Jewel's hand on hers. Jewel's face was scrunched in and her eyes blazed and she tightened her grip on Leona.

"Fight it. Leona, you need calendula. Now."

Leona felt a tingle in her hand as her sister connected with her. She calmed herself and nodded as the dark whisper cursed Jewel. Somehow she forced it back, and when it faded, she vomited into the dirt. Jewel helped her up, and together they limped back to Jewel's kitchen. She found the calendula and swallowed it as Jewel made tea.

The sisters sipped it in silence as they regained their composure. Leona shook as she buried the guilt she felt at leaving everyone and, harder still, tempered the rage that simmered within her.

T don't know about this." Jewel held up the jar and looked at it with a raised eyebrow and pursed lips. "This here ward only keeps people out. I think what we need is to keep Tammy in."

"I don't know of any white magic that will keep Tammy in. Anything that would do that is nasty stuff," Leona said.

"I don't get you, Leona. You know what we're up against. They ain't playing by no rules of fairness. They only want to kill people. We're doing it for her own good." Jewel jammed the Mason jar of red dust into her bag.

"I don't see it that way, Jewel. Maybe it's different for you, but I feel this stuff. I feel it deep down inside me, and I'm always just a knife's edge away from losing control of it."

"That's your problem. You're always worried about that. The magic knows your intent. You don't intend it bad, it won't be bad."

"That ain't how I feel, and I ain't willing to take the chance."

"Well, you might get willing when they come and try to burn us," Jewel said. "They do, and I sure won't be holding back. I need to know you won't be either."

"That ain't gonna happen, Jewel. We're gonna stop them."

"How? We're cornered, and they know it. They got their ghosts trying to bust in here and rip us to shreds. Their magic is potent enough to block us, and one of them is a filthy vampire. Unless we're willing to fight fire with fire, we're outgunned."

A rush of cold air blew in, and a bell in the kitchen rang. Cale faded into her view, and Leona's heart leapt. She smiled at him, but when he spoke, her smile faded.

"Leona, Jewel is right. You can't be picky about how you deal with them."

Leona felt her face flush hot, and a little ball of anger well up in her guts. "Not you too! Look, we'll figure out something. Jewel, just go ward the Doan place. I'll put up more circles here. Them ghosts have to go through four good solid wards to get in."

"Well, your wards ain't working so good because they've done busted in on one," Cale said. He pointed out the window to the tree line. Mary and Karla were now only about twenty yards from the house. They'd broken through one of Leona's wards in record time.

"I'm tired of this. Those two fake preachers think they're messing with some helpless girls, and we're not. Let's just go over there, curse 'em good, and be done with it." Jewel jammed the rest of her supplies into her bag and tied it shut.

"That's no plan at all, Jewel."

"Why? Because it's head on and don't require sneaking around? You're a scaredy cat, Leona. You always have been."

"And you're reckless, Jewel. How many times am I gonna have to get you out of a bind?"

"Get me out of a bind? Sister Dear, I don't need no babysitter." Jewel moved her hand, and all the pots and pans in the sink flew around the room and crashed to the floor. "I studied the magic the same as you. You think just because you can see spirits that you're some kind of special? All high and mighty cause you got a sappy ghost boy that follows you all over like a lost puppy dog? I say we walk out there and send Mary and Karla packing. It ain't our fault they got taken in by these fake Bible Beaters. Then I say we go over there to that tent, blast them boys right out of their preacher collars, and set that whole nasty place on fire." Jewel folded her arms and scowled.

"I'm not condemning those girls to eternal torment!" Leona yelled. "And have you never listened to a thing Granny Kay taught us? You think all them boys do is give the ladies a little tickle and get a charge off 'em? Levi can see ghosts. He can push. He's holding back, same as us, and we don't know what he can really do. And as for the vampire? He might be just an energy sucker, but he's strong, and we'll have to get close and nasty to kill him. His head'll have to come off. The other one will be slinging spells, and somebody will have to fight him. I say again, Jewel, we're at a disadvantage."

"Well, we need to figure out an advantage real quick. I've had just about enough." Jewel grabbed her bag and made for the door. She slammed it good, shaking everything in the kitchen.

Leona went to follow, but Cale stepped in between her and the door. "Let her cool off."

"What if she goes off half-cocked?"

Cale shook his head. "She won't. Jewel talks big, but she ain't dumb. She knows she can't just blast her way through things. Not by herself."

"She's always been rash. Quick to use the easiest magic. No thought for the consequences."

"Well, she doesn't see it like that. She's just trying to solve a problem and protect herself and her family."

"Are you defending her?" Leona scowled and put her hands on her hips.

"I guess so," he said. "Eventually, Lee, it's gonna come down to us or them. If that happens, you're gonna have to saddle up and make sure it's us."

"Of course it's us."

"Hard choices are hard. You owe Mary and Karla a lot less than Jewel. Or Peggy."

"And when you use dark magic, sometimes you don't come back!" Leona said. She slammed her medical kit shut and started for the door.

"You going to the Holler? I'll come with yo—"

Leona held up a hand. "Don't bother. I can handle myself, and I'd rather be alone right now."

"Lee, it isn't safe for you out there," Cale said.

"It's not safe for me much of anywhere. I can handle them werewolves, and those girls need looked after. Leave me be."

His face fell and his eyes searched hers. "I'm sorry, Lee, please."

"I'll be fine. Go help Jewel, since you two have such a brilliant plan."

"It ain't like that, and you know it."

"I guess I don't know much." Leona slammed the door the same way Jewel had and gunned the truck as she headed out to Nolan's Holler. In the rearview mirror, she saw Cale standing on her stoop. He had the good sense not to follow her.

39

L eona's mood had not improved when she got to the Holler. When one of the flunky wolves tried to grab her, she waved her hand and slung him across the glade into a thick elm tree. She stalked up the hill to Dora's place.

Dora sat outside, smoking. She let out a long puff of smoke and looked Leona up and down. "You sure got a bee in your bonnet."

"Mind your own affairs," Leona snapped.

"I'd say it is my affair when a pissed off witch comes a knocking.

"It don't have nothing to do with you." Leona took a breath

and calmed herself. It wasn't right to take her frustration out on any anyone else. "Any girls gone missing of late?"

Dora tilted her head and regarded her. "Girls go missing every day."

"Galen Nolan ain't likely to let his cash flow suffer from girls leaving."

Dora nodded. "No, he ain't, but surely you understand there will always be more girls out here."

Leona fumed. "What girl did he leave down by the river?"

"Her name was Roxy."

"He'll pay for that," Leona said.

Dora gave her a sad smile. "Miss Leona, I believe if anyone can make Galen Nolan pay his share, it's you. But if that's your aim, that's gonna be a rough road for you. I don't want to see you get hurt."

"How's Liza doing?" Leona asked.

Dora shook her head and looked away. She took a long drag on her smoke before she answered. "She's gone."

"What do you mean, she's gone? She wasn't in no shape to travel," Leona said. She ran up the hill to Liza's trailer. The marigolds were trampled, crushed into the mud. Leona opened the door to the trailer, and the smell of the rot gagged her. When she heard the flies buzzing, and smelled that sickly sweet stench of death, she knew still she had to see.

Liza lay in a pool of black vomit. Leona choked on the reek and waved the flies out of her face. The infection hadn't killed Liza. She was well on her way to recovery from that. A syringe lay next to the body, and Leona found a prick mark in Liza's arm. She picked up the syringe and smelled it. The vinegar smell of heroin remained. Leona threw the needle down in disgust.

She found Dora waiting outside.

"I didn't take her for an addict."

Dora shrugged. "Liza got through however she could. Lots out here do."

"I would have noticed the needle marks."

"Maybe you would and maybe you wouldn't. Don't change nothing. Dead is dead."

"Sometimes it ain't," Leona said. She went back in the trailer and concentrated. She called to Liza, but Liza didn't answer. There was no energy in the place. Leona reached out again, desperate to connect to the girl, but nothing happened. Leona sobbed as the futility of the day, and the impossibility of her situation weighed down upon her.

When she emerged from the trailer, Dora put a hand on her arm. "Miss Leona, it don't matter how she went. It was a peaceful death, considering how it could have been. You eased her pain, but once she was healed, it would have been more of the same for her. This way, she's at peace. Don't matter who gives it to her."

"He killed her, didn't he?" Leona balled up her fists and stared off down toward Galen's house as she fought back the urge to burn it all to the ground.

"Galen Nolan wouldn't waste no dope on a whore. If he'd a killed her, he'd just snapped her neck," Dora said. "She done it herself."

"She was getting well."

"Yes, and when she was well, she'd have gone right back to what got her unwell to begin with. Ain't none of us getting out of this holler alive."

At that, Leona sobbed a while. Dora left her to it, seeming to recognize her need to cry it all out.

Leona cried for Liza, but she also cried for Mary and for Karla, and for what she knew had to be done. When she got it all out of her system, she dried her eyes. A flash of gold in the fall breeze caught her eye. One little marigold remained. He had escaped the stomping, careless boots. Leona bent down and carefully dug him up, then she tucked him away in her bag. He'd have a space in her garden, and she'd make sure he grew strong. When he was ready, she'd harvest him and use him to help someone. That was the way of it. You had to know when to do what needed done.

After that, she squared her jaw, and she found Dora. "Who's gonna do for her?"

"Us girls will. We take of our own."

Leona nodded. That was the way.

She made calls to some of the other girls—a few had nasty cuts and bruises from beatings, one girl was fighting a bad case of the clap, and a few more were pregnant. Leona saw to them all, giving them all the love and care she wished she could give to Liza.

When she finished with the last girl, she noticed the new trailer at the end of the holler. It was cleaner than the rest and didn't have any green slime moss covering it, like most of the others did. The door was chained shut and one wolf, a barrel-chested giant, sour and greasy, with a long beard and enormous arms, stood out front.

"What's all that?" Leona asked.

Dora shook her head. "Leave it be."

Leona set her jaw and stared hard at Dora. "You tell me who's in there." The surrounding air swirled, and a dust devil blew up.

"Miss Leona, you know who's in there. You're the one who found her for him."

"He's locked her up? Why?"

"Because he knows she'll run the first chance she gets, and he wants what she's got."

Leona turned and marched over to the werewolf guarding the door. "Open it."

He glared down at Leona and crossed his arms. "Mind your business, witch."

Leona waved her hand, and the giant werewolf flew off the porch, whacked his head on a post, and didn't get up. Leona took hold of the chain and lock. She spoke an incantation and the padlock and chain melted, sizzling, and spilling hot metal on the cheap wood porch. She pushed out, and the door flung open. Another wolf growled and came at her. Anger coursed through her, and an invisible hand slammed him against the paneling. He grabbed his throat and choked. His face turned blue, then he passed out and slumped to the floor.

Leona walked back the hallway and in the first room, she found a small blonde, barely sixteen by Leona's eye, laying on a filthy twin mattress. Leona recognized her immediately as the girl from the locator spell. A long, angry gouge ran down the left side of her face. It was deep enough that the girl's once flawless face would forever bear the jagged scar. The girl was about six months pregnant. Her swollen belly strained against a faded calico dress and her red-rimmed eyes were full of fear and, worse, a bitter hopelessness. She cowered and pressed herself against the wood-paneled wall.

"It's all right. I won't hurt you." Leona knelt down.

The girl shied away, pressing herself tight against the wall. "No. He'll kill me."

"What's your name?" Leona asked.

The girl's eyes narrowed as if she was distrustful of a simple, civilized question. "Susan."

"Susan. My name is Leona. I can get you out of here."

Susan shook her head and put her forehead on her knees. "You can't help me. Don't matter where I go. He said the next time he'd skin me and take my baby."

The anger bubbled up again in Leona as she imagined Nolan saying those words. She knew he had. The girl meant no more to him than the animals he skinned for fun. Galen Nolan cared nothing about the cruelty or the waste. That was what made him a monster, not the fact that he was a werewolf.

She balled up her fists and pushed down the anger. It wouldn't help her now. She smiled at Susan and put a gentle hand on her shoulder. "I know things Galen Nolan don't, and I promise you, if you come with me, he will never find you or take your baby."

"How?"

Leona raised her hand, and a great blue flame enveloped them. The flames consumed nothing, they licked at them, and a pleasant cooling breeze rushed over their skin. Leona closed her fist, and the flame disappeared. Her head throbbed, and her stomach churned. She steeled herself against it and held her hand out to Susan again.

This time Susan took it.

Outside, Dora waited for them. The rest of the girls had emerged from their shacks and gathered around. They all hugged Susan and handed her little bits of money or minor items to help, toiletries and such. One girl handed her a bag of clothes. Dora hugged Susan tight then handed Susan a wad of cash and closed her hand around it.

"Girl, this time, don't you stop. Keep a going."

Two more wolves charged up the path, bellowing at them and growling threats. Leona stood between them and the girls. She raised her hands and the two men stopped, frozen in mid-stride. She concentrated, and briars snaked out from the woods. They wrapped themselves around the werewolves, binding them tightly. Leona opened her fist, then closed it again, and the briars wound up and around their faces. The men screamed as the thorns dug into their flesh, but the briars wound tighter, choking them into silence. Leona waved her hand, and the vines retracted back into the forest, pulling the wolves with them.

A wave of nausea hit Leona, and she stumbled, temporarily weakened. She sucked in a big breath and waited for the world to stabilize, then she stood up and turned back to the women, who all stared at her, fear and awe on their faces.

"There won't be any coming back, Miss Leona," Dora said.

Leona nodded. "All of you, come with me."

"You're a mighty powerful witch, but I don't think even you got the magic to hide all of us. Make sure Susie stays safe. I'll take care of these uns out here." Dora held out a hand to Leona.

Leona ignored the hand and hugged the tiny woman tight. "I'll come back for you."

Dora shook her head. "No. You might help a few, but he'll just get him some more. Start with this one. I'll do my best by the others."

Dora was right. There would never be a shortage of girls chained in this holler. She'd have to deal with the source, but right then, all she could do was save one. She'd lost two already. She wouldn't lose another.

The cloaking spell was easy enough, basic magic, but after she cast it, Leona felt dizzy and weak. She put her hand on the wall and gave herself a few precious seconds to regain her strength and balance. She took out her hidden money tin and handed the girl all the money that she had, then she drove Susan to the Sheriff's station. The deputy inside was a tall, burley boy, Daniel Newsome. He smiled at Leona.

"Hello there, Miz Monroe. How can I help you tonight?"

Leona smiled, took out a handful of blue powder and blew it in his face. Daniel coughed and sputtered, then his eyes clouded over, and he stood still.

"Daniel, you're gonna take this girl on up to Columbus

right now. Take her to the bus station, then come on home. You won't recall nothing about the trip."

"I'm gonna take this girl to the Columbus bus station," he said in a sing-song voice. Then his face scrunched up and his eyes cleared a bit. "Wait . . . I can't do that. I'm on duty tonig—"

Leona grabbed another handful of powder and doused him again. She concentrated harder before she spoke, even though her head throbbed with the effort. "Take this girl to the Columbus bus station. You won't remember anything about it."

Daniel's eyes clouded and stayed that way, and his face relaxed. "I won't remember none of this."

"That's the ticket," Leona said. She addressed Susan. "You take a bus to anywhere, but don't stop, go three or four places. Don't stay close to here. Nobody will track you. No spell will find you." Leona reached out and put her hand on the girl's belly. The baby began to move around. Leona got the image of a healthy little boy. She smiled at the girl. "You and your baby are going to be fine."

Susan cried. "I-I don't know what to say."

"Don't say nothing. Just go. Now. I got other business tonight."

By the time Leona got home, the full moon was peeking out from the clouds, and Mary and Karla had broken through all but that last ward. Mary circled and paced and Karla, big and full of rage, beat her fists ceaselessly against the ward as she screamed. The force of it pounded Leona's head and sapped her energy. Leona could feel the ward weakening as the ghosts rammed against it. It pulsed and shimmered, like a light bulb about to go out. She stayed calm and planted the little marigold in her garden.

"Odd time for flower gardening," Cale said.

He had popped in behind her. Leona patted the soil around the marigold and gave him a little drink of water. "As good a time as any. You shouldn't be here. You need to stay at Jewel's."

"I felt something off with you. What happened at that holler?"

"Galen Nolan killed that girl they found. Another girl was dead too. And I stole a girl he was keeping for her baby."

"Leona, that sounds like you antagonized that werewolf. Don't we got enough problems?"

"What problems do you got, Cale? You ain't got any I can see. You're dead. And if you'd just stay gone to Jewel's you'd be fine."

"I ain't staying over at Jewel's while you're all wound up like this. I can feel it, Lee. It tears me up inside and I—"

His speech cut off, and Leona felt a frigid blast of air as the ghost of Mary Silvus whooshed past her and grabbed Cale. Karla followed and both had a hold of him. Cale pushed back at them. He had strong energy too, but he wouldn't be able to hold both of them off for long.

Leona floundered for her bag. She pulled out a sage bundle and her bag of salt. She ran to the throng of ghosts and lit it, then she shoved it at all three of them. Cale fell backward when Mary and Karla recoiled from the burning herb bundle. Leona had only seconds. She contained the ghosts in a tight circle of salt.

"Cale, go to Jewel's. Now!" Her heart thundered in her chest as she yelled.

Cale didn't retort. The little popping sound told her he was gone. Mary and Karla raged against the little salt circle. The meager ward pulsed and throbbed with each blow and threatened to give at any second. Leona had no time to consider options. There was only one choice now. She closed her eyes and centered herself. She thought of Kay's instruction to let the magic flow and felt a trickle. It would have to be enough.

She went to her workbench and gathered what she needed: more sage, more salt, and a large, red beeswax candle. She made another circle of salt; except she left a little line crossed through it, so it wasn't complete. She set the large red beeswax candle inside the new circle, lit it. She chanted over the flame, and when it reared up, twice the size of normal, she knew the circle was primed.

Leona knelt just inside the circle. She was close enough to the circle that held Mary and Karla that she could touch it. As the ghosts beat against it, Leona felt whips of hot air against her face. She took a deep breath and ran her hand through the salt holding Mary and Karla.

As soon as it did, both Mary and Karla rushed past it and into the new circle, arms outstretched for Leona. She took two quick steps backward and out of the new salt circle. Mary's nails raked her cheek, but that was all she got. Mary and Karla ran around the circle and threw themselves toward the salt, trying to grab Leona, but the salt stopped them. The ghosts could go in, but they couldn't get out. It wouldn't hold them forever, so Leona worked quickly. She walked all around the circle, burning the sage and speaking the incantation to exorcise them. They thrashed and fell to the ground. Karla got up and ripped the thick black thread that held her mouth shut.

"Witch. Whore. You'll burn for this." Karla let out a feral scream and threw herself against the salt. She screamed again and collapsed, pulling at her hair and ripping at her skin.

Mary tried a different approach. "Please, Leona. I-I don't wanna go to the bad place. I'm a good girl. I swear, I won't hurt you no more. Please . . . it burns!" Mary fell to her knees and screamed.

They pleaded some more then screamed insults at her when the begging didn't work, but Leona kept on. The magic pulsed through her, and when it waivered, she thought of Cale and how close they had come to absorbing him. Tears welled in her eyes, and she squeezed them shut as she continued on.

Soon the beeswax candle flickered, and the ground inside the salt circle shimmered. It became red hot, and both ghosts screamed as the grass burned. Blackened, burnt hands erupted from the ground. They grabbed Mary and Karla by their ankles then dragged them down into the blazing soil. The beeswax candle went out. The grass inside the circle was black and dead. It would never grow again, and neither would anything else. Leona held back the tears and gathered her things.

She was tired, and sweat ran down her face. Leona had to pause in the kitchen. She sat in the chair and waited until the world stopped spinning and she had the energy to continue. She had to go find Jewel. It wouldn't be long before Galen Nolan came for her. She grabbed a few magical items for protection, and she jumped in the truck and headed to Jewel's place.

S he was about a mile from Jewel's place when she heard the howls. Leona gunned the engine just as an enormous black creature burst out of the brush on the roadside and rammed into the side of the truck. Leona corrected the skid and mashed the gas pedal more as the thing growled and huffed beside her, keeping pace with the speeding truck.

The throttle was pegged out. The old truck shuddered with the effort, but she pulled out in front of the creature. The engine was in the red when Leona reached Jewel's place and coughing its dying breath. She skidded to a stop sideways and scrambled across the bench seat as the monster crashed against the driver's side. Leona managed to get the passenger side door open, and she dove out of the truck and ran up the sidewalk. The snarls were right on her heels, but when she crossed Jewel's porch, she burst through the screen door and the enormous black creature behind her screamed in rage. He couldn't move past the yard, couldn't come up on the porch.

In a jar next to the door was a white powder. Jewel had refined the wolfsbane into a ward. Leona smirked at the creature and blessed Jewel's heart for being diligent about a poison.

The thing was a wolf but misshapen and hulking. It stood up on its hind legs and swiped at the air, snarling at Leona. Jewel kept a shotgun by the door. Leona picked it up, walked out on the porch and shot the creature square in the chest. The thing snarled, a noise so filled with rage there was no mistaking it, but the blast didn't move it. The great gaping hole oozed blood, but the werewolf remained unaffected. He raised his head to the evening sky and howled.

All around them, more howls sounded, and the underbrush around the house came alive with growls and snarls and werewolves. They ran at the house, but like the big black wolf, they stopped short of the yard and growled in impotent rage.

There was no escape. Not at the moment. Leona went inside in search of Jewel, and what she found chilled her blood.

The place was overturned. The furniture was busted up and strewn about, and there were blast marks and holes in the walls. In the kitchen, the refrigerator lay on its side and Jewel's magic stores were trashed. Jewel was nowhere to be found.

There had been a fight, a magic one, where curses had been slung with precision and harmful intent by all parties. Leona looked around for blood but found none. She closed her eyes and pushed out with her magic as she envisioned Jewel. Waves of thought and magic went out of her, like an ocean wave. Leona's heart leapt when the wave returned to her, stronger—

and madder. Jewel was alive. Leona smiled. That was a mistake on their part. They would pay.

Leona walked outside and glared at the big black creature. "Where is she?"

He stood on his hind legs again and laughed, an unnatural sound coming from an animal. He howled, and all the wolves echoed him.

Leona went back inside. She loaded up the shotgun and found some special rounds Jewel had been working on. She would have to wait until morning when they all changed back. They'd be weaker when they did, and when they were weaker, she'd blast them all.

Cale was nowhere to be found. Leona called to him and pushed out with magic but all she got back was a tinny whisper, muffled. Cale wasn't gone, but it was like he was trapped somewhere. She searched around, and in Jewel's bedroom, she smiled. The vanity mirror was covered by a patchwork quilt. When Leona pulled it off, she saw Cale banging against the mirror from the other side.

"All right, calm down," Leona said. She grabbed the vanity bench and slammed it against mirror, shattering it.

Cale flew out of it. He looked odd to her, less colorful, faded, and slightly out of breath.

"What happened?" Leona asked.

"Jewel put me in there. Them Walkers blasted in here. She didn't want them hexing me. Did they get her?"

Leona nodded. "Yes. But she's alive still."

"Lee, what are you gonna do?"

Leona took a deep breath and sat still and tried to tune out the relentless howls of the werewolves outside. The dark voice whispered to her incessantly now. She let it. "Make them real, real sorry," she said.

J ust before dawn, the big black creature snarled and howled. The others answered him, then all of them slunk back into the woods.

"Will they be able to cross that barrier in their human form?" Cale asked.

"To tell you the truth, I don't know," Leona said. "I ain't for sure all the ways that powder can affect them." She checked the load in the shotgun. "But leave it to Jewel to have plenty of shotgun shells, so if they try anything, we'll see how well they like a face-full of scatter shot."

"What are you gonna do about them Walkers?"

Leona shrugged. She'd been trying to center herself all night in the hopes that her magic would reset, but thus far, she'd only managed a spotty, fitful connection. She could still feel it, the magic, and it was getting stronger, but she'd never really used it so offensively before, It had taken its toll on her at a most inopportune time. "I really don't know. I ain't sure how much juice I got, but I highly doubt it's gonna be enough to take on a warlock and a vampire at once."

"Can you, I don't know, get it back faster?" Cale asked.

Leona thought of the herb of grace. It might augment her power enough to get in a solid curse if she fought dirty, but to do her any good, she'd have to take more than she had taken yet. It was dangerous. Her hand went to her stomach, which dipped and fluttered. The last dose had nearly killed her. This time, the consequences would certainly be more dire.

"I got to see what Jewel has around here. She likes a good explosion and poison. I might could make something—"

"Best get on out here, witch!"

A great graveled voice boomed from the front yard.

As the sun peeked out from the top of the hill, it shone blood red down into the little valley, illuminating Galen Nolan. He stood just outside the ward, exactly where he had stood in wolf form. He'd put pants on, but he was barefoot and bare-chested. His chest bore an angry scar, a shotgun blast barely healed over, raw and red.

Leona walked close to the ward, cocked the shotgun, and leveled it at him. "Let's us see how quick you heal without a full moon to help you."

"It's more difficult to be sure, but then how would you ever get that mouthy sister of yours back?" Galen smiled at her and opened his arms, exposing his chest and daring Leona to shoot. "You shoot me, my boys won't never let you leave here in time to get her." Galen whistled and a dozen men emerged, half-naked, fresh from the night's kills, covered in dirt and blood. They surrounded the house and kept just outside of effective shotgun range.

"What if I shoot them all?"

"You best be quick with that scattergun and hell on the reload. We'll heal up before you can get all of us, and then you'll be in a world of shit. I'll take my time with you." He grinned at her. Leona had seen his handiwork enough to know what she faced should he get a hold of her.

"What do you care if I get Jewel back?"

"I don't. But you took something of mine, and I want it back."

"Dream on. You'll never find her."

"Yes, I know. You ain't the only witch around, but you done a whammy and looks like you're the only one can undo it. So you're gonna. Or I reckon we can wait around and see how crispy them two preacher boys can fry up your whore sister."

It took a great deal of willpower not to pull the trigger and blast the smirk off his twisted, ugly face. She could empty both barrels into it, reload and blast until his head was pulp, but that wouldn't help her save Jewel. There was only one way to do that. She lowered the shotgun.

"All right. You let me pass and help me get Jewel back. I'll take the spell off."

"You'll take the spell off now."

"The hell if I will. How dumb do you think I am?" Leona scowled at him and aimed the gun at him again.

"I'll need a tracking spell. I hear your lil' sis is a sight better at that than you. She'll be safe until then."

Granny Kay had taught them everything she knew about all manner of magical beings. A great many of them were cruel and untrustworthy.

"Don't turn your back on no goblins. Always meet vampires in daylight, but don't you ever do deals with a werewolf."

Sound advice and, in Leona's limited experience, Granny Kay had been right. Jewel would be livid at having a werewolf help her, but Leona would rather Jewel be alive and mad than dead and mad. A lifetime with a mad ghost Jewel would be torment.

Galen Nolan wasn't to be trusted, not even a little bit. But at the moment, she had no choice.

"All right. Give me a minute. I need to get some ingredients."

"Hurry up about it. I don't imagine sis has too much longer."

Leona ignored him and went inside. She grabbed some more shotgun shells, a candle, a pouch of the blue memory powder, and a box of salt. She picked up the herb of grace from Jewel's stores and hesitated before she shoved it in the bag.

"Lee, what are you gonna do?"

"I'm gonna go get Jewel." She rummaged around in the icebox and found an egg.

"If you take that spell off, he'll kill you."

"Highly likely," Leona said. "But he only needs to think I took the spell off. Truth be told, I don't think I can take the spell off right now. But let's you and me keep that to ourselves." Leona set her jaw and gave Cale a little smile.

"Always. But Lee, how are you gonna—"

Leona held up a hand. "Jewel ain't the only Spencer sister that can buffalo a man."

She walked past him and out the door. Leona set her things down. She drew a circle in the dirt, put the candle in the middle and lit it. After she said an incantation, she passed the egg through the flame a few times, then kissed it, and blew out the candle.

When she stood up, she held up the egg. "That spell is now in this egg. If anything happens to this egg, the spell goes back.

When Jewel is safe, I'll give it up. Until then, I smell so much as a whiff of stink from you, sir, and I'll smash it to bits. You can do as you like to me, and you'll still never find that girl or her baby."

"You're a dirty, conniving whore of a witch," Galen growled.

"And you're a filthy, deceitful bastard of a werewolf," Leona said.

She picked up her supplies and put them in her truck, ignoring him as he growled. She got in and motioned for him to get into the bed of the truck. "Dogs ride in the back."

He growled low and mean, then he jumped in the bed, and his weight made the truck bounce and groan. A rush of cold air hit her as Cale materialized in the passenger seat.

"I think this might be the death of you, Leona." He reached his hand out and Leona felt the weightless cold press on hers.

Leona nodded. "Cale, I believe you might be right." She gunned the truck and took off toward the revival tent.

L eona killed the engine and sat still for a moment as she
studied the tent. The front flaps were pulled back, and
the lights inside were on. She got out of the truck but
didn't move toward the opening. Galen jumped down from the
truck and stood beside her.

"What are you waiting for? I smell that sister of yours, and
I smell kerosene."

Leona ignored him. She didn't need a werewolf's nose to
smell the kerosene. The place reeked of it.

"I'm going to stay hidden. He'll see me," Cale said.

Leona nodded but didn't answer him or look at him. She
didn't want Galen to know anyone else was there. Levi would

see Cale, and if Levi saw him, he could bind Cale, taking him off the table and possibly exorcising him for good.

The other issue was the very good possibility of a ward, or worse, a booby trap spell. Leona could barely feel her own magic surrounding her. It had not yet returned to full strength, and she didn't want to waste any of what she did have looking for a ward when she was likely to need it to free Jewel and defend them. Leona took a step toward the tent flap but stopped.

She couldn't chance it. If she just pushed a tiny bit, she should be able to sense a spell. Her stomach fluttered, and she felt a bit of bile rise up in her throat as a wave of sickness hit her. That wasn't how she usually detected magic, and it puzzled her a second. She took a few calming breaths, and the nausea dissipated, then she closed her eyes and reached out with what little magic she had.

She felt nothing.

Her stomach flipped again, and she doubled over as the world swirled.

Galen laughed beside her. "They must be scrambling you. I don't smell no magic."

Leona straightened up and scowled at him. It was true werewolves could smell a spell, but this werewolf couldn't be trusted. There could be magic, and she could be walking into a trap. Then a realization hit her, and she laughed.

Of course she was walking into a trap. They wanted her to come to them. If they hadn't, they would have killed Jewel and left her at the house.

"They ain't scrambling me. They want me here." Leona reached into the pouch at her side and took out a handful of the herb of grace. She had no other choice; if she didn't augment her power, she'd never be able to fight both Levi and Joshua. But something peeked out of her mind, something she couldn't quite see just yet, that made her hesitate. Her stomach lurched again, but she went with it. She shoved the herb in her mouth and swallowed it. It burned slightly, but her stomach calmed. And almost immediately she felt a little more connected to the magic. Not like normal, but getting there.

"If you know it's a trap, why are you walking in?" Galen growled.

"'Cause the only way out is through," Leona said. "And sometimes, you catch something in a trap you wasn't counting on."

They had emptied the tent of all the wooden folding chairs, but the altar remained. When Leona recognized the girl tied to it, she bowed her head and fought back tears.

Tammy Doan's body was lashed to the cross and ringed by dozens of black candles. A great sea of blood pooled beneath the corpse, sticky and congealed. Her head had been torn off and her chest ripped open, but unlike the other girls, Tammy's head was not missing. It sat on the altar, next to the decomposed heads of Mary Silvus and Karla Hupp. The black stitches sewed her mouth shut, and Leona could still see the fear in her eyes. It lingered and unnerved Leona more than the congealed blood and smell of the rotting heads.

Leona looked around for Tammy's ghost but saw nothing. The ghost's absence unnerved her further.

"Your sister's out that way," Galen growled, pointing to the back flap of the tent, which was open.

They had left Tammy's tableau on purpose. They wanted her to be afraid, unnerved, unsure. The arrogance of it had the opposite effect on Leona. Her stomached fluttered again, but rather than nausea, the little ball of anger kindled there and grew steadily in her guts. She felt it mix with the tingle of the magic, and she smiled. "Yes. I know she is. Just you remember this, mister, anything happens to her and I'll smash that egg."

"You do that, and I'll kill you both," Galen growled.

Leona smiled and nodded. "But you'll never get that baby. And I know that's what you really want."

He snarled, and his eyes flashed yellow as he drew back to hit her. Leona stood firm and stared him down. He lowered his hand and backed off. Leona pushed past him and through the tent flap.

T he Walker brothers lounged in two folding chairs, toasting each other with chalices of blood as they watched the morning sun. Blood covered their white robes, and both had blood smeared faces.

Next to them, tied to a blackened post and surrounded by kerosene-soaked straw, Jewel thrashed and cussed them both with enough vigor to make a sailor blush. When she saw Leona and Galen, she shook her head. "Goddamnit Leona, please don't tell me you came willingly with that Goddamned werewolf piece of sh—"

Levi held up a hand and Jewel stopped mid-word. "It ain't becoming of a lady to cuss like that, Sister." He grinned at

Leona. "What took you so long?" Levi slurped from his cup and grinned bloody at Leona.

"I'm itching to watch these witches burn." Joshua had pulled the hood of his robe up to protect him from the sun. His face had gone a bit red, and his lip had a cold sore. But he was otherwise unharmed by the sunlight.

"You know, I've always thought it was a shame you vampires don't just burst into flames when the sun hit you," Leona said. "It'd be a lot more impressive than just getting herpes."

Joshua fumed, and if he could have caught fire Leona thought he would have. But his brother laughed and held him back.

"Easy, Brother." Levi patted him on the shoulder, then he looked to Leona. "Sister, you're at a disadvantage. Maybe you ought not to antagonize."

Leona laughed. She felt the magic growing stronger. It swirled in her guts, and her hands began to tingle. She had to stall them a bit longer.

"You ain't a real vampire, are you? Who turned you? I know it wasn't no full vampire. If a real vampire had done it, you wouldn't blister up like that and need to siphon off the energy of old ladies."

Joshua growled and lunged, but Levi held him.

Leona laughed again. The power was coursing through her, snapping and crackling between her fingers.

"Sis, you can talk all night and all day long, but that won't help you. You and your whore sister there are gonna burn tonight. We've burnt many of your kind. I wish I could say you was special, but you ain't. No whore is." Levi said. His face soured, and for a second, his handsome features twisted ugly by rage. "We'll find you and burn you all."

"Oh, so you don't like witches. That ain't novel," Leona

said. "How come you tore up those girls then? They wasn't witches."

"They was there," Levi said. His face returned to its normal handsome visage. He smirked, and his eyes gleamed. "They don't matter, not really. We find them in every town. Girls that want absolution because they know they're whores. Abominations. Misfits. He wants sacrifices. When we get enough of them, he'll come. And when he does, you whore witches and that old bitch that hides herself away will know the meaning of the word pain."

"Who are we talking about?" Leona asked.

Levi laughed. "You'll find out soon enough." He looked over at Galen. "You took your time bringing her here.

"Well, I had to get her to take that spell off. She's a stubborn whore," Galen said.

Leona looked to Galen and smiled at him.

"Jewel, Granny Kay was right. Werewolves really are stupid," Leona said. She pulled the egg out of her pouch and held it up. "He was dumb enough to believe I could contain a cloaking spell inside this here egg." She waved her hand, and Jewel laughed, her voice back.

"You told him you put it in an egg? That's a good one!" Jewel laughed. "I don't know why anyone needs to be afraid of him. He's dumber than most."

Galen snarled, and his skin began to ripple. His voice dropped even lower into a guttural growl, and he pointed to Levi. "You best hope you can undo her spell, boy."

"Relax, friend. She'll take the spell off. She won't want to watch her sister burn. Miss Leona, undo that spell and I promise you, we won't burn your sister alive."

Joshua danced around, irate. "Oh yes, we will! Witches burn. You promised me, Levi."

Levi held up his hand. "Easy, brother. Look, sometimes we

can't know what the Dark Lord's plan is. We think it's clear, but it's beyond us. We have to trust and be justified." He patted his brother on the shoulder, then looked to Leona. "You're both gonna die today. But that could be slow and terrible, or it could be quick and as painless as I can make it. You choose."

Leona rolled the egg around her hand as she stared at Levi. His smirking face irritated her and as she stared at him, she felt the egg grow hot in her hand. She turned her head and regarded her sister.

"Jewel. It's almost always a mistake to tell you this, but I do believe you were right. I reckon we should have just come straight on out here, blasted these fellers out of them collars, and set this whole nasty place on fire."

Before Jewel could triumphantly yell "I told you so," Leona threw the egg at Joshua's feet. When it smashed, a great white light erupted from it, and Joshua screamed and fell to the ground. His robe was on fire, and no matter how he rolled, the flames would not go out.

"Brother!" Levi yelled as he threw himself on top of Joshua, desperately trying to stifle the fire. He finally managed to get the burning robe off his brother. Levi turned and hissed at Leona. While Joshua screamed and moaned, Levi muttered an incantation, and a fireball erupted from his mouth. He spit it toward Jewel.

Leona pushed out and shoved it off course. It struck several feet away, and before Levi could muster another one, Leona threw up her hands and pushed at him. Levi pushed back, and Leona felt her magic blow back at her. She dug in and pushed hard, but so did Levi. She found herself locked in a field with him and it took all of her power to keep it steady between them.

"Leona, look out for that damned werewolf!" Jewel screamed.

Leona turned her head to see Galen convulsing. He flexed his hands, and they began to elongate. Great black claws erupted from his nail beds, pushing his bloody human nails out. He stared at her and grinned, and as he did, his mouth changed. His canines grew and pushed out, and his face rippled and twitched. His skin tore and bubbled, and the bones cracked as he became a hideous combination of man and wolf. The huge man's muscles bulged and ripped, and he grew to well over eight feet tall as his leg bones cracked and reformed into hocks and his feet mutated into clawed paws the size of dinner plates. His skin fell off in great bloody patches, and black hair grew in all over his body. When the transformation was complete, the hulking monster threw back its head and howled, then turned its head to Leona and snarled.

A white-hot wave of panic washed over her as she realized that Galen was fully in control of his wolf form.

"Yes, he can change at will," Levi said. "I never knew werewolves could do that, did you?" He laughed and dropped his spell then saluted Galen. "Do what you will, friend. I'll figure out some way to break her spell."

Levi pushed out again, but Leona caught it and pushed back. She threw up her other hand and pushed out at Galen as he advanced.

The werewolf stopped as he met the invisible barrier between them and snarled at her. He threw himself against it, and the force pushed Leona back a bit. At the same time, Levi pushed, and Leona had to grit her teeth to hold off both. The magic sputtered, and she panicked, but then she heard the dark whisper. It laughed.

"*Let me...*"

Levi's push came at her, a hot, rank wave of magic, and Leona gave in. She closed her eyes, and when she opened them, she let the Whisper out.

The magic buzzed all around her, and little shocks traveled up and down her arms. She smiled and pushed back at Levi and Galen at the same time. Levi's face contorted in hatred and surprise as he slid backward ten feet before he caught himself and pushed back at Leona with enough force to meet her challenge.

Galen flew backward and hit the brush pile around Jewel. The werewolf snarled, got to his feet, and rushed at Leona again. She laughed and caught him mid-lunge. The dark whisper laughed with her and begged her to choke him. Leona nodded and closed her fist. Galen struggled and gagged as he clutched at his throat.

Next to Levi, Joshua stirred. The vampire raised himself and faced Leona. His skin was burned black in places, and where it wasn't black, was covered in yellow blisters already tight with fluid. He hissed and began muttering his own spell. As he did, Leona faltered. The dark whisper quieted. She felt weak and thin in places as the vampire drained her energy.

Levi laughed and pushed at her harder. Leona mustered every bit of rage she could and used it to push back at the brothers.

Levi countered and Joshua muttered something and she had to push a bit harder at them to keep Joshua from draining her. Galen coiled his muscles jumped at her, and Leona felt the space between them dissolve as her control of him faded. She braced herself for the slash and hoped it would be quick.

But the slash never came.

A great, frigid blast rushed past her, and Galen stopped mid-lunge. He twitched and snarled as he fell over. The monster flailed, but after a few seconds, he stood up and howled. Galen's eyes turned from hate-filled yellow orbs to a brown that she knew as well as she knew her own. The werewolf nodded at her and lumbered toward Jewel. Leona turned and pushed everything she had at the Walker brothers.

Levi's face was contorted and red with rage. He pushed back at her, and Joshua renewed his attack. A blast of hot air whipped in, and Leona felt the vampire begin to pull her energy away again while, at the same time, his brother pushed harder, advancing on her and smirking.

Next to her, Jewel's voice rang out. *"Rip et Lingua tua!"*

Levi stopped, and his smirk faded as he stared at Jewel. He lowered his hands, and his spell fizzled and died. He balled up his fists and tried to clamp his mouth shut, but it didn't help. He opened his mouth, reached in, and ripped out his own tongue.

Levi threw the bloody organ down and cried as he sunk to his knees. He looked to Jewel and Leona, then mumbled and choked, looking to Joshua as blood poured from his mouth.

Joshua's scream was rage and horror. He turned from Levi and looked to Jewel and Leona. He hissed at them and went to spring at them, but the werewolf's claw caught him by the throat. His eyes bulged as the creature dug its claws into his head and pulled. Joshua's head tore cleanly from his body, and putrid black blood sprayed from the neck.

The werewolf dropped the head and stepped back. He whined and fell to the ground. He convulsed and yelped in pain, then the big brown eyes looked at Leona.

"Do what you gotta do, Lee. He's fighting me, and I don't know how long I can hold him."

"Get clear of them two, Cale," Leona said.

He crawled away and whined as he twitched and struggled to keep possession of the creature.

Leona's hands shook and her knees wobbled. She had nothing left. Leona looked to Jewel. "Can you torch that tent? Them heads is in there."

"Gladly," Jewel said. She put her palms together and produced a fireball. When it was white hot, she threw it at the revival tent, and the canvas erupted into an inferno. She shied back from the heat. "Whew, that had a little something extry on it. I mighta got carried away." In only a few minutes, the tent was reduced to smoldering ash.

Leona and Jewel turned to Levi. He blubbered and begged

as he spit blood everywhere. Leona pulled a carton of salt from her pouch and tossed it to Jewel, then she touched the ground and concentrated. Briars and thick black roots breached the soil of the field. They snaked out and bound Levi. Jewel ringed him in salt. When the circle was complete, she stood beside Leona.

Leona took Jewel's hand and together, voices mixed in perfect harmony, they said, "*Tolle illum et veniam.*"

The ground inside the salt circle began to glow red, and Levi struggled against his bonds. Leona put her hand to her face as a wave of intense heat washed over them. Six dark hands pushed free of the soil all around him. Leona choked on the smell of sulfur as Mary Silvus, Karla Hupp, and Tammy Doan pulled themselves free of the earth. They stalked toward Levi, hissing at him. He managed a scream as they surrounded him and ripped him apart. When there was nothing left of him but a mangled pile of gore, the ground inside the circle glowed bright red.

Leona and Jewel covered their mouths and noses as the smell of sulfur and burning hair and flesh surrounded them. The salt around the circle caught fire and burned bright yellow orange. Inside the circle, the ground throbbed, and then a great red flame shot into the sky. When it retreated into the earth, the girls and Levi were gone, leaving a scorched black circle behind.

"Lee, I can't hold him!" Cale said. He let out a scream that turned into a growl, and the creature's eyes turned back to yellow. The werewolf stumbled toward them as if he were drunk, but he snarled and righted himself then closed the distance between them.

L eona pulled a jar of white powder from her bag. She
opened it and doused the creature in it. He whined
and coughed and fell over, then he began to vomit
great heaps of froth and blood.

"I sure wish you had brought my shotgun, Leona. Then we
could have killed this son of a bitch," Jewel said.

"He wouldn't let me. He ain't quite as dumb as you think."
Leona kicked Galen, who whined as he puked. He started to
shift back to human form, but he was weak. The shift appeared
to Leona more painful than anything she had ever seen. His
bones cracked and his skin bruised in huge black patches as he
reverted. Galen screamed as his spine twisted and snapped. He

threw back his head and howled as his facial bones shifted and the hair fell out.

She didn't feel remotely sorry for him.

When Galen had turned back into his human form, he hauled himself to his feet and turned toward them. Leona grabbed Jewel's hand, and they pressed their palms together.

When he saw the energy build between them, Galen turned and ran. He was well into the brush next to the field and gone before they had enough energy to blast him.

"Well, that's disappointing," Jewel said. "I reckon we're gonna have trouble with him again, Leona."

"Of that I have no doubt." Leona grabbed Jewel and hugged her tight. "I'm sorry."

"You know, Leona, I ain't one to say, I told you so, but—"

"Lee."

Cale's voice was faint. When Leona let go of Jewel and turned around, Cale was nearly transparent, and his image kept twitching.

He shook his head and flickered. "Not much time, Lee. I'm sorry."

A rush of panic and adrenaline coursed through her, and Leona stumbled toward him. "Sorry? You saved us! Don't be sorry, just hang on." She reached out to him, and her heart sunk when she realized he wasn't emitting cold anymore. She closed her eyes and called to the Whisper, begging it to come back and help her. But for once, it was silent. "No! You can't. I won't let you. You can't leave me," she screamed.

Cale reached toward her face and cupped her cheek. He smiled at her. "I never knew why I hung around that graveyard 'til I met you. Now I know." He moved closer, and the surrounding air pulsed. Cale's face screwed up in concentration, and he went solid as he bent down and kissed her.

Leona grabbed him and held tight, but it was over too

soon, and after a few seconds, her hands went through him. He took a step back and smiled at her.

"Cale, I love you," she sobbed. "Please don't—"

He twitched again, and then he was gone.

Leona fell to the ground and sobbed. She clawed at the ground and cried as she felt for him. But she couldn't sense him at all, and she knew he was gone.

This time, she didn't ask the dark whisper for the power. She demanded it.

Leona stood up. The pain and rage erupted from her and manifested as an angry red blast from her hands and eyes. She screamed and blasted the trees. They exploded into smoldering splinters, and Leona kept going. As she raged, she set the woods that ringed Old Biehl's pasture on fire.

"Leona! Calm down. You'll fry us all." Jewel yelled and rushed at her, but when she tried to grab Leona's arm, Leona jerked it back. She scowled at Jewel and sent a bolt of energy her way.

Jewel dodged it and scowled back. "Well, that's enough of that mess, Leona Jean. Stop this nonsense right now!" She moved her hands together and called up energy of her own.

The dark whisper laughed, and Leona laughed along with it.

"*Kill her . . .*"

That frightened her. Kill Jewel? That wasn't what Leona wanted. She wanted the pain to go away. The Whisper was relentless, and it screamed in her head.

"Fight it, Leona!" Jewel yelled.

"*Kill her. Now,*" the whisper demanded. Leona's hands clenched, and she shook as she struggled to control herself. But the Whisper was too strong, and she held her palms out to Jewel. The red energy cracked and swirled as it manifested in her hands. She fought to keep it in her hands, and she looked at Jewel. Tears streamed down her face.

"Jewel . . . I can't stop it. Plea—"

Jewel's blast sent Leona airborne. She landed flat on her back and struggled to catch her breath. The Whisper screamed one last time in her head, but he wasn't in control any longer. The pain was.

She reached out one last time for Cale and found she had no connection to anything to call up anymore. Not to the magic, not to Cale, not to anything. The world spun like she was drunk, and as it did, Leona gave in. She closed her eyes and lost consciousness.

When Leona awoke it was just dawn. The red light of morning made the window glow, illuminating the room in a pale pink that lent a childish delicacy to the space. When she realized where she was, the ambiance made sense.

Leona and Jewel had spent many nights in Granny Kay's spare room, with its simple maple bed frame and well-worn double–wedding ring quilt. Waking up snuggled in the deep feather tick was familiar and comforting. It was so comfortable that, for a brief moment, Leona had forgotten about Cale.

But then she remembered how the morning light had passed through him as his image flickered and faded. Her lips could still feel that last kiss, real and perfect. She licked them hoping to taste him again, but she there was nothing there. Reflexively she reached out and thought of him. She closed her eyes and concentrated on plucking that invisible string that had always existed between them. Her heart fluttered in her chest and beat erratically as she willed the pulse to return back to her as it always had.

But it did not.

The string didn't move. In fact, when she reached out to pluck it again in her mind, it seemed to disintegrate, flowing into nothingness a tiny particle at a time.

Leona sat up in the bed and screamed. She took in great huge lungfuls of air and keened. Tears of rage and grief streamed down her face, and she sobbed until her face was red and swollen. It was quite a while before she realized that she wasn't making any sounds.

It felt like she was screaming, but when she calmed a bit, she realized that no sounds were coming from her mouth. In fact, nothing was, not even air.

"Yes. That's right. It's a dream." Granny Kay sat down on the edge of the mattress and laid a gnarled hand on Leona's leg. She patted her and smiled sadly. "It's good to let it all out anyway, honey."

Leona opened her mouth to speak to Kay, but she only mouthed the words.

Kay nodded anyway. "I know. I know. He's gone now." She pulled Leona into her familiar hug. Leona clutched at the old woman and cried again. After a while the familiar clean, herbaceous scent of Granny Kay calmed her. She pulled away and wiped her eyes.

"I know it don't seem this way now, Leona, but this ain't a bad thing. Cale wasn't meant to stay here forever. He couldn't. He needed to move on."

Leona was on the verge of tears again, and in her mind, she began spewing a rebuttal to Kay's assertion. But again, no sound came out. Kay didn't need anything said aloud.

"Once you get clear of the grief, you'll see it. You've seen it before with so many others. They're free. Cale ain't no different.

"I've never seen one so intent on protecting anyone. It ain't natural, really, and I sure don't know how he was able to muster up all that energy for so long, but if nothing else, that shows you what love can do."

Leona remembered his eyes and his smile and the way his chest rose and fell on the rare occasions over the years that she had seen him sleep. He had smelled like spices and leather, and his voice had a deep, comforting musical quality to it that made her happy even when she had been exasperated by him. She relived all of these things and viciously dared them to try and fade.

"Leona, I don't think you need worry about forgetting him. That ain't a thing that can be. The grief will stay with you a good long while, and that's fine. That's what grief does."

Leona began to cry again, but Kay smiled and hugged her.

"It don't go away. You know that. That hole is always gonna be there. You travel around it, and every once in a while, you'll step in that hole, but after a bit, that pathway around it will widen, and there'll be room enough you won't step in so often."

Kay pulled away from the embrace. She used the edge of her apron to dry Leona's tears. It was a familiar gesture, and just like the feather tick and the old quilt and the smell of herbs drying, it was a thing that made Leona recall the lessons and love and safety she had always felt in Kay's holler.

Kay smiled and kissed her on the forehead, then she put a hand on Leona's stomach.

"And anyway, I don't think you'll have no trouble remembering him. Do you?"

Leona opened her eyes and blinked. She wasn't in Kay's spare room. She was in the passenger side of the truck as Jewel drove. The truck bounced along the road as it always did. The truck didn't recognize anything amiss.

It wouldn't.

It couldn't.

It was lucky.

Jewel looked over at her and opened her mouth to say something but for once in her life, Jewel had the good sense to say nothing. She just reached over, grabbed Leona's hand, and squeezed.

Leona didn't pull away. She gave a weak squeeze back, then she rested her head against the glass and closed her eyes. She laid her other hand on her stomach protectively and cried. Just like in the dream, she made no sound.

L eona set the slice of apple pie down in front of Ed Wagner and rested her hand on the small swell in her belly. It didn't really show yet in clothes, but Leona couldn't help resting her hand there protectively.

"What's this here pie for?" Ed asked. He picked up his fork and took a bite of the mysterious pie without waiting for Leona's explanation.

"It's a Christmas present," Leona said.

"I reckon I got all the presents I was gonna when we solved them murders." He smiled and puffed up slightly at the memory of his own detective prowess, a memory that Leona and Jewel had planted.

"Yeah, I'm glad you figured it all out, Ed." Leona smiled and refilled his coffee. She looked to the end of the lunch counter, and her smiled faded as she looked at the empty seat. As she always did, she reached out, looking for Cale, but felt nothing. Then her stomach did a little loop-dee, and she put her hand on it.

The bell above the diner door tinkled, and an icy blast of December air accompanied Jewel in. Her arms were filled with packages and grocery bags. She plopped down at the counter, and Leona brought her a cup of coffee.

"Whew. It is colder than a witch's—"

"Jewel Elizabeth." Leona growled.

"Anyway, it's cold. Coldest December I can recall in a while. What about you, Ed?" Jewel asked as she sipped her hot drink. "Ain't you got no whiskey, Leona?"

"No, I ain't got no whiskey, Jewel." Leona rolled her eyes. She took off her apron and put on her coat.

"I can't recall a colder December either," Ed said. "Jewel, did Leona tell you the Fraternal Order of the Police down in Charleston is giving me an award?"

"No, she didn't, Ed, but you sure did last week," Jewel said. "I reckon you deserve it though, what with all that fine detective work you done in sussing out who killed them three girls. And then how them Walker brothers killed themselves in that fire. We're all grateful, Ed."

Ed looked puzzled at Jewel's tone, which didn't sound at all grateful, unless sarcastic was grateful. His face contorted in confusion, and his eyes changed from their normal blue to black. "Well, yes, I-I did figure all that out, and now I'm being given a great honor by the Fraternal Order of the Elks over in Clarksburg and I—"

Jewel waved her hand and everyone in the room froze, save herself and Leona. Leona pulled a bag of blue powder out of her bag and blew it in Ed's face. "It's the Fraternal Order of the

Police in Charleston, Ed. And they already gave you the award. You and Donna went to the nice banquet. They had baked steak and real shrimp cocktails. The plaque is coming by mail soon."

Ed's eyes turned milky white, and he nodded and smiled. "Yes. It was a nice banquet. Real shrimp cocktail. The plaque is arriving by mail soon."

"That's the third time he's needed charmed," Jewel said. "I'm going to have to mix us up a stronger batch."

"Maybe he'd shut up if you'd stop antagonizing him. Just let him talk about it. It helps him." She patted Ed on the shoulder. "It's a good thing you done, Ed. We're all safe now."

"We're all safe now," Ed repeated.

"Well, we better figure out a way to get him a plaque or this is likely to blow up on us." Jewel waved her hand, and everyone resumed their activity. "You about ready to go, Leona?"

Leona put on her knit cap and finished buttoning her coat. "Yes, just about—"

The bell above the door tinkled again, and Dorval Ring entered, carrying a burlap sack heavy with something. Dorval was still rail thin, but his color was good, and he'd cleaned up. Like all wayward souls, time at Kay's Holler brought something out in him. He smiled when he saw Leona and Jewel, then tipped his hat to them. "Hello, Miss Jewel, Miss Leona."

"Hello there, Dorval," Leona said, smiling genuinely back. "I got some buttermilk for you, and I left a pie out back."

"Oh, that's kind of you. But I come to bring you something today. You and Miss Jewel helped me get on Old Bunky Arnold's road crew for the Township."

Leona and Jewel had convinced Bunk Arnold to hire Dorval one night at Marv's. Jewel flirted with him, and Leona snuck him an extra shot of rye, eventually convincing the Township Trustee that Dorval was perfect for cleaning up roads around

Ames Township. It hadn't been a lie. Dorval was diligent, and never had the township roads been so clean and free of roadkill and garbage.

"Well, we just put in a good word is all," Jewel said. "Glad to see it agrees with you and that you're a sight clean—Ow!"

Leona's pinch shut Jewel up. "Uh, what Jewel means is we're glad it worked out. Bunky says you're his best man."

"Yes, ma'am. Well, I got me a promotion. He made me a crew boss and got me a five-cent raise." Dorval stuck out his chest, proud of his advancement. "I been able to put a bit back, got me a couple of hogs, and this here is a ham off my new smokehouse. I wanted you to have it for your Christmas dinner." He opened the burlap sack to show them the smoked ham.

"Oh, Dorval, that's so kind of you, but really, you could sell that. You don't need to be giving us nothing," Leona said.

"Miss Leona. After all you done for me, this ham ain't hardly nothing. I owe you debts I ain't ever gonna be able to repay." He handed her the sack.

"Friends help friends. I'm sure you would have done the same," Leona said. She took the ham and then hugged him. He smelled of spoiled milk and Aqua Velva, which he had applied liberally to mask his normal odor. Leona let go of him quick and stepped back.

Dorval blushed beet red and looked at his shoes. When he composed himself enough to meet Leona's eyes, they were lined with tears. "Yes, ma'am. You can always count me as a friend." He tipped his hat to them. "Merry Christmas."

"Merry Christmas, Dorval."

When Jewel and Leona got in Jewel's truck, Jewel laughed. "Looks like you got you another boyfriend, Leona. I'm glad of it. I love ham. Maybe next time he can bring us some fresh sausage."

Leona reached out and slapped Jewel. "Don't joke about that. There ain't no new boyfriend and there ain't ever gonna be."

She stared at Leona for a second. Then her face softened. "I'm sorry. You know I didn't mean anything about Cale."

"Don't. Please. Don't say his name. Don't joke. Don't say nothing, Jewel. I just can't. I can't."

Jewel started the truck. "You gotta stop with all this, Leona. It ain't healthy for you. It ain't healthy for that baby."

"Stop what?"

"Stop all this moping. Cale went out protecting us. He loved you, and it don't stop. But you can't spend your life pining over a ghost. It ain't natural. And you can't keep punishing yourself by cutting off the magic."

"What are you talking about? I do magic."

"You make up potions and tinctures. Sachets and root magic. You don't do no charms or spells. You haven't since that day. I thought maybe it was the effect of the herb of grace and the calendula antidote, but that's long gone now. It's your choice."

"I ain't one to use magic every time I get a fart wedged crossways, Jewel. Unlike you."

"I ain't offended. I like magic. It solves a good deal of my problems. It could solve a lot more of yours, too, if you'd let it."

Leona crossed her arms and turned toward the side window. "Well, I won't. I can do it myself. And anyways, it's gone. I-I can't really feel it anymore. I let myself go, and that's what happened."

"Oh, bullshit, Leona. You used it to save our lives. You're hurting because Cale's gone, and you've constipated yourself. Work it out. It's dangerous to be all bunged up like that. When it busts loose, it's libel to be explosive." She pulled up in front of Leona's house.

"Well, thanks for that dirty talk, Jewel. I know I can always count on you for colorful commentary." Leona got out and slammed the door. Jewel opened it.

"That don't offend me neither, Leona. Just don't be so hard on yourself." She held out the ham. "You want me to bring the bread and cranberry sauce for Christmas Eve?"

"Yes. And a few quarts of the green beans you put up." Leona took the ham and slammed the door again. Jewel honked a few times then gunned the truck and spun gravel in her usual manner.

Leona rolled her eyes and shook her head as she brought her load into the house. The truck was not in the drive, and that gave her a bit of relief as that meant Bob was not home. But her relief was short-lived when she walked in the kitchen to find Bob sitting at the table, a dozen empty Stroh's cans strewn about and the kitchen in disarray. Every cabinet was open, and the contents kicked around.

"What happened in here? And where's the truck?" Leona put the ham down on the counter and began picking up pots and pans. She never saw the blow from the chair that hit her in the head and upper back. Leona screamed and fell to the floor.

Bob stood over her with the chair. He tossed it aside, then grabbed her by her hair. He pulled her to her feet then slapped her hard enough to knock her down again. "Never you mind where my truck is. Where's the money hid?"

"Bob. I really don't—" Leona had gotten to her knees, but a punch to her face knocked her off her feet again. She scooted away from him, her back against the sink, and instinctively covered her stomach with her hand.

"I want that money. Now," he said.

In that instant, Leona knew why Bob wanted money, and she knew that her life was never going to be free of Galen Nolan.

Bob advanced on her and slapped her again. "Now you tell me right now where you hid that money. I swear to you, Leona, I will kick that bastard baby right out of—"

He drew back his foot and aimed a kick at her stomach, but it never landed. The air around them swirled, and all the pots and pans and kitchen things levitated. Leona pushed out with her palm, and Bob Monroe flew across the room.

His body made a man-shaped dent in the wall. It knocked the breath out of him, and he choked and sputtered as he struggled to catch his breath. Leona got to her feet. Her right eye was rapidly swelling shut, but her left was open and blazing green, filled with hatred for Bob Monroe. He wouldn't quit, and he would hurt her and the baby he knew wasn't his.

Leona closed her fist, then she raised it to eye level and twisted it. Bob's head rotated 180 degrees on his neck, and the crack of his neck breaking filled the room up with sound. He went slack, then fell to the floor.

"Mama?"

Peggy croaked out the word, then she looked to Bob and screamed.

Leona scooped her up and hugged her, but Peggy kicked and screamed.

"Shh . . . baby it's all right."

"What happened to my daddy? He ain't moving!"

"He got sick, and he—"

"You're lying. You hurt him. He said you'd do it. He told me!"

"Peggy, sweetheart, calm down. I didn't—"

"Yes, you did! You did it."

Peggy screamed and kicked Leona in the stomach. Leona dropped her and bent over double as the jolt went through her abdomen. When she righted herself, she found the blue powder in her stores and blew a pinch of it into Peggy's face. The little girl stopped screaming, and her eyes clouded over.

"Peggy. Darlin'. Calm down. Your dad . . ." Leona stopped and began to cry. She took a deep breath before continuing. "Your dad went away. I don't know when he will be back."

"Daddy went away, and we don't know when he will be back." The little girl parroted the sentence back, but she screwed up her face as if she were working something out in her mind. Leona took another pinch of the blue powder and blew it in her face.

"That's right. Daddy went away, and we don't know when he's gonna be back."

"We don't know when he'll be back," Peggy whispered.

Leona mixed up some milk and Ovaltine. She added a bit of sleeping draught to it and got Peggy to drink it down, then she tucked her in bed. Leona sat by the bed and sobbed, ashamed of what she had done.

52

That was where Jewel found her when she arrived about thirty minutes later.

"Leona."

"I done it." She stood up from Peggy's bed and went out into the kitchen with Jewel. "I-I lost control. He went to kick me . . . said he'd kill the baby, and I just lost it."

Jewel hugged her, and Leona melted against her, sobbing.

"It's what he deserved, many times over. You ain't got to feel bad about Bob Monroe getting what he had coming."

Leona shook her head. "Peggy saw."

"Shit."

"I charmed her. My own child. I confuddled her. My baby. She wouldn't stop screaming."

Jewel picked up an overturned chair and steered Leona into it. She touched Leona's swollen face. She ran a towel under the cold water and held it to Leona's face. "What's done is done. Peggy is better off not knowing any of this, and she's gonna be a sight better off not having Bob Monroe around no more."

"Jewel. I killed a man. Her daddy. I-I can't justify that."

"The Hell if you can't. He'd have killed you, and because of him, we're never gonna be shut of that damned werewolf. He's lying low because he knows we'll hex him good, but he'll be back. This is all Bob's fault. Good riddance."

"Jewel. I used magic—"

"To protect yourself and your family. Did you intend it any other way?"

"No . . . I-I don't think so."

"Well, I know you didn't. Bob Monroe was a worthless son of a bitch, and there ain't nobody gonna miss him."

"Somebody might," Leona said, pointing at the body. "What am I gonna do about that?"

"Yeah, I think we can count on a friend to help us."

Christmas Eve broke cold and overcast. Leona and Jewel were both exhausted, but they had cleaned up the house and set everything right. They bundled up the sleeping Peggy and took her to Ida Mae's, who had been happy to have the little girl to dress up on Christmas Eve and agreed to bring Peggy home for dinner that evening.

Then they had wrapped Bob Monroe up in a sheet and drove him out to Dorval Ring's farm.

Dorval was pleased to see them. He beamed with happiness when Jewel got out, but his happiness dissipated when he saw Leona's swollen face. His thin features colored in rage, and his eyes glowed yellow.

"Miss Leona, who done that?"

Jewel opened the tailgate of the truck and gestured to the body. "He done it. Listen, Dorval, I'm gonna get right to it, we need you—"

Dorval held up his hand. He grabbed Bob's body and slung it over his shoulder like it weighed nothing. He carried it past his pigs and disappeared into the barn. When he came back, he gave them a little bow.

"He won't bother nobody ever again. And if you ever have more trouble, you just—"

Jewel held up her hand. "No need to say nothing else there, Dorval. We got it."

Leona walked over to Dorval and hugged him tight ignoring his stench. "You are a true friend."

Dorval awkwardly patted her back and pulled away, flustered at the affection. "Always, Miss Leona. Always." He tipped his hat to them. "Merry Christmas, now. Best you get on home. I believe it's gonna snow today." He pointed to the low gray clouds.

They got in the truck, and when Leona looked back, she saw Dorval scratching his big sow behind her ear. He stood up and smiled at her as he waved. Leona couldn't seem to muster much of a smile, but she tried as she waved back, then she turned around and laid her head back against the seat and closed her eyes.

Her stomach fluttered, and for a second, she thought she felt a wisp of cold air and heard a whisper, but it was gone. The only sound was the wheels of the truck on the gravel as they bounced over the rough road. She put her hand over her stomach, cradling it, then she slept.

"Is Aunt Ida gonna carry me over to the Halloween Party?" Peggy skipped around the driveway in her cat costume. Leona had made ears and a tail out of felt and painted a black nose and whiskers on Peggy's face. Peggy picked up a few pebbles and threw them at Leona's truck. The truck wasn't in good enough condition to worry about anything the pebbles might do to it, but Peggy's surly throws couldn't go undisciplined.

"You quit chucking them rocks, Peggy, or nobody is gonna take you. I'll cut a switch and the only place you'll go is to bed early."

The baby fussed, and Leona picked him up and bounced him. He was agitated and had been for a few days, just like her. She'd put up wards, but the dread she normally felt on Halloween had been much less this year. Ghosts didn't appear quite as frequently as they once had, and when they did, they were just indistinct blobs who whispered a few words to her before they faded away, like black smoke on the wind.

When Jewel's truck pulled up, Peggy stomped and threw a handful of pebbles at the house. "No! I want Aunt Ida to take me!" She stuck out her lip and crossed her arms.

"What did I say about chunking them rocks?" Leona yelled. The baby cried, and she cuddled him close.

"Well, Margaret Jean, you'll be happy to know I ain't taking you nowhere except over to Ida Mae's. Go on and throw a fit over there and see if you don't get pinched." Jewel stuck her tongue out at Peggy, who reciprocated.

"Don't call me Margaret!" Peggy yelled. She marched over to Jewel's truck and got in, then slammed the door.

"Maybe you need a switch too," Leona said.

"It's too late for that kind of training. I'm hopeless," Jewel said. She smiled at the baby and tickled him under his chin. He giggled at her, his big brown eyes happy to see her. "Jackie, you little devil. You're gonna have all the ladies chasing you. Why is she so surly?"

"We've all been a little off. I figured on account of tonight." Leona sat down on the porch and tucked Jack's blanket around him.

"Yeah, maybe. You been seeing more people?"

"A few more. They're louder too. I put up a few extra wards."

"You want me to do the cloaking spell for the night?" Jewel asked.

Leona shook her head. "I don't need it no more. The wards should be enough. I don't feel it as strong anymore."

"Someday you will," Jewel said. "Once you feel better about things."

Leona shook her head. "No, Jewel. A little root and bone magic is one thing, but I don't know if I can ever do the other ever again."

"It's a part of you, Leona, and when needed, it'll come back."

They both looked up as a police car pulled into the driveway. Sheriff Ed Wagner got out. He set his hat on his head and walked up to the porch, then he took his hat off nervously and fidgeted.

"Evening, Jewel. Evening, Leona."

"What are you doing out here, Ed? Ain't you supposed to be manning the apple bobbing down at the Knights of Columbus Hall?" Jewel asked.

"Ah, yes, I am. Well, in a bit, I reckon. Anyway, I had some business, and I needed to see about . . . Well, I wanted to know . . ." He danced around from foot to foot and passed his hat back and forth in his hands.

"How can we help you, Ed?" Leona asked.

"I come to ask if you two could come down to my office tomorrow. A girl's gone missing over in Shadyside, and their sheriff asked me to consult on account of last year, and I-I just thought you all might could—"

Leona held up her hand and smiled at him. "We'll be there after my shift at the diner, Ed."

"Ah, oh, thank you, Leona. You know, I just want to find out if, you know, you can help . . . well . . ." Ed jammed his hat on his head, then he gave a little bow. "Enjoy your evening."

Jewel laughed as he drove off, his red taillights mirroring the glow of the red sunset and the autumn leaves falling all around them in that last twilight of October. "I guess we're crime fighters now," she said. "He might need another dose of confuddlment."

Leona shook her head as she stood up and put the baby on her hip. "No, leave him be. We'll help him any way that we can—"

Leona turned her head sharply toward the tree line when she heard the crash and growl. Jewel did the same. Leona tucked the baby close to her, and her heart thundered. She held up her palm. A faint red light began to form around it. Jewel did the same.

Two enormous yellow eyes appeared, and the creature snarled from the underbrush. The energy of their hands grew, Jewel's a bit brighter than Leona's, but Leona could feel the power percolating, the old sensation of connection coming to life as the werewolf stalked just outside the ward of wolfsbane she put out religiously.

He stared at them and pointed with a claw. "That little bastard don't belong to Monroe," the creature said, its voice a strange mixture of human and guttural growl. "Maybe I'll take him in payment."

"Try it and I'll end you," Leona growled back. This time she wanted the Whisper, but it was gone.

"I want what's mine," Galen snarled. "Where did you send the girl?"

"Nothing is yours. You can't own babies. That poor little mite is going to raise her son in peace. Far away from trash like you," Leona said.

"Son?" Galen said. For a second, Leona saw disappointment flash across his dark face, but then it was gone, replaced by his usual mask of casual cruelty and indifference. His lips curled back in a sneer, and he gave a strange, guttural laugh. "We'll see how it all ends up, witch. We'll see." The werewolf was still laughing when he stepped back into the underbrush. Only his yellow eyes were visible now.

"Stinking coward of a werewolf," Jewel yelled. "Too chickenshit to show yourself and have a fair fight." Jewel flung her ball of red energy into the brush, but the yellow eyes were gone.

"None of that dirty talk, Jewel. Galen Nolan doesn't ever fight fair. Of that, I am absolutely certain." Leona saved her energy, tucked it away. She'd need it soon enough. She thought of the young mother with the little boy, Galen's little boy, and she hoped they were far away and safe. Jack giggled in her arms, and she held him closer and kissed the top of his head.

"I can't wait to blast that werewolf someday." Jewel sighed as she walked back to the truck. "Be careful tonight."

Leona gave her a little smile and nodded. "You too."

"I always am," Jewel said.

"You never are," Leona retorted.

"You're right. I never am." Jewel waved, then got into the truck and spun gravel as she left.

The baby giggled loudly and pointed toward the porch swing. It creaked gently, even though there was no breeze. Jack pointed again and laughed louder as he smiled.

Leona could just make out the outline of someone on the swing, a man, and for a second, she grinned broadly as hope kindled in her heart. But as the man became more solid, he had a bowler hat and a handlebar mustache. Leona's smile faded, and she closed her eyes. She reached out, feeling for a familiar energy, but connected only with the man sitting on her porch swing.

She opened her eyes and gave him a polite smile and waved. "Hello there, Mr. Barrows. I've got to put the baby to bed, so I hope you all will be quiet and stay out here tonight, please. I do hope you have a pleasant night."

The man tipped his hat to Leona and waved at the baby again, who giggled and waved back.

Leona went inside, put Jack to bed in his crib, then she made herself a cup of tea and went back out onto the porch.

Where she waited all night.

ACKNOWLEDGMENTS

This book is about strong women and I couldn't have written it without a ton of them. First, my Nan who like Leona, was ahead of her time. Thanks to all her sisters for giving me hugs and support all through the years, especially my Aunt Midge. Thanks to my Aunt Bun for being an aunt, a mom, and a friend. Thanks to my second mom growing up, Linda Miller for always showing what hard work and being of service to others looked like. Thank you to my stepmom, Lynn for all your support and cheering. Thank you to the members of my critique group: Allorianna, Julie, Beth, and Jae. This book wouldn't have been finished without you and your thoughtful feedback. Lastly, thank you to my editor, Kelly. This book shines now.